Julie is a former NHS administrator whose first novel, *Long Shadows*, was published in 2015. She was walking in the Lake District last summer and taken by surprise when *Evil Echoes* embedded itself, as she hadn't planned to write a Victorian prequel. She is married and lives in West Sussex.

This novel is dedicated to the memory of Elizabeth Kate Kealey – a lady's maid. Having lost her fiancé in the Great War, Lizzie remained in service for her entire working life. I hope she would be pleased with the fictional story her great-niece has weaved around some of her below-stairs tales from the viewpoint of the hierarchical life of a servant.

Julie Haiselden

EVIL ECHOES

AUSTIN MACAULEY
PUBLISHERS LTD.

A CIP catalogue record for this title is available from the British Library.

ISBN 9781786294777 (Paperback)
ISBN 9781786294784 (E-Book)
www.austinmacauley.com

First Published (2016)
Austin Macauley Publishers Ltd.
25 Canada Square
Canary Wharf
London
E14 5LQ

I would like to thank Clive for again tolerating an eclectic bunch of imaginary people who moved into our home and for reading my manuscript.

I would like to thank Emily for checking the accuracy of the medical bits, Sarah for her creative artwork which influenced the cover design and Phil for ensuring my details are easily found on the internet.

I also very much appreciate the encouragement of Graham, Heather and Will whose unremitting belief in their mother's ability to spin a yarn has motivated me immeasurably.

Chapter 1 – The Big House

July 1877

Lizzie Tester awoke at dawn. She saw the sun's early morning rays make patterns on the rough surface of her bedroom wall. From its position she estimated the time was a little after five o'clock. It was Saturday; normally part of the weekly wash would be done this day with Lizzie helping her mother manoeuvre the heavy copper which had to be carefully positioned on the range. Today was different. Today Lizzie made the transition from eldest daughter of Frederick and Rebekah Tester, scholar and surrogate mother to her younger siblings, to assistant laundry maid at the big house.

Her heart thumped in her chest as she thought with trepidation about her future. She knew this day would come; her mother Rebekah and maternal aunt Phily had planned it for ages.

Philadelphia and Rebekah Crittle were sisters. They had both worked at the big house, Lizzie's mother was a nursery maid but had left to marry Fred Tester the assistant game-keeper with whom she currently had six children. Phily on the other hand had remained in service, worked her way up the pecking order and was now a lady's maid.

Lizzie fondly remembered looking forward to the fortnightly visits from her aunt and thought she must be a grand lady, as she wore expensive-looking clothes and smelled nice. She had her hair piled high on her head in a tight bun and made a striking contrast to her sister Rebekah who hadn't time to concentrate on her appearance with a horde of children and a husband to care for. She did her best but her fair hair escaped from its confines at every opportunity, hanging in strands and sticking to her face or tumbling round her shoulders and down her back.

Aunt Phily always brought with her a large wicker basket which contained all manner of delights: bread; cheese; ham and sometimes the remains of a game pie. Once there was a pot of lemon curd with a piece of coloured cloth covering the lid. Lizzie looked at it in wonderment. To think some people ate this sort of thing for tea every day! In late summer there were apples and pears from the fruit trees in the grounds of the big house which the gardener sent for them.

Whilst there was never an abundance of luxuries, Lizzie's childhood had been predominantly happy and she willingly helped her mother with the younger children. She currently had four brothers and a sister. Although her mother hadn't said anything, from the thickening of her waist it would appear that another one was due in a few months' time. When Lizzie was small she couldn't work out why at times her mother appeared to be tall and slim and at others to be extremely plump. The plumpness always seemed to result in the arrival of another baby, after which her figure would return to normal for a while; until the next time.

Her mother never complained but equally never looked cheerful. She smiled at times but the smile never reached her eyes. As she got older, Lizzie wondered if maybe her mother had suffered some sadness in her life and asked her about it once.

'How could I not be happy, Lizzie my love, I have you and your brothers and sister, what woman could want more than that?'

Lizzie didn't know; she couldn't really see the attraction of procreating every couple of years if it made you look so exhausted and careworn but then that was probably because she wasn't grown up or had fallen in love.

When she asked her mother how you knew when you had met the right person and wanted to marry them, Rebekah had adopted a distant far-away look in her eyes.

'It's the most incredible feeling in the world, Lizzie, and somehow you just know. I hope you will be as fortunate as I and experience it one day.'

Lizzie couldn't really reconcile that idyllic concept with the day-to-day drudgery that made up her mother's life but she had no more time to think of it at present as the sun was creeping round and filling the room with early morning warmth. That meant it was time to get up to face the day.

She crept softly out of the bed with the straw-filled mattress which she shared with her sister Rose and noted that the indentation her body had made remained in place. She straightened her petticoat which doubled as a nightdress and pulled on the cotton print frock her mother had given her to wear today. It was an old one of her own that she had cut down to fit Lizzie, although if truth be told they were nearly the same height and it only had to be nipped in a bit at the bust.

How she wished she could stay there in the warmth and safety of her family home. But she was thirteen. Old enough to be earning her living and contributing to the family finances. She would earn twelve pounds per year all found; with deductions made for gluttony, excessive use of soap or beer intake. No more the familiar walk to school with her brothers and her sister. She loved to learn; knowledge was there to be explored, devoured and enjoyed. Her teacher, Mr Hawes, said she was very bright and had wanted her to stay on. He had spoken to her mother but Lizzie knew it was not to be. Girls of her class could not expect a protracted education. Aside from the financial implications, it would not be fitting.

Lizzie learned to read and write with ease. She noted the look of panic in her father's eyes in the rare event that a letter arrived and would sit with him while he attempted to read it but if the "print was too small" she would read it to him. She loved words, thought of facts as her friends and the more she could internalise, the happier she was. She also liked to draw; "doodle" as her mother called it and to sew. Aunt Phily said this latter accomplishment would be useful as she made her way in life.

She walked down the open wooden staircase, out of the back door and across the yard. After going to the privy or "lavatory" her mother told her she should call it at the big house, she walked over to the water pump and washed her hands and then splashed water on her face.

This did not cause her to wince as the morning breeze was warm and welcoming; unlike in winter, when she could put off "visits" for hours on end rather than go out into the cold.

Her mother appeared in the kitchen of the cottage and waved to her as she walked back towards the door.

'How are you feeling, my lovely?' she asked as she put her arm around Lizzie's waist.

'I'm fine, Ma; don't worry; Aunt Phily will be there to look after me.'

'Don't forget you have to address her as "Miss Crittle" at the big house. She can only be "Aunt Phily" here. Even if you think you are alone, from my time in service, I can tell you walls-have-ears.' She tapped her nose cryptically as she studied Lizzie's appearance.

'Well at least that frock looks nice, although you will be given a uniform I'm sure, working in the laundry. We will set off in about an hour; it won't take us long to walk there.'

The big house was situated about two miles away and the cottage in which Lizzie and her family lived was in a row of terraced dwellings attached to the estate. It had two rooms downstairs, with two on the first floor and an attic where her four brothers slept. She and Rose shared the small room on the same floor as her parents.

Lizzie helped her mother prepare the porridge for breakfast as her brothers tumbled down the stairs. Rose appeared on the third time of calling.

'That child would sleep her life away if she could,' her father commented as he walked into the kitchen and sat down at the wooden table.

Lizzie didn't really listen to the chatter as they all sat round for breakfast. She was consumed with overwhelming sadness that this was not something she would ever be part of again, in future she would be a visitor.

Afterwards her father said that Rose could see to the washing up and silenced her with a look before she protested yet again that it wasn't fair that the boys never had to do it.

'Women's work,' her father had stated many a time.

Her mother got her comb from a vase that stood on the mantelpiece over the range and tugged it through Lizzie's long thick dark hair. She then weaved it into a single plait and secured it with her own blue ribbon.

'No, Ma; Dad got you that when he went to Tonbridge, it was a present, I can't take it.'

'You're right it was a present, so that makes it mine to do with as I wish and I choose to give it to you,' she whispered into Lizzie's ear as she held her gently by the shoulders.

After Lizzie collected her shawl and few possessions which were wrapped in brown paper, her father stood up from the table and awkwardly gave her a brief hug.

'Take care of yourself girl; know that we're all proud of you,' he mumbled almost inaudibly into his moustache.

She didn't want a fuss but they all came and stood outside of the cottage as she left, as did their immediate neighbours. Everyone called out their good wishes for Lizzie's future. She forced a smile but couldn't trust herself to say anything for fear that the bubble of emotion welling up inside her would burst from her body.

Mother and daughter walked in silence for much of the time, each submerged in their own thoughts. The tree-lined path was not unfamiliar; she had been to the grounds of the big house previously but only when there was an event to which all the estate workers were invited. She had never before been inside.

Just before they got to their destination her mother stopped and stood directly in front of her. 'Remember, Lizzie, you are a very special person; you are cherished more than you can ever know. My thoughts will be with you every single minute of every day, so you will never be alone.'

Rebekah then enveloped her firstborn in her arms and squeezed her until Lizzie thought her lungs would never be able to fill with air again. They parted without further words and wiped the tears from their eyes as they continued their walk.

As they approached, the building looked grand and imposing. It was brick built with windows on every side and several chimney pots sprouting up from the roof. They skirted round the front of the building and walked through the kitchen garden and yard to the back door.

Rebekah tapped lightly on the door and as if by magic it opened almost immediately. A liveried footman looked enquiringly at them both for a brief moment and then smiled at Rebekah.

'This is Lizzie Tester,' said Rebekah, 'she is expected and is to start as a laundry maid today.'

'Come in, Mrs Tester. You don't remember me do you?' said the footman as he opened the door wide enough for them to be admitted. 'I'm Horace and I used to be the pageboy.'

'Oh my word, Horace, it's wonderful to see you! You were so small but of course that was ages ago wasn't it? You have certainly done well, congratulations; you look splendid in your uniform.'

'I'm head footman now, Mrs Tester, and don't worry I'll keep an eye out for Lizzie. I remember you being very kind to me when you worked in the nursery and I was the lowest of the low.'

Rebekah seemed about to reply when a very important-looking lady appeared from the passageway leading off the back door. She was of average height and wore a black dress with a white lace collar. She had a gold locket round her neck and a huge bunch of keys suspended from the belt at her waist. She made a swishing and jangling noise as she walked. From her mother's previous description, Lizzie thought this must be the housekeeper.

'Hello, Mrs Luck,' said Rebekah deferentially, 'It's very nice to see you again.'

'Mrs Tester, good morning to you. This must be Lizzie, welcome to Westden Chase, Lizzie.'

'Thank you, Ma'am,' said Lizzie bobbing a curtsey.

'You may address me as Mrs Luck, you will save "Ma'am" for Lady Constance, your mistress, in the unlikely event that you meet her. Now we won't detain you, Mrs Tester, I'm sure you want to get back to that ever-growing brood of yours,' she said looking pointedly at Rebekah's midriff.

'Come along, Lizzie, let's get you settled,' she said briskly as she took Lizzie by the shoulders and tried to steer her away from her mother.

Lizzie wriggled free so that she and Rebekah could exchange the briefest of hugs. With that she was recaptured firmly by the imposing black figure and whisked along the passageway with her mother looking despondently after her.

Lizzie had never felt so forlorn and vulnerable in her life.

The passageway was painted cream at the top with dark brown below the dado rail and had cream skirting boards. As well as the swishing and jangling, Mrs Luck's footsteps echoed as she walked on the flagstone floor. She led Lizzie up two narrow flights of stairs to the top floor and turned to the left. This was the female staff quarters she was told. She would be sharing with Gertie, the kitchen maid. The room was small and under the eaves of the building. There was a double bed in the centre with a washstand to the left side. On the right there were two lines suspended from the wall, one for each of them to hang their clothes. There was also a chest of drawers for them to share. Lizzie would be allocated two uniforms and underwear to be changed weekly. She would also be given a pair of leather shoes.

'You're a lucky girl; in many large houses junior domestic employees have to sleep in the kitchen or under the stairs. Mr Knightley and her Ladyship are generous to their staff and committed their welfare,' announced the housekeeper proudly.

'Yes, Mrs Luck,' said Lizzie solemnly, feeling suitably grateful.

The housekeeper looked at her closely. Without warning, she lunged at Lizzie, pulling her plaited hair towards her. 'Lice! And I suspect fleas,' she stated firmly. 'We need to get that addressed before you infest the whole place.'

'Please, Miss; my family are clean. My Ma would never allow parasites,' Lizzie looked shocked at the suggestion.

If Mrs Luck was surprised that Lizzie would know such a word she gave no indication of it.

'One doesn't "allow parasites" you silly girl. They are endemic among people such as you,' she said grimly. 'Sally will attend to you, come with me.'

Sally turned out to be a "useful" or "helpful" maid who looked at Lizzie with disdain. After a brief discussion with Mrs Luck, she steered Lizzie towards the scullery and produced a jar from a cupboard. Armed with a bucket of water filled from a kettle on the range in the kitchen, a lemon, the mysterious jar, some vinegar and a comb, she marched Lizzie into the back yard and stood the bucket in the water trough.

Once Lizzie was in position over the trough, Sally added some of the contents of the jar to the warm water and without warning, plunged Lizzie's head into it; Lizzie screamed and tried to pull herself upright by putting her hands on the sides of the bucket for leverage but Sally's strong hands held her down. She looked through her wet hair in dismay as the treasured blue ribbon floated on the water, sodden and ruined. She was thrashing around for what seemed like an eternity when she heard a familiar voice.

The pressure from the hands that were pushing her head disappeared and she was able to stand up. She gasped for breath as her bedraggled hair dangled in front of her face and dripped down her back. Lizzie coughed and spluttered as she tried to wipe the water and tears from her eyes.

'It's alright, Sally, thank you; I will attend to this now, I think Mrs Reader wants you; she said you have a way with a milk jelly which is unparalleled, so please could you help her in the kitchen.'

'But, Miss Crittle, the new girl has head lice and probably fleas into the bargain; Mrs Luck said I was to de-louse her and put her clothes out for burning,' said Sally in justification of her actions.

'Don't worry, I think I can remember how to treat such problems; leave it to me I'll take care of her,' said the tall authoritative lady.

Sally marched off clearly none too pleased to have been dismissed. Philadelphia Crittle waited until Sally had entered the house and shut the door before putting her arms around her frightened niece and hugging her tightly as Lizzie sobbed silently.

'Aunt Phily, you'll get soaked; I mean, Miss Crittle.'

'Never mind, Lizzie, I'll dry out quick enough. Now we need to finish off your hair and don't worry about your clothes; I'll see to it they are not incinerated. Bessie in the laundry, whom you will be assisting, will be happy to treat your things for bugs.'

'But I don't have any bugs honestly; you know my Ma wouldn't allow it,' repeated Lizzie. Even her aunt thought she was infested!

'It isn't your fault you sleep on a palliasse mattress made of straw which harbours bedbugs, lice, fleas and all manner of things. The solution already applied to your hair is made up of baking soda and warm water. Next we need to comb it through, after that we will apply lemon and comb it again; after that cider vinegar will be the last application and you will have wonderful shiny clean hair.'

Philadelphia Crittle continued to work on Lizzie's hair as she talked in a low soothing voice. At the same time she unobtrusively retrieved the soggy blue ribbon from the bucket of water.

'After we have finished I will get the page boy, John, to bring some warm water to your bedroom and you can have a strip wash and put on one of your new uniforms; I will borrow the key from Mrs Luck and get what you need from the linen cupboard. I know it all seems strange now, Lizzie, but being in service is a good life; you will never be hungry or without a roof over your head. An intelligent girl like you will always be in demand for the skills you already possess and those I know you will learn.'

An hour and a half later, after washing and changing, Lizzie was taken down to the servants' hall by her aunt and left with Gertie to have dinner which was to be served at twelve thirty.

Her hopes were dashed when she suggested she would eat with her aunt, as Philadelphia advised her that the senior servants took their meals in another room, separate from the junior staff. However she promised to try to see her later in the day or the following day.

Horace the head footman sat at the top end of the table in the junior staff dining room and passed round the plates having cut a luscious smelling large pie into slices. Potatoes and turnips were placed in serving dishes in the centre of the table. Horace introduced Lizzie to the others with a pleasant smile and several nodded in her direction. She sat with Gertie at the bottom end, as befitted her status. The pie turned out to be some sort of fish which was tasty and filling. This was followed by currant dumplings with custard. Gertie whispered to Lizzie that the cook, Mrs Reader made dinner for the family and senior servants and her assistant Aggie, made their dinner.

Afterwards Sally the useful maid took Lizzie across the yard to the laundry room which was a medium-sized brick building with work tops on three sides accommodating various wooden tubs, washboards and handwringers. The fourth wall housed the brick built copper. Lizzie was pleased to see that she would not be required to heave the copper onto the range, as this one appeared to be a large cauldron under which a fire could be lit. Above them racks for drying the laundry were suspended from the ceiling.

'Bessie will be along in a minute. She doesn't live in; she goes home for dinner to check on her mother. How do you know Miss Crittle, she doesn't usually get involved with the junior staff?'

'Shall I wait here for Bessie? Is there anything I could be getting on with until she comes?' asked Lizzie ignoring Sally's question.

With that, a small round lady of middle age appeared in the doorway. She looked red in the face, sweating and breathing heavily, as she pushed her mousy brown hair streaked with grey away from her face.

'Sorry, Sally; me Ma was playing up a bit; didn't like the dinner I gave her. Hello, you must be Lizzie.'

'Yes, Miss,' said Lizzie.

'I'll leave you,' said Sally as she walked out of the door, clearly rather annoyed to be none the wiser regarding Lizzie's connection with Miss Crittle.

'Take no notice of that one; full of herself. A "useful" maid apparently! Useful my eye; work-shy more like and you don't need to call me "Miss" – I'm Bessie! I don't live in as I share with me Ma. We live in a grace and favour cottage about half a mile away. Ma used to be the laundry maid here before me but she's ailing these days so I need to keep an eye on her.'

'I hope I won't be a hindrance to you, Bessie,' said Lizzie sincerely.

'Of course you won't; I'll show you what you need to know. You will be doing the servants' washing to start with and then when you know what's what, well perhaps you can move on to the family's laundry.'

The rest of the day was taken up with Bessie showing Lizzie the ropes with regard the equipment, materials and methods used to tackle the ongoing fight against grime, dirt and stains.

Tea was taken at five thirty. This consisted of bread, cold mutton and cheese with homemade preserves. The tea was brewed and served and Lizzie was mindful not to accept seconds when asked if she would like more mutton or another cup of tea, lest this might come under the heading of "gluttony".

After tea there was mending to be done and the fact that Lizzie had just arrived clearly didn't excuse her from the task.

'Do you know how to sew, Lizzie?' asked Sally.

'My Ma taught me to do plain stitching as well as basic embroidery and I can learn other things if I'm shown,' offered Lizzie trying to appear keen.

'The senior servants look after the family's clothes and the housemaids do most other things but you have to pull your weight if you are to be employed here. You need to be able to turn sides to the middle; do you think you can do that?' Sally said without offering further explanation.

'Yes, that will be fine. If you show me which sheets you would like me to adapt; I can get on with it.'

Sally looked rather annoyed; clearly disappointed that she wouldn't be called upon to furnish an explanation regarding her rather cryptic comment but said nothing.

She gave Lizzie two sheets which were tired and worn in the centre. The middle of each sheet had to be cut out and the sides attached to each other thus making a useable, if somewhat smaller, sheet. These would be used for the servants' beds, being of no further use to the family. She had helped her mother with this task on many occasions and was grateful to be doing something familiar which would occupy both her hands and mind.

She hadn't seen Aunt Phily again but she hoped she might see her tomorrow, for she had heard from the chatter at the table, the family were shortly leaving for Highfields House. When she tentatively asked Gertie where that was, she was told it was the family's home in the north of the country. They would be leaving on Monday and staying for several weeks. As a lady's maid, Aunt Phily would be accompanying her mistress. Lizzie was terrified at the thought of being alone until she returned.

Horace sought her out before she went to bed to ask if she was settling in. He seemed nice and Lizzie hoped she could take him up on his promise to her mother to look out for her, particularly with Aunt Phily being so far away.

Gertie smiled at her as they climbed into bed. 'You'll be alright, Lizzie; Bessie's a good sort, she'll show you the ropes. Stay out of Sally's way as much as you can because she's unkind to new staff.'

'What is a "useful" maid?' Lizzie asked Gertie, as this had puzzled her all day.

'It's one who thinks she is too grand to get her hands dirty or speak to likes of us unless she has to! No, really it's a funny sort of position. She was a parlourmaid and now she is understudying Miss Crittle so that in time she can become a lady's maid. She's supposed to help out all over the house and run errands on behalf of the mistress. They tend to choose people who look smart and can talk proper. Maybe you will be a useful maid one day as you're tall and nice-looking and you know ever so many clever words. What was it you said to Sally; something about the sheet?'

'Oh you mean when I asked her if she would like me to "adapt" it; I wanted her to know I understood exactly what she meant. If I do ever become a useful maid, I'll make sure I'm nice to people. My Ma said; "if you can't be sweet be silent". I think that's a good philosophy,' said Lizzie as she smiled at her companion.

'Well I'll be jiggered! I've never heard of that before, fil … what? Please will you learn me some words so that I can talk like you?'

'I'll "teach" you anything I can. "Philosophy" in that context means "approach to life". I had a wonderful school teacher who used to lend me books to help widen my vocabulary. Words are wonderful things Gertie. What time do we need to get up?'

'The family don't rise until eight-fifteen. The senior servants are up by seven but it's four thirty for the likes of us, Lizzie, my love!'

Lizzie settled down into bed and wondered what the coming days would bring. She felt she had made a friend in Gertie and hoped she could do her job well and not let her parents down.

When she looked back later in life she realised this was the first time she had heard mention of Highfields. Little could she possibly realise what a fundamental part that place would play in her future.

Chapter 2 – Consolidation

May 1879 - January 1887

Almost two years had passed since Lizzie entered service. For the most part her life had been uneventful. She had completed eighteen months in the laundry under the tutelage of Bessie.

After her initial training, they had fallen into a comfortable routine with Lizzie sorting the laundry and, once it was established that her reading and writing far outstripped anything Bessie could manage, she entered each item into a wash-book so that they could be checked off after washing, drying, ironing and airing. When each item had four ticks it was returned to the linen cupboard and once again became the responsibility of Mrs Luck who kept everything under lock and key.

When she first arrived all the linen and garments had symbols sewn into them. As she gained in confidence Lizzie suggested it might be easier if they embroidered individual names into the garments and colour coding for the linen to denote if it belonged to the family or staff. Bessie at first looked uncertain;

'How the Dickens will I know which is which?' she bewailed.

But when she saw how Lizzie could embroider she came round quickly, particularly when Lizzie also gave her word associations to recognise the letters which made up each name.

The third day she had been at Westden, she realised that horror heaped on horror, Horace had left with the family for Highfields House in the Lake District along with Phily! She had hoped he would be there to look out for her but now what was she to do? As it transpired, it was all rather fortuitous as with the family and lots of the servants absent, she and Bessie did not have so much pressure to get the laundry turned round in a few days.

'We take the chance when the family's away to have a good sort through the linen and wash the antimacassars, curtaining and nets. We also wash all the bolster pillow cases which again don't get done as a rule.'

It seemed this was a common theme at Westden, as the remaining maids also took the opportunity available to give the house a good deep clean, which was not possible with people living in it all the time. These tasks were all completed under the ever watchful eye of Mrs Luck, whom it seemed missed nothing.

Lizzie had been a willing pupil and had quickly understood the processes needed to successfully run the laundry function at Westden Chase. She attacked each allocated task with vim and verve, sometimes a little too enthusiastically. Inevitably this led to a few blunders in the early days and getting streaks of blue dye on the whites was probably the biggest fundamental error of which Lizzie was guilty.

'Oh lummy,' Bessie had wailed when she had seen it and tutted at Lizzie but in a kindly way.

However, being an old hand, her mentor made sure Lizzie did not launder anything of importance until she was confident Lizzie had become competent in each area; what Bessie lacked in literacy, she made up for with her abundant knowledge of fabric care.

As time went by, they forged a strong friendship and made an impressive team. Lizzie noticed that some of the other servants made fun of Bessie at times because she appeared a little slow on the uptake. Lizzie became her staunchest supporter and strongest advocate. She soon silenced the mockers with her able use of syntax and lexicon so that it was they themselves that ended up looking foolish. She delighted at the look of joy on Bessie's face whenever she stood up for her; over time Lizzie noticed it happened less and less and then not at all.

During the summer months the job was made easier by the warm, drier weather. In the winter the task of getting washing dry was well-nigh impossible. The warmth from the fire under the copper only served to add to the condensation. There were days on end when the walls teemed with water and though the laundry was clean it was far from dry and aired when it was returned to Mrs Luck.

'Don't worry, lovey,' said Bessie, 'everything gets aired in front of the fire before it's used. They know we can't do aught about the weather.'

It wasn't just the laundry that was damp; it seemed to Lizzie that she went for weeks without being completely dry herself. Her hair frizzed up each day as a result of the water vapour in the air and it was still damp when she went to bed in the evening, such that she shivered herself to sleep many a night.

Occasionally she managed to get close enough to the fire in the servants' hall to dry her hair but then it ended up smelling of smoke and when she went to bed, her pillowcase got caked in grime and started to smell.

Her clothes never dried out and she flinched each morning when she had to get dressed with the feel of the cold damp material against her skin. Thankfully she had a strong constitution and did not succumb to coughs and chills, though she looked forward in eager anticipation to the warmer weather to come in the spring.

She was entitled to one afternoon off a fortnight and one Sunday a month.

On one such occasion, Bessie had invited Lizzie to tea to meet her mother. Mrs Kemp had given her a warm welcome and the visits became a regular occurrence. Lizzie also visited her former teacher, Mr Hawes at his invitation. He had told her when she left school that she would be welcome to go to his home and borrow books and discuss any questions her enquiring mind was bound to throw up.

'Just because you are no longer at school Lizzie, doesn't mean you will stop learning. Someone such as you with a thirst for knowledge will continue to absorb information until the day you die and I hope to steer you in the right direction for as long as possible.'

Lizzie also visited her parents' cottage to see her family. Rebekah had given birth to another boy, Harold, who was now over a year old. This time however she hadn't recovered from her confinement as she usually did. She still looked tired and drawn and was wan and lethargic. If Lizzie was honest, she was worried about her. She had spoken to her father who told her to stop fussing, her mother was as strong as an ox but Phily clearly shared her concern and made extra visits to the cottage when she could, to help out. The social visits to Mrs Kemp and Mr Hawes had to be put on hold when it became clear that her mother needed more support to look after the family.

If they could organise it, Phily and Lizzie visited together so that Rebekah managed to have several hours' respite. She could give the house a lick-and-a-promise until her sister and daughter visited, safe in the knowledge that they would give the place a thorough clean every couple of weeks. Phily and Lizzie cooked, cleaned and changed the beds. Lizzie was now a dab hand at stain removal, using the copper and managing the wringer.

Rose was chivvied into helping out more however, as Philadelphia said quietly to her sister on one visit; 'she's clearly not cut from the same cloth as Lizzie, is she?' Rebekah shook her head sadly with a small ironic smile. Lizzie didn't think she was supposed to have heard that and said nothing. Nonetheless it was a curious remark.

As was often the case in the world of service, vacancies opened up in various areas of the house as maids moved on to gain promotion. It was common practice for servants to stay anywhere from a few months to a couple of years in each situation. So it was, when a vacancy arose, Lizzie came to be offered a job as an under-house parlourmaid. It was impressed upon her that the duties would be just as arduous and the hours as long but Lizzie's bright nature and freshness of spirit were not lost on the senior servants. Mrs Luck the housekeeper and Mrs Reader the cook had apparently confided in Philadelphia that they were both of the opinion that if things panned out, Lizzie could potentially be trained as a lady's maid in years to come. Firstly, though, at the age of fifteen she would need to continue to learn her trade by working her way up over the next few years. Not for her the opportunity to move on to a better position at another house as she would not leave her mother until her health improved.

'To be honest, Mrs Reader, I'm worried about my sister, what she clearly doesn't need is another pregnancy,' confided Philadelphia in hushed tones one afternoon when she and the cook were having a cup of tea together. Lizzie remained out of sight and fervently hoped her aunt was speaking hypothetically and that Rebekah was not with child again. Surely her body couldn't withstand another confinement? She made up her mind to ask her mother about it next time she was home; after all she was an adult now.

In the meantime, Lizzie was slowly getting to grips with the duties of an under-house parlourmaid. It was clearly preferable to work in the house rather than the laundry however she still rose at four thirty and undertook some of the more physically demanding tasks.

She cleaned the fireplaces daily, along with the fenders and irons. The emery paper she had to use on the rust spots ripped her fingernails to shreds within days

33

and she found herself wondering more than once if she had made the right decision to leave the security and safety of the laundry room. She missed Bessie's gentle kindness and her company and took every opportunity to pop into the laundry to say hello after trips to the privy, or rather, lavatory.

Thankfully she did not have to clean the range as that was the domain of the kitchen maids; however she did have to black-lead the fireplaces with a paste-like substance which was an extremely messy process. Many a day she had to change her apron before she could resume her duties. This done, she then swept the rooms. It was common practice to use cold tealeaves on the rugs and carpets as this trapped the dust which could then be swept away and burned in the range. She used cold tea on the windows as well as vinegar and these were cleaned once weekly, one room at a time.

On balance, Lizzie thought her position was preferable to that of the chambermaids, although sometimes she and her colleagues were expected to assist them, particularly if there was a house party in residence. On those occasions it meant getting up even earlier.

After laying the fires ready for the family and their guests in the reception rooms, Lizzie went upstairs to help the chambermaids with the additional bedrooms. Once these were vacated, the slops needed to be emptied. There was a housemaid's sluice cupboard on the landing that led to the family's quarters. This contained a high mounted lead-lined sink. When empty, chamber pots, or "sanitary-ware" as they were tactfully called, were rinsed with warm water and soda. After returning them to their cupboards in each bedroom, the beds needed to be aired and then changed or made up. She also lent a hand once a month when the mattresses needed turning.

They were fortunate at Westden to have the services of a page boy which meant the chambermaids did not have to carry coal for the fires or water for the family's ablutions. As time went by, they had what Mr Hemsley the butler referred to as "new-fangled pipework" installed with running water which meant that there was no need to lug heavy buckets of water to and from the rooms for bathing. They also had flushing sanitary-ware installed for the family and later in the privy – lavatory – in the yard for the servants.

She no longer had to spend her afternoons and evenings engaged in turning "sides to the middle"; now that she was working in the house, she graduated to the mending of clothes. When her dexterity came to Mrs Luck's attention, she was tasked with turning shirt collars as well as cuffs on the servants' uniforms. Aunt Phily undertook all the mending and goffering for her Ladyship but as time progressed, Lizzie was given some of the less complex sewing for the family.

During the morning, prior to any visits by callers, Lizzie or one of the other under-house parlourmaids had to sweep and scrub the front steps. This required the use of a bleaching agent, whitening and pipe-clay which made Lizzie's hands rough and sore. For that reason she hated the task but took her turn as was expected. Once the mixture was dry it had to be rubbed off and then brushed. Her knees ached from the continuing toil but she knew she was more fortunate than many to have a secure job, a roof over her head and food to eat. In fact so good was her nutrition that she gained several inches in height and her figure filled out to fulfil its flattering potential.

Lizzie in her lowly station was not supposed to be seen by the family so she needed to make sure she was not sweeping the main staircase when any of them descended for breakfast. Should she hear someone coming she needed to exit via the nearest backstairs door. If there was not time for this, she must face the wall and make no sound, presumably in the hope that she would look like part of the pattern on the wallpaper or a hat-stand.

She had never seen any of the family until she started to work inside the big house. All the time she was in the laundry, she only saw the carriages clattering along the cinder drive leading to the house but never the occupants.

However her acquaintanceship with her employers increased significantly in the winter of 1881 during an outbreak of smallpox. Several of the staff succumbed to the infection but mercifully in no case did it prove fatal. Aunt Phily became ill but her condition manifested like an episode of mild influenza and she only had a handful of pustules. Sally the useful maid saw her opportunity and stepped into Phily's shoes with unedifying delight.

Lizzie in the meantime was deputising for the parlourmaid and, in the absence of the ailing butler, showed guests into the morning or drawing room, depending on the time of day. In addition she was assisting Mrs Reader in the kitchen. The family curtailed their entertaining during this time, as did many other households, so it was a question of keeping the house running until things returned to normal. True to her reputation of having an iron constitution, Lizzie didn't as much as sneeze during the whole episode.

Some of the servants blamed the outbreak on "drains". The instillation of running water in the house was thought to be the source of all ills.

'Miasma,' said Sam the new page-boy, John having been promoted to the position of junior footman. 'That's what my grandad says.'

'That was a popular theory in bygone days, Sam,' opined Horace, 'however I think it is commonly agreed now that germs spread disease. Waterborne illnesses are transferred by the water itself and not the smell coming from it.' He looked very pleased with himself as he glanced towards Lizzie.

Lizzie nodded approvingly in his direction. They had formed a close friendship over the years she had been at Westden Chase. He was soon to leave his position of head footman as he had gained a promotion and was to take up the duties of butler to a wealthy family in Sevenoaks. She would miss him tremendously but understood his desire to better himself. If it had not been for her mother's health, she too might be on the look-out for another situation.

Rebekah had indeed been with child again but had miscarried at the end of her first trimester. On one of their regular visits, Phily had taken her brother-in-law Fred firmly by the arm and led him outside. Lizzie managed to position herself by the window so that she could hear as Philadelphia told him she held him entirely responsible for this situation and if he knew what was good for him, he would ensure that such an event never occurred again. If he did not, she was confident he would be widowed within the year. Clearly he took this to heart as although her mother remained weak, she never again fell pregnant.

Lizzie found herself thinking about her parents as she sat in the yard outside the laundry room one evening just after the smallpox outbreak was over. Horace broke into her chain of thought as he sought her out. After asking her permission, he sat down next to her on the bench.

'I'm pleased to have found you, Lizzie, as there's something I would like to ask you,' he said hesitantly.

'Really, what's that?' Lizzie asked enquiringly.

He suddenly stood and looked rather awkward.

'Well I'll come straight to the point; we get on very well don't we? As you know, I'm to take up my new position shortly and to be frank I wondered if you would consider doing me the privilege of coming with me, as my wife I mean. As butler I will have my own quarters and you would not be expected to undertake any heavy duties; in fact when the children arrive, you wouldn't be asked to do anything at all. My new employer is very enlightened and feels employing a married man is desirable as he will be more likely to stay put.'

Lizzie looked up at Horace in stunned silence. Marriage and children; looking like her mother within ten years. To be fair, maybe not that bad as Horace, or Mr Blackford as he would be when he took up his new situation, would certainly be a better provider than her father. However, at seventeen, the thought of such a life was not one that filled her with joy.

She called upon all her skills of articulation as she formulated a gentle rebuttal of his proposal. She too rose and addressed him; she was as tall as him and looked him straight in the eye.

'Horace, I have to say that I am truly taken aback by this turn of events; in my wildest dreams I never for a moment thought that you would consider me as an equal and choose to bestow me with such an honour. If I were a little older I would be delighted to consider your proposal but in truth, I fear my inexperience and youth would be disadvantageous as you make your way in the world. I could never forgive myself if my very presence was to prove a burden and prevent you from further forwarding your career.' Lizzie opened her eyes very wide and hoped she looked convincing.

He spent several minutes trying to get Lizzie to change her mind. Her deft responses were equal to his appeals and eventually he accepted the inevitable.

'My dear girl, only you could be so selfless. Maybe in a year or so …'

'I could not possibly ask you to make such a sacrifice on my behalf. You must follow your destiny, Horace. Please feel free to leave here without the weight of a promise to me. Now I'm feeling chilled, I need to return inside before the cold gets right into my bones but thank you, my dear friend for caring about me so much.'

So it was that Lizzie turned down her first proposal of marriage. She wondered later in life if she had accepted Horace how differently things would have turned out.

As it was, a month later Horace Blackford left Westden Chase accompanied by Phoebe the parlourmaid who was to become Mrs Blackford prior to Horace taking up his new position. Lizzie felt a little peeved that she was so easily replaced in his affections but accepted that maybe it was the need for a spouse that had driven the proposal rather than any deep affection for either herself or Phoebe.

Fortuitously this paved the way for a vacancy as a parlourmaid for which Lizzie applied and was duly offered. There was a little muttering that an under-house parlourmaid should make such a leap in such a short time but she had more than acquitted herself during the smallpox outbreak.

She easily adapted to the task of greeting visitors when Mr Hemsley the butler was otherwise engaged. She sometimes had to make the decision whether a caller should be announced as a guest to her Ladyship or if it was a non-social caller such as a seamstress. She then needed to politely leave the caller sitting on a chair in the hall while she informed her mistress of the arrival without causing offence. She also had to decide whether or not to take the visitor's outer garments. This also denoted the importance of the caller. Those of lower standing were not relieved of their vestments. Having been a parlourmaid herself, Phily was a source of great knowledge and advice regarding this and Lizzie called upon her experience many times.

She was now in receipt of eighteen pounds per year and under her white apron, wore a cotton print or plain woollen dress in the mornings, depending on the season and in the afternoons, changed into a black dress with white collar and cuffs. She wore her thick dark hair in a tight bun tucked under a small white cap with ribbons down the back. She had maintained her reputation for hard work and knew her colleagues held her in high regard.

By now she was able to put a name to each of the family and had even been spoken to by some of them. Lady Constance was the daughter of the sixth Earl Kingsbury and the wife of Mr Herbert Knightley whose family had made their money in merchant banking and Mr Knightley himself was now an MP sitting in the House of Commons. His uncles were firmly in control of the banking business and endowments from this furnished Herbert Knightley with a handsome income each year. This contrasted significantly with many old established families who found their finances dwindling and their estates having to be reduced or sold off altogether to keep the bailiffs at bay.

The fortunes of the Knightley family on the other hand rose steadily and so it was that they had been able to move from their first home, a villa near St John's Wood in the north west of London, to Westden Chase, a moderately sized Georgian mansion near Tonbridge in Kent.

They had been blessed with four children. Lizzie's mother Rebekah had been a nursery maid to the two oldest girls, Miss Prudence and Miss Anna. Both had married into well-established families and no longer formed part of the household. Mr Donald was the son and heir and currently a bit of a tear-away and Miss Sophia was the youngest child.

Lizzie continually marvelled at the amount of possessions the family owned. Furniture was crammed into every available space, nowhere more so than in the drawing room, which was located on the first floor. It was the grandest room in the house with panelled walls encrusted with gold beading. The wallpaper itself was deep red in colour and had a raised flowery pattern stamped on it. The curtains were of a similar colour with blinds fitted into each window. Everywhere a dust trap, Lizzie thought grimly. There were three sofas, two ottomans, several upright chairs to accommodate the ladies with their full skirts, bustles and crinolines and lower easy chairs for the gentlemen, six stools, two occasional tables, two bookcases and a piano, with every surface covered in knickknacks and ornaments. However, it was the photographs that intrigued Lizzie in particular.

There were likenesses of Lady Constance's mother and father, the earl and countess, riding and playing tennis as well as more formal portraits. In addition, on another table, there were some of the master's family; in one they were enjoying a picnic and in another Mr Herbert Knightley was standing in formal pose behind his parents, with his younger brother who now lived abroad, next to him. There were also photographs of the children at various ages and Lady Constance and her sister Lady Nora as girls.

Lady Nora lived with them permanently now. She had stayed intermittently for many years but after the death of their father, she made her home with her sister and family. She was a semi-invalid with a hip problem. Lizzie had heard that her legs were different lengths which made walking difficult; poor thing. She managed quite well indoors but used a wheelchair when she wanted to go out. She had a footman allocated for her personal use. He was of strong disposition and carried her to her room each evening. She declined the use of a downstairs bedroom, as she hated to be stigmatised and defined by her condition. Lizzie admired that. She had spoken directly to Lizzie on two occasions and seemed to study her closely if their paths crossed.

Lizzie's new role was physically less arduous as there were now others to fulfil her previous duties but nonetheless her days were still full. Everything had to be dusted each day. Any stains from the lamps had to be cleaned and it was her duty to ensure that each room was ready for the family to enter at any time.

Life carried on in uneventful fashion for the following few years; Lizzie accepted the status quo and tended not to think too far ahead, as her main priority remained her mother's delicate health.

However her situation changed on a cold January morning in 1885 when Lizzie was called to Mrs Luck's private sitting room and offered tea; a privilege indeed.

'Are you happy here, Lizzie?' Mrs Luck enquired as she sat down opposite Lizzie, jangling as she did so.

'Yes thank you, Mrs Luck; I have everything I need,' replied Lizzie, appropriately.

'As you know Sally has now left us and we have a vacancy for a useful maid. You have always shown yourself to be a helpful girl and Lady Constance is particularly pleased with you. We would therefore like to offer you this position with a view to becoming a lady's maid in the future.'

Lizzie absorbed this information solemnly. This would be a very good opportunity for her; she would get the chance to run errands on behalf of the cook, housekeeper and butler, as well as get a fuller understanding of the running of the whole house. In years to come, she would possibly get the opportunity to become a housekeeper such as Mrs Luck.

Of course if that should be the case she would be addressed as Mrs Tester. "Mrs" was an honorary title bestowed on cooks and housekeepers when in truth very few were married. Mrs Luck certainly wasn't; Lizzie found herself wondering if there was actually any man alive who would be equal to the task of standing up to her but doubted it, even Mr Hemsley the butler kept out of her way. She brought her thoughts back to the present and hoped that she had taken enough notice to be able to undertake her new role.

It soon became apparent that being a useful maid suited Lizzie down to the ground. She had twenty pounds a year, a new uniform and most importantly was learning transferrable skills which might not be of use now but in time, when she was no longer bound to stay in the area, she could look for a suitable situation. There were advertisements in the newspapers every week for lady's maids and housekeepers; but not while her mother needed her.

In particular she enjoyed the days when she was travelling in the carriage as Miss Sophia's chaperone. In fact she was only a few years older than Sophia Knightley but their upbringings had been so diverse that she felt many years her senior. The youngest child in the Knightley family had been cossetted all her life and had never learned to do anything for herself. The plan was for her to "come out" for a season in the hope of attracting a suitable husband. Miss Sophia told her that if this went to plan, Lizzie would accompany her to her new home as her personal maid. Lizzie explained about her mother but Sophia dismissed her concerns in an instant.

'Lizzie, I always get what I want, Papa makes it happen, so whatever the situation with your family, Papa will make it right. He will give them money or something or maybe send someone to the cottage to help out. If I want to take you with me then that is what is going to happen, so there's an end to it.'

Lizzie remembered thinking how simple life was when one was born into the upper echelons of society; how different things would be for Miss Sophia if her family were not wealthy. Not for the first time Lizzie pondered the inequalities of life.

Whilst there were several suitors, none were quite to Sophia's liking; until she met Joshua Montgomery. Mr Montgomery was a very presentable young gentleman whose family had made their money from journalism. Mr Hemsley said haughtily they were "nouveau riche" and not "old money" as would be preferred. However, when Miss Sophia had made up her mind, she would not be swayed. If the family had any doubts about the match, they kept it to themselves. All was going swimmingly with the engagement announced and the marriage planned for the following March.

Lizzie was to go with Sophia to her new home in Orpington which would mean that she could still visit her mother regularly, as Sophia had decreed that a carriage would be made available for Lizzie on her day off each week.

Six weeks before the wedding disaster struck when Joshua Montgomery was found dead near the railway line between Tonbridge and Tunbridge Wells. He had been playing cards the previous evening with some friends at a private gathering in Southborough and he had left to return home to his lodgings on the outskirts of High Brooms. He had lost at the poker table and had been drinking heavily. It was later revealed that his gambling debts were substantial.

Embarrassment compounded tragedy three days later for both the Montgomery and Knightley families, when a rather brassy-looking woman calling herself Mrs Montgomery arrived on the doorstep of the Montgomery family home in Chislehurst. Their housekeeper was heard to refer to the poor unfortunate creature as a slattern.

The coroner recorded a verdict of accidental death in the case of Mr Joshua Montgomery.

Sophia's humiliation was complete when it was discovered that, unbeknown to his family, her intended had been living openly with his common-law wife and child. Finally pecuniary circumstances had led him to adhere to his parents' wishes to marry his way out of potential financial ruin.

After days of refusing to come out of her room, Sophia had asked her father if she could spend some time at their holiday home in the Lake District to get away from the scandal. This was agreed but only if Lady Nora accompanied her, as it wasn't fitting for a young lady to be travelling alone, albeit with her maid. A fortnight later they were on their way.

And so it was that Lizzie first visited the Lake District with its breath-taking scenery. She was awestruck by what she saw. She couldn't possibly know what life in this seemingly idyllic place would throw at her in the coming years.

Chapter 3 – Highfields House

February 1887

If she felt resentful at being asked to accompany her niece to the family holiday home in the Lake District, Lady Nora Kingsbury gave no sign as she sat in the first class carriage of the train that was speeding them on their way.

Life was not easy for someone in her situation. She was the daughter of a peer but without much of a dowry. However that had not stopped her elder sister Constance marrying well but Constance had one advantage, she was not crippled.

In fact, for anyone that was interested, Nora's legs were the same length, she knew because she had measured them. It was her hips that were out of alignment. "Asymmetrical" was the word the doctor used when he told her mother it was unlikely she would ever walk. Well she had proved them all wrong. It was ungainly that was true but she could get along under her own steam, after a fashion.

Of course the fact that she was an invalid meant that she was treated differently. "Not quite the ticket," her father had said quietly when describing her to a friend. No coming out ball for her. Sometimes she was taken along, presumably out of pity, so that she could sit at the back and watch as the other young people laughed and danced and flirted. No-one took much notice of her. Well almost no-one. For a time she had wanted to shout at them; "I'm the same as you; I have feelings, I can converse, play the piano, embroider, speak French ..." but no-one was listening. Well almost no-one.

The years passed and as Nora got older, she went to stay with married friends and acquaintances and often spent time with Constance and her growing family. Constance had been the golden child; the favoured daughter. She was bright, intelligent, vivacious, captivating and above all physically fit and strong; woe-betide anyone who fell short of perfection in the Kingsbury family. "Put her away" had been the advice when Nora was a child and it became clear her disability was not something she would grow out of. However her mother had flatly refused to give up on her second child and kept her at home, adapting the nursery and school room to accommodate her needs.

Their mother had died when she was seven and her father professed himself broken-hearted. Clearly this grief-stricken state was quickly outweighed by the need for a male heir as he remarried within two years and her half-brother Hugh was born a year later. Her father subsequently died when she was twenty-eight and her half-brother inherited almost everything. In common with a lot of the aristocracy of the time, Hugh's mother had found him a rich American bride whose family bought her the title of countess in exchange for a substantial dowry; clearly not a coincidence when one of the oldest families in the country was facing financial ruin as a result of an extravagant lifestyle and poor investments.

When Hugh married at the age of twenty-one, he had said Nora could remain at the house but it was clear that Mathilda, her new sister-in-law along with her step-mother the dowager countess, were having none of it. They could just about tolerate each other as they had no choice but they both drew the line at the half-sister being in residence too. They decided Nora would be far more comfortable in a small cottage near the gatehouse. So it became clear that to maintain any dignity at all, she had no choice but to leave the family home in which she had been born and throw herself on the mercy of her sister.

Constance had been kind, thoughtful and accommodating but at the same time rather patronising and condescending. Nora was made fully aware that she was not quite her sister's social equal. When they entertained, people were polite to "poor Nora" as she had heard herself described on one occasion. Herbert was civil; he was never unkind, just indifferent. He was consumed with his work and left all the domestic arrangements to Constance. Therefore, if Constance asked Nora to accompany Sophia to the Lake District, she actually had no real choice in the matter.

As it was, she went willingly. The lakes held a secret for her, one which she shared with someone special and she would see him soon.

Her disability meant nothing to him. He cared for her just the way she was and she him. She hoped he would be there when she arrived. The journey seemed to be taking an age but they were nearing Keswick and a carriage would meet them to complete their journey to the small hamlet of Rowendale. The family retainers, Mr and Mrs Field, were aware that they were on their way and a cold supper would be waiting for them. Yes, this trip really was the answer to her prayers.

*

Back in a third class carriage, Lizzie and Lady Nora's footman George sat facing each other. George had travelled this route before but normally in the company of a whole host of other servants when the family went on retreat to Cumberland. With only Lizzie for company he appeared ill at ease and slightly uncomfortable. He wore the livery of a footman, covered with a good quality top coat and bowler hat. Lizzie thought he looked very smart and could see why several of the female servants at Westden Chase were smitten.

For her part, Lizzie's only brief encounter with affairs of the heart had been the proposal by Horace the head footman. For this she was extremely grateful, as she had firmly decided she wanted to control her own life and not be the chattel of any man. Clearly her very presence had rendered her travelling companion speechless as he had hardly said a word all journey. Very different to when he was holding audience in the servants' hall at Westden.

As they travelled north Lizzie found herself worrying about how her mother would cope without her. She had Philadelphia of course but she understood they would be away for at least a month or until Miss Sophia felt able to hold her head up in society again. Currently she declared her life "over" and "wished she was dead".

Lizzie felt a little disappointed to be going away, as she would miss the hustle and bustle of Westden when the family were entertaining. With Mr Knightley being an MP there was a myriad of social gatherings which he and Lady Constance attended and many invitations sent out in reciprocation.

Lizzie had been rather hastily advanced to the position of assistant lady's maid a few weeks previously, prompted by the situation which had arisen as a result of the "Montgomery Scandal", as the servants had taken to calling it. It seemed only Lizzie could manage Miss Sophia in the aftermath. So grateful was Lady Constance to have a buffer between herself and her irate and self-absorbed youngest daughter that promoting a servant was a small price to pay.

In reality even whilst she was still classified as a "useful" maid, Lizzie had been performing the duties of a lady's maid for months as Miss Hill, the personal maid who looked after Miss Sophia and Lady Nora, was in poor health. As she was nearing retirement it was decided the trip north would be too arduous and it was to be Lizzie that accompanied the ladies to Highfields House.

She was now in receipt of an annual salary of twenty-three pounds. She had the natural advantages of height and deportment and she was intelligent with a good command of English. Even so, she was an eager pupil and readily absorbed all that her aunt could teach her. She had just started taking her meals in the upper servants' dining hall and was waited on by the junior staff as befitted her status, which was still rather strange.

She enjoyed the challenges that looking after two such diverse ladies brought. Sophia was self-centred but not too difficult to manage, if one knew how to handle her. Lady Nora on the other hand was an enigma. She was compliant with the family's wishes on the surface but Lizzie felt somehow she kept her real personality hidden. It was almost as if she were an actress playing a part.

She had questioned Aunt Phily about Lady Nora's disability. Apparently it was something she was born with and incurable. She found herself wondering if Lady Nora could actually do more for herself than she chose, as on more than one occasion Lizzie had entered her room to find that Lady Nora had managed to get a garment out of the wardrobe by herself, when the hanging rail was supposedly out of her reach.

George had told her that Lady Nora spent hours by herself in the wood at Highfields, the family's home near Rowendale. Lizzie wondered what on earth she found to do there as she chose to go at all times of the day and evening. George left her on a path about a quarter of a mile into the thickest part of the wood and always collected her from the same place, usually after about two hours.

'So where does she go after you leave her, George?' enquired Lizzie on one occasion.

'She just wheels herself round for a bit I suppose. She said she likes to think and the wood is the only place she feels at peace. Can't begrudge her that can we, poor thing,' George had said but without too much interest.

'Have you ever followed her to see what she does?'

'What? No of course I haven't; none of my business is it? Besides, she often goes about lunchtime so I manage to slip off to the Blenny for a quick half.'

The Blenny was apparently the name the locals used for the Blenthorne Inn which was the only hostelry for miles around. Not that it was something that bothered Lizzie in the slightest, alcohol held no interest for her and her beer allocation always remained untouched.

Lizzie was looking forward to seeing the house for the first time. She understood that Mr and Mrs Field would be opening up some rooms for their use over the next few weeks but it would be nothing like the normal visits that the family made in late-July to late-September, and at Easter.

Philadelphia had told her there weren't as many rooms as Westden but then as it was only a holiday home that was to be expected.

Apparently there was a drawing room, a dining room and a morning room. In addition there was also a billiard room and a small library which doubled as a study. The family and guest bedrooms were on the first floor and the servants slept on the top floor. Entertaining was kept to a minimum but there would be the occasional weekend party, usually during September for partridge and grouse shooting.

Mr and Mrs Field lived in and when the family were in residence, several servants were drafted in from the local area. This and the servants that accompanied the family, including the butler and cook, made up a full complement to staff the house.

With only Lady Nora and Miss Sophia on this trip they would need no more than three additional girls from the village who would not live in. George would assist Mr Field with any manual tasks and Lizzie would help Mrs Field in the kitchen if needed. She was grateful for this opportunity as her culinary skills were her one weakness. If she was to be a successful housekeeper in years to come, she would need a full understanding of every aspect involved in running a large establishment, otherwise a cunning cook would run rings round her.

Lizzie spent the early part of the trip going to and from the first class carriage at every stop, as Miss Sophia found a hundred and one things she needed but she fell asleep by the time they reached Birmingham and Lady Nora seemed lost in her own thoughts. The remainder of the journey was relatively peaceful for Lizzie and she herself dropped off until she was gently shaken by the shoulder as they neared Keswick.

'Wake up, Miss Tester, we're only one stop from Keswick; no doubt Miss Sophia will want to look her best for alighting from the train, even if she has got a broken heart.'

Lizzie ignored the sarcastic comment. If truth be told she was still getting used to being addressed so formally; she had been "Lizzie" at Westden from the time she started there in the laundry. She had asked her aunt if it would be appropriate to tell the servants to continue to call her by her Christian name but Phily had been resolute in her answer. Standards had to be maintained and "familiarity bred contempt". Well far be it from her to breed anything, so "Miss Tester" it was. She straightened her uniform and flattened her thick hair which often had a mind of its own as she alighted from the carriage and once again made her way along the platform to her mistresses in first class.

*

Two hours later, having settled the ladies and loaded the luggage aboard the carriage, they rattled along to their destination. Protocol had been suspended for practicality and it was decided as there were only four of them in total, it was an unnecessary extravagance to send two carriages to meet the party just so that the family and servants could travel separately.

Lizzie and George had faced the two ladies during the journey. Lizzie thought Miss Sophia seemed very quiet whereas Lady Nora seemed quite excited and looked a little flushed.

It was twilight when they reached Highfields House. Lady Nora smiled when the house came into view. Miss Sophia glanced out of the window with disinterest. George had seen the place before so didn't even bother to look. Lizzie on the other hand took in everything as she peered towards the house. Without warning, she felt a small involuntary shiver pass through her and couldn't understand why.

The building was made of stone and was approx.-imately two thirds of the size of Westden. It looked imposing at it stood in the fading light against the backdrop of the distant fells.

The entrance was quite grand with pillars to each side of the porch and the building looked symmetrical at first glance. As the carriage approached, two people appeared from inside the front door. This would be Mr and Mrs Field, Lizzie surmised.

George jumped out as soon as the carriage stopped and helped Miss Sophia down first. A wheelchair was waiting for Lady Nora at the left side of the front door and George deftly and with a minimum of fuss transferred his mistress from the carriage to her chair. Lizzie brought up the rear.

Mr and Mrs Field greeted both ladies with deferential respect. As she was now senior in rank to George, Lizzie introduced herself after she alighted from the carriage. They all filtered into the hall with Mr Field enquiring as to the journey. Lizzie assured him it had been uneventful and followed as Mrs Field led the way upstairs.

The hallway was large and quite dark with a central mahogany table on which stood a vase of dried flowers. The floor was made up of flagstones with a patterned rug underneath the table. Lizzie well remembered when it would have been her job to be up before five in the morning scrubbing such a floor at Westden.

There was a long vertical mirror on the right hand wall with a table in front of it upon which stood a large brass bowl containing an aspidistra, along with a brass salver for any letters or personal cards. A dado rail divided the walls, under which was dark wood panelling. Above was heavy-looking brocade damask wallpaper. There were windows to both sides of the front door with a chair in front of the one on the left. This would be for guests of indeterminate class. Presumably it would be Mr Field as senior male servant in the absence of Mr Hemsley to decide if a caller should be introduced to the family. The hallway seemed to head off in different directions, presumably with doors situated along it leading to the reception rooms. At the end of the hallway a passage disappeared towards the back of the house which in the normal planning of things, would lead downstairs to the servants' hall and kitchen.

Framed pictures were hung from a rail, presumably of relatives of Lady Constance and Lady Nora, as the house had been in their mother's family for generations, prior to being bought by Mr Knightley from his brother-in-law when the earl needed to free up some capital. The hallway was dimly lit by wall lighting and a chandelier suspended from the ceiling. Lizzie again shivered.

The staircase was also made from dark stained wood and had a central runner in a similar colour to the wallpaper with brass rods to keep it in place on each stair.

They all followed, with George carrying Lady Nora to her room on the first floor. After settling both ladies, Lizzie was shown to her own room by Mrs Field. It was a pleasant surprise after the dark heavy surroundings downstairs. The room was situated on the left back corner of the building and had dual aspect windows set under the eaves of the house. There were two single beds with eiderdowns covering blankets. The linen looked fresh and clean, as did the curtains. Mrs Field obviously ran a tight ship; Mrs Luck would be proud. There was a washstand with a matching bowl and pitcher. There was also an oak tallboy in which to store clothes. Half was shelved and the rest hanging space. This would do very nicely she thought and her mood lightened a bit. She hoped that when the family were in full residence, she would share this room with her aunt.

She and George were to take their meals in the kitchen with Mr and Mrs Field and the ladies would use the dining room. The long table would easily seat twelve and Mr Field had laid both ladies a place at the fireplace end, facing each other. Neither sat at the head of the table as that was reserved for the master of the house, even if he wasn't in residence. It seemed to Lizzie that Mrs Field served the same cold buffet to both the ladies and themselves but neither she nor George minded about this and she was sure neither Lady Nora nor Miss Sophia gave any thought to what the servants were eating.

As she settled herself into bed, after seeing her mistresses had all they needed for the night, Lizzie thought that maybe this wouldn't be so bad after all. It did seem that she would have some spare time on her hands so maybe she could explore a little of the area. From what she had seen from the windows in the train and then again when they were in the carriage, it looked like an amazing place. So many mountains, lakes and rivers – fells, tarns and becks she corrected herself – it would be unforgivable not to take advantage of the surroundings on offer.

*

It was eleven thirty in the morning; not too early for her to set out. She rang for George. He came quickly and found Lady Nora already in her outdoor coat waiting to be taken for her walk. He carried her downstairs and settled her into her chair. After collecting a package from Mrs Field they were on their way.

As George pushed her through the grounds Lady Nora's heart was pounding.

It had been several months since she had seen him; he would not be expecting her as she normally only visited him when the family was in residence. She hoped he wouldn't mind the intrusion as he was a very private person.

George left her as planned in the depths of the wood to the right of the estate, leading in the direction of Blenthorne. He promised to return for her in two hours.

She wheeled herself for several hundred yards until the path petered out. Then she put on the brake and levered herself out of the chair. Henceforth, she had no choice but to hobble along on foot, however ungainly the sight. He didn't mind of course; he didn't even seem to notice. She leant heavily on her stick and her progress was laboured and slow as she struggled along with her package under her arm. After a few minutes she reached her destination and tapped lightly on the door. He opened it within seconds. He was wearing very casual clothes; he had no interest in his appearance. His shirt was open at the neck and his corduroy waistcoat unbuttoned. His hair was falling into his large brown eyes as usual. He looked at her enquiringly for a moment as he had few visitors. When he realised who it was his face lit up and he scooped her up in his arms and swung her round in delight.

She felt the air leave her lungs and thought she might never breathe again; to be honest she wouldn't care if she didn't as all she wanted in the world was right here – with him.

'But what are you doing here, Nora? I wasn't expecting you for ages. Are you real or am I dreaming?' he asked showing puzzlement and delight in equal measure.

Nora laughed; a laugh that she kept under wraps for most of her life and reserved just for him.

'No; I'm real enough,' she said breathlessly and she went on to explain the reason for their unscheduled visit to Cumberland.

'So Sophia's determination to get her own way has really backfired this time then!' he said with a small smile, 'May I get you some food; I don't have much in the larder as I wasn't expecting company, as you can see,' he said as he gestured around the room with his hand.

'Not a problem we can get this place tidied up in an instant,' said Nora as she set to work picking up clothes and plates from the table, 'And don't worry about food, I have some, look,' she exclaimed as she unwrapped her parcel. 'We have cold meat and cheese, as well as bread and a bottle of wine, so we can dine in style!'

'You truly are a wonderful woman, my dearest Nora,' he said with feeling, 'how I miss you when you are away.'

When she thought back over the time they had spent together after she returned to the house, she realised they had talked and talked as if they had never been apart, somehow the months just slipped away and it was as if no other life existed outside his home. They had arranged to meet again tomorrow and the day after and the day after; Nora realised she wouldn't mind if she never returned to Kent.

*

After five weeks of self-imposed exile, Miss Sophia declared herself ready to face the world again.

'They will all be laughing at me, Tester; but I'm a strong resilient woman,' Sophia announced resolutely.

Lizzie kept her face straight, 'Yes, Miss Sophia,' she replied implacably.

If she was honest, Lizzie herself would be very sorry to leave the area. She didn't like the house but the setting was breathtaking; many acres of land encompassing fields and the wood as well as a beck and formal gardens. Open grazing for the farmers to run their sheep added to the ambiance. She had explored quite a lot of the grounds and also ventured onto the fells but was always slightly worried about getting lost. Lizzie thought herself to be a sensible woman; she was certainly well educated for her class however a sense of direction was the one thing that had always eluded her.

She had walked into both Rowendale and Blenthorne in the other direction. Rowendale would be considered a hamlet she supposed and Blenthorne a village. Each had things the other lacked and once she had got used to what facilities were located where, she thoroughly enjoyed exploring both places.

It would be difficult to get back into the formal routine of life at Westden however she was employed to go where her mistresses commanded. There were few large houses in the vicinity so not much hope of finding a local situation. Besides, there was her mother to consider.

No point in dwelling on it; she would just have to pack and look forward to coming back.

*

Lizzie wasn't the only one who was disappointed to be leaving. Nora was bereft at the thought of going back to the day-to-day routine of her life. He had begged her not to go. They had spent practically every day together, sometimes he cooked a simple meal for them or sometimes Nora took their dinner or supper with her. Neither cared what they ate. They could have survived on fresh air alone if need be.

The day before they parted he had told her just how much she meant to him.

'You are my life; I couldn't go on without you.'

She would remember those words until their next meeting. It wasn't much of an existence; the chair that imprisoned her and everyone treating her like a freak but knowing they would be together again in a few weeks meant the world to her. It was the only thing that kept her sane, without that to look forward to ...

They travelled back as uneventfully as they had arrived. Mrs Field had seen them off and said she would be looking forward to their next visit. Not half as much as Nora would, she thought ironically as they reached Westden once more.

Chapter 4 – A Horrifying Happenstance

Late August 1891

The morning dawned bright and pleasant in Cumberland. Lizzie had attended to both Lady Nora and Miss Sophia. She had helped them bathe and dress and had styled their hair to their satisfaction. Until recently, everything took much longer than at Westden Chase as Highfields didn't have access to the modern amenities the property in Kent boasted. The lighting was fuelled by oil and the only running water in the house was via a tap in the scullery. However the introduction of plumbing achieved through the modification of some of the dressing rooms to bathrooms, meant the house was one of the few in the area which enjoyed such creature comforts. Nevertheless, life at Highfields was taken at a gentler pace and the family seemed more relaxed. Apart from Miss Sophia who was as wilful and skittish as ever.

'Tester, I do wish you would stop being difficult; you must come with me when I marry Sir James and move to this area, even Papa is happy with the arrangement. They can find someone else to look after Lady Nora. Maybe Nanny could do it. I mean it's not as if Lady Nora goes out anywhere much so she doesn't need a lady's maid of your calibre. I, on the other hand, must have you with me. You really need to understand that; you are the only person that suits me. No-one else can set my hair as you do and you are so very clever with your needlework. You have such an eye for the right accessories. So it's settled then, you'll come.'

As she combed her mistress's long fair hair, Lizzie spoke gently but firmly.

'The thing about Nanny is that she is really getting on now, Miss; she looked after you and your mother and aunt and I believe started as an assistant nursery maid in your grandmother's time, so she is long past retirement. It really isn't fair for her to be pressed into service once again. She was never trained as a lady's maid and you cannot expect her to learn a new role at her age. She does lots of things anyway; she mends clothes, sorts the laundry and helps Mrs Reader. Being a lady's maid is hard work, even though Lady Nora rarely goes out, people come to the house and she needs to be well-presented. She deserves the same respect and attention as Lady Constance.'

'Well alright; Crittle then, she could do it,' said Sophia Knightley petulantly.

'No, Miss, she could not. She is fully taken up with looking after her Ladyship. With respect, Miss Sophia, I don't think you have any idea what the work entails. At home in Kent, Miss Crittle is up before seven and doesn't retire until well after Lady Constance; so if the master and mistress have been at a formal function it can be after midnight when they return. Miss Crittle spends her days attending to her Ladyship's clothes and personal requirements; she is always there waiting to help her Ladyship undress and check if there's anything she needs. Sometimes Lady Constance wants warm milk after a long evening of socialising. Cook and all the other servants have gone to bed so it's Miss Crittle who sees to that.'

'Oh for goodness sake, Tester, you do go on! A lot of mistresses would not stand for such a contrary attitude from a servant. You are very lucky that I am so tolerant.'

Lizzie smiled to herself at the thought of the young lady in front of her being tolerant of anything or anyone.

'Yes, Miss,' she said deferentially. They had had this conversation a dozen times since the engagement and Miss Sophia's desire to be near her latest intended was such that they had already spent many weeks at Highfields House this year.

Lizzie had been promoted to the position of lady's maid nearly two years ago, Miss Hill having retired to live with her sister in Hastings. Lizzie was now in receipt of twenty-eight pounds a year and yet another new uniform. Her dresses were black, slim-fitting and made of good quality cotton in summer and a woollen mixture in winter. She was permitted lace at her collar and a necklace, as long as it wasn't too ostentatious. She wore her hair in a tight bun at the nape of her neck and was no longer required to wear a cap. Her shoes were good quality black leather with a discreet low heel and a bar across the forefoot fastened with a button to the side.

Each time Lizzie returned home she was no less worried about her mother. Rose was working at Westden as a kitchen maid and she was visiting in Lizzie's place during her absences but Rose seemed to have inherited her father's casual attitude towards life. She needed "a stick of dynamite up her derriere" as Aunt Phily had said to Lizzie when she was last home in Kent. Thank heavens for Philadelphia.

Having completed her morning's duties, Lizzie had volunteered to walk into Blenthorne to buy some stamps. Clearly George could have done it but she enjoyed the fresh air and took the opportunity to leave Highfields whenever possible. She loved the area but for some reason still hated the house. She had been visiting it for four years now and the feeling she had the first time she saw it remained with her. It had a sort of depressing melancholy air hanging over it; as if it harboured a sinister secret. She had spoken to Phily about it but she had said Lizzie was being fanciful. After buying her stamps and having a pleasant conversation with the post mistress, she walked along the gentle sloping road back towards Rowendale with the sun warmly resting on her shoulders, her shadow playing out in front of her.

As her feet trod on the rough path she knew there was no question of her leaving Kent to remain in the employment of Miss Sophia after her marriage. Her mother relied upon her too much. She was pleased that her mistress had finally found a suitor who passed muster. Of course she was very lucky to have made such a good match because she had "missed the first boat" as Mrs Reader put it in a confidential chat with Phily one day over an afternoon cup of tea when she thought they were alone.

It took about eighteen months for her to be completely rehabilitated into society after the "Montgomery Scandal". She had now accepted a

67

proposal of marriage from Sir James Fryer who was a widower with two young children and a large fortune made from the textile industry. He had been a guest at a shooting party at Highfields a year ago and lived near Carlisle. There was no way on earth that Lizzie could move there. Aunt Phily was wonderful but it wasn't appropriate to leave everything to her, besides … a noise intruded into her thoughts at that moment.

A panting sound came from behind her with soft padding on the ground. Lizzie looked round and as she did so a dark shape leaped at her back but she was quite unable to comprehend what was happening. She fell to the ground and instinctively put her hands to her head as she tried to roll into a ball. Whatever the creature was, it was incredibly strong. It was on top of her, trying to bite at her head, growling and slavering around her and she could feel its hot rancid breath on her neck.

She heard someone screaming and hoped they would help but then realised with growing terror that the noise was coming from the depths of her own being.

After what seemed like an eternity when she truly thought she would die, she heard another noise. It was a man's voice shouting, followed by a thudding sound and a jolt which seemed to travel through her whole body. The creature let out a yelp and suddenly the weight was lifted.

Lizzie stayed cowered in a foetal position for some moments until she felt safe to look up. She saw a large man with his back to her looking down the road. He turned and faced her. He seemed familiar but Lizzie was disorientated and couldn't place him.

He moved towards her and knelt down next to her quivering body.

'Are you alright, Miss? My apologies; that was a darn silly thing to say, of course you aren't. Excuse my language, Miss. Can you sit up? Let me help you. Take your time.'

He had a gentle calm voice with a soft local accent.

Lizzie pushed herself into a sitting position and after a minute or so held her hands towards the man and he pulled her gently to her feet. She noticed her gloves were ripped to shreds. Her hair was cascading down her back and her bonnet was lying in tatters on the ground with her shawl next to it.

'It's Miss Tester isn't it, from Highfields? I thought the family were in residence as I've seen Mr Donald Knightley at the inn.'

So that's who this gentleman was, Obed Daniels the innkeeper, she had seen him at a distance when she had visited Blenthorne village previously.

'Mr Daniels, I can't thank you enough. I believe you have literally just saved my life. What was that animal; where is it now?'

'I suspect it to be a bull-terrier, Miss. They shouldn't be kept as pets and I don't know anyone that has one. Mind you, I think some might be used as fighting dogs and kennelled at one of the local farms. I'll alert the constable once I have taken care of you.' He paused as Lizzie looked with slight alarm towards the thick wooden baton in his hand.

'I keep a club about me, not that I need it at the inn as a rule. They're peaceful people for the most part but there's the occasional one who can't hold his liquor and gets a bit beyond himself, so I always have this behind the bar. Force of habit, I put it in the cart when I travel and good job I did today. I got in a strong blow, sufficient for the animal to run off but not enough to mortally wound it. But it will likely be even more dangerous now.'

'I am very grateful to you, Mr Daniels; I'm quite alright now, I can be on my way.' Lizzie attempted to take a couple of steps and immediately felt faint. Her heart was pounding in her ears and her legs felt like they were made from jelly.

'No indeed, Miss Tester, you're certainly not going anywhere under your own steam and that should go for anyone else who is thinking of venturing out until that beast is caught. Now we're less than a quarter of a mile from Blenthorne, let me take you to the inn so that you can rest a while and I will take you back to Highfields this afternoon after the dinnertime customers have gone.'

For once in her life Lizzie didn't argue. The whole episode had shaken her up more than anything she had ever experienced. Mr Daniels helped her up onto the seat behind the horse and climbed aboard the cart next to her, taking the reins. She declined the blanket he offered and pulled her shawl around her shoulders, however within moments it became apparent that she was shivering uncontrollably and without a word, her companion intuitively placed the dark green cover gently over her. With a slight flick of his wrists and a small clicking noise made between his tongue and teeth, the horse moved off slowly towards Blenthorne retracing the route she had taken just a few minutes earlier.

Lizzie's heart was still beating wildly and she was finding it difficult to breathe evenly, she felt intermittently faint and admonished herself for being so weak. Clearly seeing her distress, Obed Daniels talked gently to her, asking her about Highfields and how she liked the Lake District. Realising her answers were monosyllabic, he told her about his daughters and his nephew who lived with him at the inn. She wasn't really listening closely as she was feeling strangely emotional and it was taking almost all her powers of concentration to stop herself from weeping out loud.

After a few minutes they stopped outside the inn. It was a large building and had been a coaching hostelry previously. Mr Daniels said it had been extended by the previous owner and now had a second bar and upstairs there were sufficient rooms to accommodate guests.

He helped her down gently. He was tall and broad with copper coloured hair and a full beard. Lizzie estimated he was probably between thirty-five and forty years of age. If she had to describe an innkeeper, Mr Daniels would exactly fit the bill. He led her in the backdoor through the scullery and kitchen, then across the hallway into a living room. There was a settee along one wall and he directed her towards that. A skinny teenage girl appeared in the doorway.

'May, this is Miss Tester; she met with an accident along the road. Fetch me some warm water and the iodine bottle. She has a few cuts and grazes.'

May bobbed a courtesy to Lizzie and disappeared towards the scullery.

'She's my elder girl, Miss, and has the makings of an excellent cook; she does a few mutton pies for the dinnertime trade as well as baking some cakes. I'm mindful not to put too much on to her though; she's but thirteen.'

'Your wife, Mr Daniels, I'm sorry you may have told me but my thoughts were taken up with my situation earlier, is she no longer alive?'

'No indeed, Miss, she died about eighteen months after Lily was born; she's my younger daughter. My sister-in-law moved in here with her son Ned about seven years ago, that was after my brother passed away but sadly she too was taken last year.'

May returned with a steaming bowl of water and a brown bottle on a tray with a towel and some white bandaging material.

'I didn't know if the lady needed any wounds dressed, Dad.'

'Thank you, May; I think it's only scratches, thankfully your gloves and bonnet saved you, Miss. Oh, May, could you take some water up to the best guest room for Miss Tester to use when I have finished here.'

Lizzie was about to protest but thought better of it. This kind man had gone out of his way to help her and it would be churlish to rebuff his generosity; he wanted to look after her and the least she could do was to let him, certainly for the time being. It was a novel experience as she was never ill nor in need of help so just for once it was nice to be cosseted.

Obed Daniels deftly attended to the grazes on Lizzie's hands for a couple of minutes. When she questioned his dexterity, he explained his brother had been a prize fighter and he himself had worked his corner for several years. Sadly, after one particularly brutal encounter in the ring, his brother had taken a nasty blow to the head and died a few days later; leaving a widow and a teenage son. Obed's nephew Ned, now helped him run the inn.

Lizzie refused the offer of food and assured him she was able to make her own way upstairs to the guest room.

'Take your time, Miss. If you want to have a rest on the bed it's all clean and made up, so please do so. I will send May along with something for you to wear; your frock has been torn.'

Until that moment Lizzie hadn't noticed the rip to the front of her uniform a few inches up from the hem.

Lizzie found the room she had been directed to and went to the washstand in the corner near to the window. She looked in the mirror and on touching her hair was alarmed to discover that some came away in her hand. The dog had clearly come very close to inflicting significant damage to her skull but thankfully she couldn't find any abrasions on her scalp. She turned to check the door was firmly closed before stripping to her chemise to wash her face and upper body.

As she went to pull her dress back up over her shoulders she realised there were puncture marks to the back. She turned to look at her back over her shoulder in the mirror. Thankfully only a little red marking denoted the area where the dog had pounced on her. If Mr Daniels hadn't happened along when he did … that really did not bear thinking about. She looked out of the window towards the fells in the distance.

There was a little light cloud high in the otherwise blue sky, a soft breeze ruffling the leaves on the trees and the distant bracken swayed gently. What a truly wonderful place this was and she knew she was a very lucky woman to be alive to appreciate it. Again she felt a little shaky.

The room was very pleasant and airy with a high ceiling and architraves. It had pink and green flowery wallpaper and mounted wall lights. There was a writing desk against one wall with a chest of drawers next to it and a wardrobe on the wall next to the washstand. Each side of the double bed there was a small cabinet with an embroidered doily centred on top. The bed had a crocheted counterpane over it with a pillow on each side and a double length bolster running underneath. Everything looked clean and tidy. Mr Daniels was certainly a man of high standards she thought approvingly. He probably had someone in to "do" for him.

In spite of her assertion that she was fine, she decided it wouldn't hurt to rest for a few minutes. She removed the counterpane and climbed on top of the comfortable-looking bed. She relaxed as the soft eiderdown seemed to wrap itself protectively around her.

She awoke with a start some time later to find May standing next to her holding a garment in her arms.

'Sorry, Miss, I was just checking on you, I didn't mean to startle you,' said the girl somewhat nervously.

For a moment Lizzie was completely disorientated. She sat up and looked around her. This was not her room at either Westden or Highfields. Then she remembered what had happened earlier in the day and looked at May.

'What time is it, do you know? I must be getting back.'

'It's a little after four, Miss. They know where you are; my cousin Ned went to Highfields to tell them. They sent someone to get you but you were sleeping so Dad said he would take you home before teatime. I'll let you get up, Miss. Do you want some more water; can I fetch you something to eat?'

'No, May, thank you; you are a very attentive girl and I appreciate your concern. I'll just straighten my hair and I'll be down.'

'I hope this fits, Miss; my mother wasn't as tall as you so it may be a bit on the short side but it will do to see you home.'

Lizzie took the grey dress being held out to her. She was deeply touched by the kindness of this family and thanked May, who turned and left the room. She put on the dress which was indeed a little short. Scarcely decent in polite society as it barely reached her ankles but in the quiet sleepy backwater of Blenthorne, she thought she could get away with it albeit just for the journey back to Highfields.

She tidied her hair as best she could without the use of a comb and made her way downstairs. Obed Daniels was doing some ledger work at the desk in the living room where he had first taken Lizzie.

He looked towards her and smiled at her as she entered the room.

'Mr Daniels, I can only apologise; I have impinged on your hospitality for far too long. I only meant to lie down for a few minutes and then fell asleep for hours.

Please forgive me. Thank you so much for the loan of this dress, May said it belonged to your late wife. I'm truly humbled by your generosity. I will launder it and return it by the end of the week.'

'No rush, Miss, you are welcome to the gown. I went along to the police house and spoke to the constable about the dog and he's going to put up some notices. Word is being spread around the surrounding hamlets about not going out alone until it's caught. I also bumped into the village doctor who said to let you sleep as long as possible as it was the best remedy for shock. George arrived an hour or two ago and I told him I would take you back to Highfields as soon as you were ready.'

'Do you know George, Mr Daniels?'

'Yes, Miss, he's a regular when the family are in residence. No inn at Rowendale you see, so he makes his way over here quite often. Not that he overindulges, Miss; I wouldn't want you to think that.'

Lizzie smiled as Obed Daniels stood up. In spite of her height, he towered over her and made her feel quite small. She was very grateful for his strength earlier in the day and wished there was some way she could repay his kindness. When she mentioned this he shook his head vehemently.

'Anyone would have done the same. No thanks or repayment necessary. Now I'll get you home.'

True to his word, he helped her back on board the cart and with a gentle click to the horse they turned towards the road for Rowendale. Lizzie received a few stares along the way from interested parties which had probably happened on the way to the inn but she had been too distressed to notice.

Upon arrival at the backdoor of Highfields Mr Daniels took his leave after turning down the offer of refreshment from Mrs Field. However before he could escape, Mr Knightley himself appeared from around the side of the house and thanked Mr Daniels, shaking him by the hand.

'Miss ... um ... well, she means a great deal to my sister-in-law and daughter as you can imagine, Mr Daniels and we are truly in your debt.'

The innkeeper removed his bowler hat in deference to the master of the house and looked a little embarrassed. Having been sent by his wife Lady Constance to thank the innkeeper, Mr Knightley left as quickly as possible and returned in the direction he came.

Lizzie saw Mr Daniels on board his cart and watched as he disappeared into the distance.

An unnecessary fuss was made by the cook and Mrs Field and word had already gone round that no one was to leave the vicinity of the house alone until the animal was caught. Lizzie left the ladies and went to her room to change the borrowed dress.

The grey cotton fabric was of good quality and the stitching was neat and even. Mrs Daniels had obviously been a fine needlewoman thought Lizzie approvingly. The dress looked as clean as when she had put it on and it still smelled slightly of lavender. She made up her mind to wash it herself; the skills of a laundry maid were never forgotten.

The following Sunday George accompanied Lizzie to the inn so that she could return the garment. He was no doubt grateful for an excuse for a small libation.

However the main reason for her need of a companion was that worryingly the animal had still to be caught.

Word had reached Highfields that three sheep had been found slaughtered during the week and then yesterday a sheep from the Highfields estate had been savaged, the poor thing had been brought to the yard. Lizzie initially recoiled in horror when she saw its pitiful wretched little body but getting over her repulsion, she looked more closely at its wounds which penetrated to the bone in places. That could have been her. She very much hoped the dog would soon be caught as it was clearly causing great concern among the farming community. The official instructions were for it to be shot on sight should the opportunity arise.

George went into the public bar on arrival at the inn and Lizzie walked round and tapped lightly on the backdoor. May let her in almost immediately and greeted her warmly. She took the package containing her mother's dress from Lizzie and called her father through from the bar, leaving them alone in the living room.

Mr Daniels seemed very pleased to see Lizzie again and enquired as to her recovery.

Lizzie assured him she was completely well and over her ordeal. She thanked him and again asked if there was any way she could be of service in return for his kindness and generosity to her.

He paused for a moment and then said in a rather embarrassed tone;

'Well, if you're really sure? I don't know if I should ask, Miss Tester, but if I might impose on you … do you think you might … well I hardly like to … but it's the girls, I know nothing about material and the like, well

they both need new clothes ... since their aunt died ...
You see the local women, well I don't like to ask, I mean
it doesn't take much to give some of them the wrong
idea, if you know what I mean.'

Lizzie thought that Mr Daniels would indeed be a
good catch for a hopeful spinster and could sympathise
with his predicament.

'Oh, Mr Daniels, I would be delighted. There is a
draper and haberdashery establishment in the village is
there not? I would be more than happy to help them
choose dress material. I have some spare time while we
are in residence at Highfields, so I can make the girls
some new dresses.'

'No I couldn't impose, Miss; I mean ... I couldn't
ask you to actually make the garments.'

'It would be a pleasure; the family don't entertain
lavishly at Highfields as a rule so my duties are far
lighter than when we are at home in Kent. I'll see the
girls later in the week if that suits you? I'm sure George
can be imposed upon to bring me into Blenthorne if that
wretched animal is still at large.'

Obed Daniels smiled and his whole face softened.
He wasn't an unattractive man Lizzie thought and
immediately admonished herself. She was completely
indifferent to men and assumed she must be suffering
from some sort of delayed shock.

During the week there was another report of a sheep
attack and the constable reminded all the residents of
Blenthorne, Rowendale and the outlying areas to remain
vigilant. George duly delivered Lizzie to the Blenthorne
Inn on the following Wednesday afternoon and both
May and Lily Daniels were eagerly awaiting her arrival.

They spent a happy couple of hours being measured and going off to look at material in the shop in the village. They chose from bolts of cotton and woollen material for summer and winter wear. Lizzie had patterns stored in her head; she knew how best to make use of the material and was confident they had spent Mr Daniels' money wisely. The fabrics were wrapped into two brown paper packages and Lizzie promised the girls she would see if she could have something ready for a fitting of one pinafore dress each the following week.

On their way back through the village Lizzie saw a man entering a cottage just along from the green. He looked familiar and when he turned his head a little she could see that it was Mr Donald.

'May, do you know who lives at that cottage?' asked Lizzie as she inclined her head towards the building she had seen the son of her employer enter.

'That's Mrs Cork's place, Miss Tester. There's always folk coming and going.'

Lizzie was none the wiser and made up her mind to ask Mr Daniels. It certainly seemed an unlikely place for Mr Donald to be visiting.

Lizzie posed the question to Mr Daniels upon their return to the inn. He looked rather uncomfortable and replied rather hesitantly.

'Well, Miss, Grace Cork is a widow from what I understand and she has lived in the village for a few years now.'

He didn't seem inclined to elaborate upon what he had said. Maybe she ran a tea room or a tailoring service but then if that were the case, Mr Daniels would surely have said.

Obed Daniels took Lizzie home and she told him she had promised the girls she would see them the following week.

Just before her next visit to the inn it was reported that a bull-terrier had been sighted worrying sheep and had been subsequently killed by the farmer. The residents of Blenthorne and Rowendale breathed a sigh of relief that the whole episode was over and Lizzie was pleased she would no longer have to be accompanied every time she left the house.

What no-one knew at that stage was that before succumbing to a bullet, the bull-terrier had apparently claimed one last victim, with tragic consequences.

Chapter 5 – Injudicious Suppositions

September 1891

Thankfully the "Beast of Blenthorne" as the dog had been dubbed, had been caught and no-one was more delighted than Lady Nora. At last she could venture into the wood unattended.

He would be wondering where she was. No doubt he had heard about the dog, so maybe he wouldn't be surprised that she had not been to see him but still, knowing she was in the vicinity, yet unable to go to him must be tormenting him as much as it was her.

Her heart beat wildly as George left her at the usual place and she wheeled herself as quickly as possible to the end of the path. With difficulty, she put on the brake and managed to get up out of her wheelchair. With the aid of her walking stick, she made her way as quickly as she could to his home which stood before a backdrop of deciduous trees beginning to display their autumnal hues.

The silence was only broken by a slight rustling of occasional falling leaves and the gentle soporific sound of bird song. She reached the wooden door, making sure not to drop the bread, cheese and wine she had bundled up in a cloth tucked under her left arm. It was as if he had been waiting just inside because he flung the door open before she could knock, sweeping her off her feet and swinging her round. The stick was discarded in the excitement as he kicked the door closed behind them with his right foot.

She laughed in pure delight to be with him once more as they again transcended into a world where no outsider could intrude.

*

On the same day as Lady Nora went for her first unaccompanied walk in the wood after the dog was killed, Lizzie visited the Blenthorne Inn as agreed with Mr Daniels and his daughters.

May and Lily were delighted to see her. She had cut out the material for a pinafore dress for each of them from the dark blue cotton print. They squealed with delight as they tried on their new clothes, held together with tacking stitches and Lizzie got busy with pins, tucking the material in here and there and measuring for the hems. She planned to be as generous as possible to allow for growth and would show May where to loosen the seams so that the dresses would fit for a year or two. The air was filled with happy excited voices and the girls' eyes shone in a way that Lizzie hadn't seen before. Her heart went out to the two delightful children so cruelly denied a mother's love and attention due to her untimely death.

As they were finishing the fitting in the bedroom the girls shared, they heard a noise in the yard downstairs. Lizzie glanced curiously towards the window to see what was causing the commotion. A wagon had pulled in with two men aboard and a bundle in the back. One of the men jumped down and she recognised him to be Ned Daniels, the nephew of the landlord. He raced off in the direction of the village. The other went to the backdoor of the inn and banged loudly, shouting as he did so. Clearly Mr Daniels opened the door quickly as the man disappeared from her view.

'What's happening, Miss Tester?' asked Obed Daniels' younger daughter as she walked towards the window to look out.

'I've no idea, Lily, just a lot of noise and fuss and then your father let in the man from the wagon. I didn't recognise him. Ned was with him but he just jumped down and ran towards the village. I expect we will know shortly.'

Lizzie was aware that she needed to get back by eleven thirty as Miss Sophia had accepted an invitation to luncheon issued by the Misses Mackenzie who lived in genteel retirement in a cottage near to the vicarage where their father used to be the incumbent. Lizzie would need to be on hand in case Miss Sophia needed anything before she left Highfields.

A few minutes later when the dress fittings were complete, they all went downstairs and Lizzie saw Obed Daniels as he came in from the scullery.

'Mr Daniels? What has happened?' asked Lizzie as she stood in the kitchen, pulling her shawl around her to prepare for the journey home.

'A bad business, Miss Tester, and that's for sure. A body has been found out on the fells. Jem Mitchell stumbled across it and then bumped into Ned, who came for the wagon. Ned's gone for the constable.'

'Do you know who it is?'

'Well I think it's most likely Grace Cork as she hasn't been seen for a few days.'

'But what on earth would she be doing out on the fells by herself? And why is there doubt as to her identity?'

'Well, I'm no doctor but it looks like she was attacked and slaughtered by the beast; she has lacerations and other injuries particularly around her neck, so I suppose she tried to run and stumbled. She must have lost a lot of blood so she wouldn't have got far. She has taken a nasty blow to the head.'

'Oh yes I can see how that would be possible. I got caught up in my dress and tumbled over immediately when the dog attacked me but if I had had a bit more warning, I too may have run and then fallen. Poor lady, does she have any family? I mean, she seemed very popular, there were always people going in and out of her cottage.'

Obed looked uncomfortable.

'Well, yes I think she was popular in a manner of speaking. As to family, I don't believe so. Freda from the village does for her several days a week, so she may know about the possibility of relatives.'

'Where is she now, Mr Daniels?'

'In the barn, Miss; the constable will need to contact the police force in Keswick. I expect they will send over an inspector; poor old Tom Cummins will be way out of his depth with this. Once reinforcements arrive and the village doctor has seen her just to confirm death, well maybe they will want to move her but until then, she's in as good a place as any.'

May appeared in the kitchen at that moment and had clearly been listening to the conversation between her father and Lizzie.

'Dad, what about Mrs Cat and her kittens; they have their basket in the barn. Can I go and get them?'

Before Obed could answer his daughter's question, there was a knock at the back door. He turned and walked through to the scullery, reappearing almost immediately with a flustered-looking Constable Cummins who nodded in Lizzie's direction and then followed the innkeeper through to the living room.

Not getting an answer from her father, May turned to Lizzie. 'Do you think I can go and get the basket, Miss Tester? I can't leave them in the barn not with … a body in there,' she finished in a whisper.

'I'll get them and put them in the scullery; I'm sure your father won't mind,' said Lizzie kindly.

Lizzie swallowed as she walked purposefully towards the barn. It was only a body and she was certain it would be covered up so how could it harm her? She reprimanded herself for being so foolish.

As she opened the door, the contrast between the bright light of day and the dark interior of the barn was striking. She looked round as her eyes acclimatised to the dim light. She saw movement out the corner of her eye and located Mrs Cat and her kittens almost immediately.

She walked over to them making soothing cooing noises which she thought cats would probably like and was just about to pick up the basket when her eyes were drawn to the bench on the other side of the barn and the pitiful bundle it bore. Mrs Cork's body was lying under some hessian sacking. Lizzie tried to look away but was inexorably drawn towards the bench and its sorry burden.

As she approached she looked towards it and in horror saw that an arm had escaped its cover and was hanging down from the bench. Lizzie's heart went out to this poor unfortunate woman who was clearly a very giving and generous soul, her popularity gave testimony to that. She deserved better than ending her days on a bench under a rough cover with her left arm dangling from its resting place. But for Mr Daniels, this could so easily have been Lizzie herself.

Lizzie said a prayer as she lifted up the sacking sufficiently to place Grace Cork's arm back next to her body. As she did so she looked at the hand. It was not the hand of a working woman. Both sides were smooth and soft. Her nails were neatly manicured and clean. The skin was not discoloured from peeling vegetables or rough from manual work. Lizzie looked at the wrist and forearm. It was pale and smooth for about two inches, above which were laceration marks, presumably made by the dog, but all the same …

'Miss Tester; are you alright? What are you doing in there? Can I come in?' May's voice interrupted Lizzie's thoughts and she hastily replaced the sacking having tucked the arm firmly back in place.

'Coming, May, just rounding up your cat family. No, my dear, don't come in, it's no place for either of us.'

Lizzie picked up the basket and was still thinking about Mrs Cork's arm as she walked towards the backdoor of the inn. She placed the basket in the scullery; both May and Lily were delighted to have their cat and her two kittens away from the barn.

Obed Daniels appeared from the living room with the red-faced constable and led him through the kitchen and scullery, across the yard in the direction of the barn. Lizzie was well read and knew in principle what should happen henceforth. The constable would inform the Cumberland Constabulary in Keswick, a post mortem would be conducted by a police surgeon and the coroner would be informed so that an inquest could be convened.

Lizzie walked back quickly to Highfields with the pinafores wrapped in brown paper, having made arrangements with the girls for their next fittings. She asked May to apologise to her father for leaving without saying goodbye however Miss Sophia would be in a tither if Lizzie was not there when she needed her. She was still thinking about Mrs Cork's hand and arm. She would talk to Mr Daniels next time she saw the girls. In the meantime, she needed to get back to her duties and tried to put all thoughts of the poor unfortunate lady out of her mind.

*

Over the next few days Lizzie had little time on her hands. The Knightley family had decided to invite some friends from London and there would be ten in the party arriving at the weekend. Most would be bringing their own personal servants with them and they would need guidance from the resident staff so Lizzie's time would be at a premium. Miss Sophia was always difficult when there was competition in the form of other attractive young ladies present. Her clothes weren't right, her hair was a mess and she hated all her jewellery. Lizzie's diplomatic skills were tested to the full as she conciliated, cajoled and calmed her mistress. Lady Nora was just irritated at having to be in attendance when she would far rather be wandering off in the wood.

After one particularly stressful day when Miss Sophia had been at her most demanding; Lizzie collapsed into a chair next to Philadelphia in the servants' hall. It was late in the evening but Lizzie's mind was buzzing.

'There's tea in the pot if you want one, dear,' said Philadelphia gently.

Lizzie nodded and Philadelphia rose to pour her niece a large beaker of tea with a dash of milk.

'You haven't been to see the Daniels' girls yet this week have you?'

'No, with everyone here, there hasn't been time, which is a shame as I promised them I would get their pinafore dresses done. I'm nearly there with them and I've cut out and tacked their long sleeved winter dresses, so they need fitting. However it's actually Mr Daniels that I particularly want to see.'

'Really!' said Philadelphia with a smile, 'well that's a turn up as I thought you were indifferent to men!'

'What? No, no I don't mean I want to see him for any romantic reason. He is very kind of course and I respect him immensely for the way he is bringing up his daughters but I'm not interested in anything like that, as you well know. I do like being with the girls though; May in particular is very bright as well as having practical skills and I would like to encourage her to fulfil her potential, whatever that may be. No, I need to speak to Mr Daniels about Mrs Cork,' Lizzie paused and then made a decision.

'Aunt Phily the more I think of it, the more confused I am. You see everyone just seems to be happy to believe she was killed by the dog that attacked me. From what I hear, it sounds like the inquest will be a foregone conclusion. No other possibilities have been considered and I think they're wrong.'

'Other possibilities, what do you mean? Presumably if it wasn't the dog, it was an accident?'

Lizzie shrugged.

'Or … if it wasn't an accident, well then what … you think someone actually killed her?' asked her aunt incredulously.

Lizzie was shocked to hear her worst fears expressed out loud and then focused on her aunt's voice once more.

'Why are you sure they're wrong? After all, the police are experienced when it comes to investigating causes of death and presumably a doctor has confirmed how she died. You can be rather fanciful at times Lizzie, just look at how you reacted to Highfields when you first came here, you said it was sinister or some such. What a load of nonsense; I think you are letting your imagination run wild again.'

90

Lizzie didn't look convinced as she sipped her tea. Her aunt looked at her closely.

'Alright, why do you think the police are misguided in their assumption that Mrs Cork was killed by the dog that attacked you?' asked Philadelphia finally.

'That's just it, it's an assumption. Because the dog had attacked me and killed some sheep, they assume it then killed Mrs Cork but the marks on her body are not right. Well, to be honest I have only seen her arm but that was sufficient for me to question whether the wounds were made by a dog.'

Lizzie paused but her aunt did not speak.

'Firstly there were no defence wounds to her hands, which seems odd. The first thing one does, out of instinct or self-preservation or whatever one likes to call it, is to put one's hands up to protect one's head. That's what I did and my gloves were ripped to shreds. Secondly, I saw one of the slaughtered sheep when it was brought back to Highfields and it had deep puncture wounds, penetrating its muscles and exposing the bone in places where the dog had torn into it. Mrs Cork's wounds looked like grooves scratched into the flesh, almost like they had been done by some sort of implement.'

Lizzie paused and then thought of something else;

'Thirdly, no-one has explained what she was doing out on the fells, by all accounts she didn't leave the village as a rule, so why all of a sudden when there was a dangerous dog on the loose and everyone had been advised to stay away from open countryside, did she suddenly decide to go walking alone?' Lizzie stopped and shook her head;

'Oh goodness, maybe I am just being fanciful as you say. I didn't know her of course but she must have been a popular lady to have had so many friends, I remarked on that to Mr Daniels. I think if she was killed, well she deserves justice.'

'So what did Mr Daniels say when you described Mrs Cork as a popular lady?'

'What, um, I'm not sure he said anything … Oh yes, he said she could be described that way "in a manner of speaking". She did have lots of friends though; in fact I even saw Mr Donald going into her cottage one day. I did wonder if she ran some sort of service … tailoring or something, I mean there's nowhere locally is there, if a gentleman wanted to get some buttons sewn on, or had a snag in a tweed jacket but then I would have thought Mr Donald would have asked us to repair his clothes … Aunt Phily what are you smiling at?'

'You, for goodness sake, Lizzie, for an intelligent woman you are incredibly naïve. Just think about it; you say she had lots of friends, how many times did you see women entering or leaving her cottage? I would hazard a guess and say never. She provided a service alright but I venture it had nothing to do with tailoring! How do you think she managed to live so well and maintain her home, it's not exactly a two up and two down is it? Also where did she get the wherewithal to pay for a servant girl from the village?'

'Well I assumed she had private means, a widow's pension or some other form of income …' Lizzie paused while the truth dawned on her gradually, 'you mean she was a … common prostitute? Good Lord! But how do you know; I mean, I don't think Mr Daniels knows, he didn't tell me if he did.'

'Well he wouldn't would he; he was sparing your blushes! You daft girl, of course he knows, the whole village knows, in fact I'll wager that half of Cumberland knows, apart from you it seems! Goodness me, Elizabeth Tester, sometimes you don't have a ha'penny worth of common sense.'

Lizzie put her head on one side for a moment and then said; 'so thinking about it, if she was a lady of … ill-repute as you say, well that could be a reason for a person wanting to get rid of her couldn't it? I mean maybe she was blackmailing someone.'

'Well you do have a point there I suppose,' Philadelphia paused and seemed to make up her mind. 'In fact, Lizzie, I agree that you should talk to Mr Daniels, after all he saw the body didn't he and he also saw your wounds, superficial though they were. See what he thinks. If he believes there is any merit in what you say, he will be the right person to speak to the police, before the inquest is held. Do you want me to come with you?'

'No, no, I will be fine. I believe that's a good plan. I will put my thoughts before him and if he thinks I am misguided, I will respect his opinion and let it rest. However if she was murdered, she deserves justice, just the same as anyone else, Aunt Phily.'

'It's a nice idea my girl, but if you think everyone is equal in this world, then you are even more naïve than I thought.'

*

The following day after the house guests had left and Lady Nora had slipped away to the wood, Miss Sophia announced herself exhausted and decreed she would

93

spend the day in her room to recover from the rigours of entertaining.

As she was not needed at Highfields, Lizzie took the opportunity to go to Blenthorne. May opened the backdoor when Lizzie knocked and her face lit up upon seeing who it was. She looked hopefully to Lizzie's left and right to see if she had a parcel with her which might contain the much longed-for completed pinafore dresses but was disappointed to see that she had no more than her felt purse.

'May, I have been so busy with the house guests that I haven't had time to complete your dresses this week, but I really need to see your father if he is at home please.'

May showed Lizzie through to the living room behind the public bar and went in search of the inn landlord.

Obed Daniels appeared in the doorway within seconds it seemed. He smiled when he saw Lizzie.

'Miss Tester, this is a pleasant surprise; May said you wanted to see me, how can I be of assistance to you?' Obed wiped his hands down the side of his brown corduroy trousers which were held in place by a wide belt at his waist with the rather superfluous assistance of a pair of dark coloured braces. He was wearing a blue serge shirt open at the collar and she could see a small amount of copper coloured hair protruding from the top.

Lizzie was not at all sure why she had noticed this.

'Please do take a seat. May I offer you some tea?' asked Obed looking at Lizzie enquiringly.

She snapped out of her disturbing thoughts regarding chest hair.

Lizzie sat down on the settee. 'No thank you, Mr Daniels. You really must excuse this intrusion; I know you are a busy man with a living to make however there is something which is worrying me. After discussing it with my aunt, Philadelphia Crittle who is Lady Constance's personal maid, we both thought you would know the right thing to do.' Lizzie realised she was flustered as the words came tumbling out of her mouth far too quickly. She fixed her eyes on the ceiling so as not to let them wander back in the direction of Mr Daniels' neck.

She took a deep breath and told him exactly what had passed between her and her aunt the day previous.

'Do you think I am quite mad, Mr Daniels, or do you think there could be some merit to my concerns? I mean regardless of what we think of her morals, Mrs Cork didn't deserve to end her days like that, always supposing that I am right.'

Obed Daniels sat quietly looking at Lizzie for what seemed like an age. He finally spoke in a measured tone.

'Miss Tester, I don't think you're mad, far from it. I think you are a very intelligent lady who has given this matter a lot of thought and on the face of it yes, I believe there are questions that need to be answered. If I am honest, it was bothering me as to what Grace Cork would have been doing out on her own on the fells at all, let alone when there was a dangerous dog on the run.

'I did see some of her wounds; however I mainly took note of the damage to her head and throat, so I suppose I didn't think too much about the other injuries.'

'But if you wanted rid of someone, Mr Daniels, wouldn't it be the perfect time to take advantage of the situation? The dog was a perfect scapegoat, if you see what I mean.'

'You certainly have a point there,' said the landlord with a smile. The inquest has been set for Friday next week. I think it best if I contact Constable Cummins, tell him of our concerns and request that he contacts the inspector in Keswick; he can take the credit if he wants, just as long as the matter is looked at again. If after that nothing comes of it, we shall have done our best for her.'

Lizzie sighed, she noted with relief that he had said "our concerns".

'Oh my goodness, Mr Daniels, I am so pleased that you don't just see me as a foolish woman.'

'No indeed, Miss, anything but,' came the reply.

Lizzie thought of something else she wanted to ask the inn landlord. Still directing her gaze to the ceiling she said; 'May I ask you something else, Mr Daniels? It may be that I'm being fanciful, my aunt says I can be at times, particularly with regard to my feelings surrounding Highfields House, you see I have always hated it from the very first time I saw it. I have no idea why but it somehow feels sort of sorrowful, almost like it's harbouring a sinister secret. You're a local person, do you know of anything strange in its history?'

'No I can't say I do; it's a large estate with acres of land and woodland. There are probably several old buildings scattered around. I think there might well be former crofters' dwellings that were absorbed into the estate years back and an old folly in the grounds somewhere so I believe, although I've never seen it. Are you sure I can't get you something to drink, Miss; lemon cordial maybe?'

Lizzie thought for a moment and relented. After getting them both a glass of cordial, Obed Daniels sat down opposite her again and continued his recollections.

'Highfields has been in Lady Constance's mother's family for generations. The earl and countess spent more time here than the Knightley family currently do but of course that's to be expected with Mr Knightley being a Member of Parliament. From what I understand, Lady Constance and Mr Knightley did a lot of their courting hereabouts before they were married so it must hold special memories for them. Mr Knightley's younger brother used to come for the house parties too, before he left to live abroad but I can't recall his name.'

'Yes that would be Mr Charles. I have seen his photograph in the house here and also at Westden Chase in Kent,' confirmed Lizzie.

'That's about as much as I know, Miss Tester. No mysteries or tales of gruesome goings on that I know of; if there had been, you can be sure the whole village would have made much of it.

'In all honesty, I think we have enough going on, Miss, with Grace Cork in the here and now, don't you?'

'Yes indeed, Mr Daniels, thank you so very much.' Lizzie finished her drink. 'I will see the girls in a few days and maybe you can let me know how you get on with the constable?'

In fact Lizzie didn't have to wait until her next visit to Blenthorne to get news about Grace Cork's death, as

Detective Inspector Albert Bishop arrived at Highfields House three days later to interview her.

No one could have predicted how that event would impact on the small village of Blenthorne and in particular, the residents of Highfields House in the not too distant future.

Chapter 6 – A Fresh Pair of Eyes

September 1891

Inspector Albert Bishop settled into the carriage for the journey from Keswick Police Station to Blenthorne. So much for a nice straightforward case he mused. On the surface, it looked cut and dried. Dog attacks woman then kills sheep, subsequently attacks another woman who bled to death out on the fells from the wounds to her neck.

He rummaged in the pocket of his jacket for his pipe. His teeth seemed to fit together better when he had it in place so he stuck it in his mouth without filling it.

Constable Cummins was sweating like a pig by all accounts when Albert's colleague, Inspector Sidney Huggins had arrived in Blenthorne shortly after the body was first discovered. He had made some enquiries and purported to be satisfied that the evidence was consistent with the information gathered at the time. Unfortunately poor Inspector Huggins was subsequently found to be suffering from a peptic ulcer, so it fell to Albert Bishop, who had been drafted in from Carlisle to Keswick, to re-examine the case.

From what Albert had heard of the constable in Blenthorne, he was not renowned for being a bloodhound when it came to the detection of crime so it seemed strange that he suddenly wanted to take another look at the evidence. Albert would bet his bootlaces someone had put the idea into the constable's head, he would never have thought of it for himself.

Albert's housekeeper had packed him a bag that morning, grumbling and bemoaning the fact that he needed enough clothes for over a week. Nevertheless, she found sufficient collars, cuffs and underwear to see him through to the inquest and beyond if necessary. He could also send home for more when he got settled in Blenthorne or maybe the landlord where he was staying could recommend a local woman who took in laundry.

He looked at the notes he had been given on the case. Grace Cork aged thirty-two, purported to be a widow but no evidence of any marriage certificate had been found. Moved to Blenthorne four years ago and made her living discreetly, apparently on immoral earnings. Kept a clean and tidy house and gave little trouble to anyone. She employed a local girl to come in usually four times a week. A cursory search of her house revealed nothing of significance. No information contained in his case notes indicated that Inspector Huggins had deemed it necessary to visit the site where the body was found. The police surgeon raised no concerns and his report stated that her injuries were consistent with a frenzied animal attack. There was no reason to believe her death was anything other than a tragic accident.

Albert needed to question Tom Cummins closely regarding his newfound suspicions and their origins; wild goose-chase probably but all the same. He had asked the doctor to take another look at the body just to confirm the findings of the original post mortem. Albert was unable to shake the thought that they had all been guilty of an over-willingness to believe that the cause of death could be attributed to the dog attacks which preceded it. On the face of it, serious crime didn't happen in such places as Blenthorne; poaching and a bit of stealing were usually as bad as it got in these rural areas.

The inspector nodded off intermittently and eventually reached his journey's end with the carriage rolling into the yard at the Blenthorne Inn. Obed Daniels the landlord came out to meet him and took his bag as he stepped down from the footplate.

They went in through the front door of the inn and Albert readily agreed to a bottle of brown ale prior to settling into his room. He then planned to see the village constable to discuss his newfound concerns regarding the Cork case and the landlord's nephew Ned Daniels was dispatched to fetch him.

An hour later Tom Cummins was sitting in the back room of the Blenthorne Inn facing the inspector. It took less than five minutes to ascertain that in fact it was Obed Daniels who had drawn the constable's attention to possible inconsistencies in the evidence, prompted it seemed by the lady who had originally been attacked by the dog. Rather wearily, Albert called the landlord through and asked for a few minutes of his time. His back was stiff after the long journey from Keswick.

Obed excused himself from the bar, leaving Ned in charge. It seemed like a fairly quiet time at the inn but interest was certainly raised by the unexpected presence of the new inspector.

Obed came through to the living room behind the public bar with a tray containing two bottles of brown ale and a couple of mutton and tattie pies.

Albert Bishop thought his enforced sojourn out in the sticks might not be so bad after all.

*

It was an hour and a half later and Ned had provided another couple of bottles from the bar. For good measure, they also had a slice each of Simnel cake baked by May earlier in the day. The inspector tucked in with gusto as he took the landlord briefly through the events of the last few weeks. The settee was comfortable and his back was no longer giving him jip so he was in no hurry to move.

'So then to sum up, Landlord, the lady who was originally attacked, Miss Elizabeth Tester from Highfields House, came to you because she had seen Mrs Cork's body and was not convinced that the wounds were consistent with those inflicted upon herself and wanted your opinion, you having seen the body also.'

'Miss Tester's wounds were only superficial. I arrived before the dog could do too much damage. It mainly ripped her gloves and clothing. She had a few scratches to the backs of her hands. When she inadvertently saw Grace Cork's left arm, she felt the wound pattern didn't look consistent with the puncture wounds she had seen on a sheep that had been killed and then taken to Highfields. However, I think her main

102

point was that Grace Cork's hands were free from defence wounds.

'I specifically noticed the neck and head wounds when my nephew Ned and Jem Mitchell brought the body back here. Mrs Cork had been savagely attacked, particularly around her throat but since speaking to Miss Tester, I have wondered if her injuries were inflicted by a dog. It didn't seem to have actually bitten her anywhere else; there were just deep grazes on her arms. Miss Tester said it looked like some sort of tool might have been used to give the impression of a mauling but obviously neither she nor I have enough expertise to speculate any further.

'Also several people have remarked on the fact that Grace Cork was not given to walking out on her own on the fells, it was totally out of character. So taking these points into account, we decided on balance we should speak to Tom Cummins and see if he thought we had a point and if so, to pass that on to the constabulary in Keswick, Inspector Bishop.'

'I have instructed the doctor to take another look, particularly at her neck to see if he might have missed something the first time. It did seem cut and dried, so it's possible that he only found what he was looking for, if you see what I mean. That's to stay between us for now of course, Landlord,' said the inspector quietly.

Obed nodded his consent. 'Will you be speaking to Miss Tester, Inspector?'

'Yes I think that would be a good idea; plus the body was found near the boundary of the Highfields estate. Maybe someone saw something, who knows what I might glean if I pay a visit to the house. Are the family all in residence do you know?'

'I imagine so; I saw Mr Donald Knightley, that's the son and heir, in the village the other day. Miss Tester said she had spoken of her concerns to Lady Constance's lady's maid, so clearly her Ladyship is staying there at the moment. Of course Miss Tester herself would not be present if Lady Nora and Miss Sophia were not there. She looks after the two of them from what I understand.'

'So you said you found Miss Tester on the road being attacked by the dog, that would be two or three weeks ago wouldn't it, so forgive the indelicate question, but your continuing connection with her is ... what?' asked the inspector, clearly intrigued.

'Well, Inspector, after finding her and bringing her back here due to the shock, my daughters have struck up a friendship with her and she is making them some new clothes. I asked her to as a matter of fact. It's difficult for someone in my situation as you might imagine. The girls have no female presence in their lives, if you will. Miss Tester was here the day the body was brought in from the fells and placed in the barn.'

The inspector pulled his watch out of his waistcoat pocket and after opening the cover, looked at it contemplatively. Too late to go to Highfields today, better to wait until he was fresh and clear-headed in the morning. He agreed to a nightcap before turning in and accompanied Obed Daniels through to the public bar.

*

The following morning, after inspecting the area where the victim's body was found, Inspector Bishop made his way to Highfields House. He declined

Constable Cummins' offer to accompany him and sent him back to the village in the pony and trap. The weather was set fair with no sign of the intermittent rain of recent days and he decided the walk would do him no harm after everything he had consumed the previous evening. He was reliably informed it would take no more than ten minutes to get to the house by following the track from the fell.

Upon reaching the front door, he wiped his boots on the brush provided and pulled the brass chain which would announce his arrival. He was rewarded with an almost instant response.

The door was opened, quite majestically, by an imperious-looking servant whom the inspector thought must be the butler from his projected air of self-importance. He looked the police officer up and down with evident disapproval but managed to restrain himself from directing Inspector Bishop to the backdoor.

'How can I help you ... Sir?' he enquired with an edge to his voice and his nose turned up slightly.

The police officer introduced himself and proffered his badge for the butler's inspection, 'I would like to see Miss Elizabeth Tester please; I believe she is employed here as a lady's maid?'

There was a pause before the butler deigned to speak again. 'Step this way if you please.'

Inspector Bishop was led into the hallway and asked to sit on an upright chair facing the central table. The butler did not offer to relieve him of either his topcoat or hat.

'Do you have a business card ... Sir?'

Albert thought that rather a supercilious request but nonetheless, delved into his suit jacket pocket and produced a small oblong printed card which he placed on the salver shoved under his nose.

The butler disappeared into a passage which led off from the hall; returning a couple of minutes later.

'Follow me please ... Sir; I'm to take you to the morning room,' he said with no further explanation but a most definite inhalation of breath.

Inspector Bishop followed the butler down the passageway into a grand-looking room with a high ceiling.

'Inspector Bishop, my Lady.'

He was just getting his bearings when a smartly dressed lady rose from the sofa.

'Thank you, Hemsley. Inspector Bishop, I'm Lady Constance Knightley, I understand you have requested to see Tester, may I enquire why? It is highly unusual for us to be visited by the constabulary and more so when it concerns a member of staff. Do you suspect Tester of being in some sort of trouble? If so, I can assure you, you are mistaken as my sister, Lady Nora Kingsbury and my daughter, Miss Sophia Knightley, trust her implicitly.'

'Please rest assured, Lady Constance, she's in no trouble,' Albert Bishop looked uncomfortable, he had not been asked to sit down and was feeling rather warm, as he was still wearing his coat and holding his hat.

'You may know of a tragic death in the area recently of a villager Mrs Grace Cork; well that is my reason for calling. It has been assumed that the lady in question was attacked by a bull-terrier and, as I'm sure you know, Miss Tester was attacked by such an animal a few weeks previously. That is what I need to speak to her about. Is she available at this time please?'

'Wait here,' commanded the mistress of the house as she swished her way out of the room, leaving the inspector standing in front of the empty sofa with only the lingering smell of her perfume for company.

He wandered round the room a few times, looking at photographs that were much in evidence. His attention was drawn to one which featured the lady who had just cross-questioned him. It was obviously taken on her wedding day and she was standing next to a tall slim young gentleman. That must be the Right Honourable Herbert Knightley MP as he now was, although presumably at that time he was still working for his family's bank.

He heard the door open and straightened himself up as he turned to see who had entered the room. He was a little annoyed to see that rather than it being the woman he had come to see, it was in fact Mr Knightley himself.

'Inspector … Bishop is it?'

Albert Bishop wondered if the MP had trouble reading. After all, his name was clearly printed on the card that he had been asked to provide upon arrival. All part of the game he supposed to make sure he stayed firmly in his place.

'Yes, Sir; as I explained when I arrived, I need to speak to Miss Tester whom I understand is employed by yourself in the position of lady's maid. I am looking into the death of Mrs Grace Cork and I believe Miss Tester may have some information pertinent to that enquiry.'

'Do you indeed! Well I can't imagine what that could be. My wife feels that if you wish to question a member of staff to whom we have a duty of care, I should contact our family solicitor.'

'I don't want to formally question her; I would like to speak to her regarding the dog attack she suffered a few weeks ago as it may be relevant to our enquiries.'

Mr Knightley appeared to consider this proposal for a full minute before nodding his head. 'Very well, Inspector, but I shall be present.'

'There really is no need for that, Sir. I'm not going to interrogate Miss Tester. I just want an informal chat with her. She may be … well … inhibited to divulge certain information if you are present. She may not feel she can be forthcoming with her employer there.'

'Nevertheless, those are my terms, Inspector. If you are unhappy with that, I'm sure I can have a word with my close friend, Sir Stanley Blake.'

So, thought Albert, he's playing the "guess who I know" card already, he must be rattled about something, but what? He assumed he was supposed to be impressed and also a little intimidated by the mention of someone as exalted as a police commissioner.

'Please do; Commissioner Blake was in touch with my office the day before yesterday asking how things were proceeding with this case.'

Thankfully it would take a few days for the gentleman before him to ascertain that the statement he had just made was untrue. By which time he should have the doctor's revised report which he hoped would clear things up one way or another. In fact his interest was becoming aroused by the minute as to why the Knightley family should be so worried about him interviewing Elizabeth Tester.

Finally, a full hour after his arrival, the inspector was taken downstairs and shown into a small sitting room which apparently belonged to the couple who worked as retainers when the family weren't in residence. Feeling uncomfortably warm, the inspector took off his coat and put it over his arm.

After a couple of minutes a tall slim woman, probably less than thirty years of age, entered the room. She was wearing a black dress with a small brooch at her throat and her dark hair was pulled into a bun at the nape of her neck. She had large intelligent but gentle eyes and she looked composed and dignified; she was certainly striking he thought as he rose to greet her.

True to his word, Mr Knightley himself settled down into the most comfortable chair and crossed his legs. Clearly he was not to be moved so Albert decided to make the best of a bad job.

*

Lizzie was surprised when Mr Hemsley told her that an inspector of police wanted to see her. She had been cleaning some of Miss Sophia's pumps in the boot room. She immediately felt nervous though had no idea why. After washing her hands and removing her apron, she made her way to Mr and Mrs Field's sitting room where she found not only the unfamiliar policeman but also her employer, Mr Knightley.

The master of the house immediately took control of the situation. 'Now, Tester, there's nothing to be alarmed about, this gentleman is a police officer who wants to speak to you about the attack you suffered on the road to Blenthorne a few weeks ago. I will remain here with you throughout. Just answer his questions honestly and it will only take up a few minutes of your time,' he said patronisingly.

Lizzie was irrationally annoyed with Mr Knightley; she was perfectly able to acquit herself. He knew nothing of her; he never acknowledged her presence if she was with her mistress when he entered a room. However he had now made an erroneous judgement that she was some sort of dolt that couldn't string a sentence together and needed to be chaperoned.

The inspector moved forward with a smile and introduced himself, offering his hand as he did so.

Lizzie grasped his hand firmly and decided, regardless of any personal cost, to be completely candid with him and not be intimidated by the presence of her master.

'Please sit down, Inspector; it's a pleasure to meet you,' Lizzie was impressed with how confident she sounded. 'Allow me to take your things.' She deftly relieved the inspector of his coat and hat.

If Mr Knightley was surprised by the maid's self-assured demeanour he managed to hide it quite well but looked at her sharply. She wondered if, in all the years that he had employed her, he had ever heard her speak before. She returned immediately after taking the inspector's outer garments to hang up on the peg rail in the passageway, incurring a glare from the butler in the process.

The inspector outlined the reason for his visit and Lizzie repeated her conversation with Obed Daniels. He took her through the events of the day of the dog attack and her reasons for believing that Grace Cork's death was unrelated.

'It's my belief, Inspector, that Mrs Cork's death was made to look like the results of a fatal dog attack. She was a lady of … ill-repute as I understand it. A motive could be found for wanting her dead I'm sure and the dog attacks gave her killer the perfect opportunity to seize his chance.'

'Good God, Tester! That is a preposterous thing to say; where did you get such an absurd notion? If this is the result of fraternising with villagers, which I understand you have been doing, then clearly it's inappropriate and you are to remain within the grounds until further notice. Now get back to your work.' Mr Knightley stood up. 'Inspector Bishop, I have afforded you an audience, treated you with civility and courtesy but now this vulgar business needs to be brought to a close.'

'One moment if you please,' the inspector stood up and faced the master of the house. 'Miss Tester is a material witness in a possible murder investigation and as an officer sworn to uphold the law, it is for me to decide when an interview is terminated. Also begging your pardon, I would have thought surely it is impossible to ban her from leaving the grounds in her own time. She's an employee not a serf, unless I am mistaken, Sir?'

Lizzie wanted to hug him but remained seated demurely with her hands folded in her lap; they could have no idea that her heart was beating fit to burst out of her chest.

'Report to me in my study, Tester, as soon as you are finished with this … charade.' Herbert Knightley turned abruptly and left the room without any further acknowledgement of the police inspector.

The inspector returned to his seat. 'Miss Tester, I'm sorry if I have caused problems for you with your employer; I don't understand his animosity to my interviewing you. I explained it was an informal meeting for the purpose of gathering information, no more.'

'No, Inspector Bishop, I too am at a loss to understand his reaction. I will see what he has to say shortly, as you heard I have been summoned to attend his study.'

'I hope to have some further information later today and then we will know if Mrs Cork actually was murdered, but I wouldn't be here, Miss Tester, if I didn't think there was merit in your theory.'

'Will you return to Blenthorne now, Inspector, to await the information you need?'

'Yes, I'll have a look at Mrs Cork's cottage in the morning and maybe see if I can trace any of her um … clients. I understand that while she was a discreet woman, there was a steady stream of gentlemen callers; I'll see what they know in the Blenny.'

'Well I'm in enough trouble anyway, so I might as well tell you, I saw Mr Donald, that is Mr Donald Knightley, the master's son, going into Mrs Cork's cottage a while ago. Of course I had no idea why at the time.'

'No indeed of course not, Miss, nor would I expect you to,' replied the inspector maybe a little too quickly.

'Thank you though; I won't pursue that today but I will certainly be speaking to him in the future should the need arise and rest assured I won't tell him who gave me this information.'

'I suspect most of the village knows who visited Mrs Cork. It seems I was the only person in the whole of Cumberland who thought she was running a tailoring service.'

The inspector laughed heartily as he looked at Lizzie with a kindly smile that seemed to light up his whole face.

'And well you may, Miss Tester,' he replied regaining his composure. 'Please let me know if I can be of any service to you, with regard your employer I mean.'

'Well, even if they let me go, I hope I can be assured of a good reference. There are always vacancies for servants, Inspector. With new factories being built all the time, fewer and fewer people want to go into service.'

She went on to tell the inspector about the situation at home with her mother and her reasons for staying with the same employer for so long; she was not sure why and how it was relevant but he was a good listener.

She found herself idly wondering how old he was; mid-thirties she would surmise but then she was in her late twenties herself. He was of medium height and build for a man and clean shaven with brown wavy hair. She admonished herself; the other day she had stared at Mr Daniels' chest hair and now she was wondering about the inspector's age and weighing up his appearance. It seemed that whenever a man was kind to her, she started to have all sorts of improper thoughts. She felt suitably shameful.

'One final thing, Miss, do you know if any of the other servants might have seen anything around the time Mrs Cork died; I suppose I mean what's the gossip in the servants' hall about all this?'

'We were advised not to go out while the dog was free so none of the servants ventured far from the house after what happened to me. If anyone had any information you can be sure they would not be keeping it to themselves … unless they were where they shouldn't have been of course …'

The inspector seemed to be digesting this information as they left the warmth of the sitting room and he was reunited with his outer garments. Lizzie saw him to the backdoor; neither wanting to incur any further wrath from Mr Hemsley.

Lizzie made her way to the study as instructed after she had seen the inspector on his way. She tapped lightly on the door and entered when commanded to do so.

Mr Knightley was standing behind the desk with his back to her, looking out of the window.

'Well, Tester, what do you have to say for yourself?' he demanded, making no attempt to hide his anger.

'I don't understand, Sir. I have done nothing wrong,' Lizzie said honestly.

'Excuse me, Madam!' He turned round, his face flushed in a rage such as she had never previously witnessed. She would have considered if asked, that her employer was the most mild mannered of gentlemen and almost devoid of emotion.

'Sir; I saw Mrs Cork's body and the wounds to her arm did not look consistent with the wounds I saw on the sheep or I had sustained myself.'

'If you had concerns why didn't you bring them to me as any responsible servant would have done and then be guided by my judgement? No, you wilfully brought scandal to my door, upsetting me and my family and for what; to draw attention to yourself presumably, just who do you think you are?'

'I have brought no scandal to your door. If Mrs Cork was murdered she deserves justice like any other human being. I would have thought you would have been in favour of that, Sir, being a man with a strong sense of honour and duty.'

That was clearly the last straw.

'Have you quite finished Tester? In fact let me answer for you; yes, you have quite finished. Not a hint of contrition. In fact I think you are quite proud of yourself! Well let's see how proud you are when you find yourself unemployed and homeless. Pack your things and leave this instant.'

Herbert Knightley was spluttering and spitting as he hissed at her and gesticulated towards the door. He clung on to the back of the desk chair for support and Lizzie feared he may keel over. He retrieved a trail of saliva that had escaped his mouth and was falling in the direction of his chest.

She thought about objecting, arguing her corner but what power did she have; a servant versus a master, no matter how unreasonable, she had no channel of redress.

'As you wish, Sir; am I dismissed now? May I help you into your chair before I leave as you look unwell?'

'Get out. Get out. You will leave here without a reference.'

'I see; thank you,' she replied demurely and dropped a small curtsey.

She turned and left the room, feeling nowhere near as calm as her demeanour suggested. She was a well-trained servant and she knew how to hold herself in check no matter what. Actually that really could not have gone any worse. She had lost her job; her home and sadly most of all, she would not see the Daniels' girls again. She made up her mind to go into Blenthorne to say goodbye at least and apologise for not being able to complete their dresses.

She went to her attic room and was pulling open the drawers to put her few possessions into her soft carpet bag. The door was flung open and her aunt rushed in.

'Lizzie, is this true? Mr Hemsley just told me he was instructed by the master to order the carriage to take you to the railway station. You have been dismissed?'

'Oh goodness if he is arranging my travel, he must be desperate for me to leave the area. As I am no longer employed by him, he cannot dictate where I go. I will choose my own time. I am going to Blenthorne in the short term.'

'I'll come with you,' said Philadelphia with resolve as she sat down firmly on Lizzie's bed.

'No, Aunt Phily, there is no reason for us both to be jobless and indeed homeless. I'll write to you and let you know what I am doing. I will go home to see mother before I decide anything. I have enough savings for the time being. I …'

They were interrupted by a terrible noise coming from the floor below; a shrill scream that deafened them both.

Shortly afterwards, Miss Sophia came flying up the servants' staircase and flung open the bedroom door without knocking.

'Tester; whatever has happened?'

'I have been dismissed by your father, Miss Sophia, for contacting the police regarding Mrs Cork's death.'

Sophia Knightley left as suddenly as she appeared.

Lizzie and Philadelphia looked at each other in confusion. They were just preparing to go downstairs when Hemsley appeared at the door with a message from Lady Constance telling Lizzie to remain in her room.

So Lizzie and her aunt sat in virtual silence for over two hours, just waiting. Cook sent some tea up to them on a tray. They could hear muffled voices wafting up from the floors below.

At six-thirty Lizzie was summoned to the morning room. Lady Constance sat on her sofa, looking in the direction of the window. Lizzie wondered if her ladyship had noticed her presence.

Finally she spoke; 'Tester, first let me say that I do not condone your behaviour of earlier today. However both Mr Knightley and I feel we would be harsh employers indeed to dismiss you for an honest misjudgement. Now kindly attend to your duties; we are eating informally this evening and Lady Nora wants to dine in her room so will not need you. Miss Sophia is waiting for you to attend her. We will say no more about this. The whole unfortunate matter is closed. Send Crittle to me please.'

*

However, the matter was far from closed as at the same time that Lizzie was being reinstated, Inspector Bishop was taking delivery of a report from the police surgeon regarding his latest inspection of the injuries to Grace Cork's neck.

As usual there were a myriad of medical terms. Amid all the jargon, carotid arteries and jugular veins and the like, Albert found the part he was looking for.

"In conclusion, it is my considered medical opinion that whilst the deceased had suffered a blow to the head, possibly consistent with falling, it was not of sufficient severity to kill her. The fatal wound was inflicted with a small thin blade, which severed both the external and anterior jugular veins, causing exsanguination." Albert knew that to mean immediate and extensive blood loss sufficient to extinguish life. *"Further examination of that area and also the upper limbs now reveal linear markings, most likely inflicted post mortem. The injuries had been difficult to determine during the first examination due to oedema and erythema ..."* blah, blah, blah, yes you cover yourself mate, Albert thought grimly.

So Lizzie Tester had been right. Grace Cork had been killed and they had a murderer in their midst.

Chapter 7 – Uncertainties and Lies

September 1891

Herbert Knightley stood in his book-lined study looking out of the window leading onto the terrace, beyond the indiscernible ha-ha to the sheep grazing in the distance, heads down, not a care in the world. He had learned something yesterday. He could command respect from his peers on the Privy Council, he could represent his constituents' interests in a variety of areas and he could stand up in Parliament to deliver an authoritative speech, holding his own in any heated debate that followed.

However, when it came to his family, was he master in his own home? The simple answer to that was no.

He could barely think of the events of the last twenty-four hours without his heart-rate increasing and the pressure in his temples creating the feeling his forehead would burst open like a virulent pustule.

He expected to be vexed by life events in London, in fact when the House was sitting late he often stayed at his club where he could dine and unwind without Constance bearing witness to the strain he was under.

When the family retired to Cumberland for their twice yearly holidays that was a time to relax, no pressure of work, no enforced socialising; house parties made up of friends, held out of choice not political necessity. There would be no strife, no discord, just fresh air, good food and above all, a time to think and reflect. But no more it seemed. His sanctuary, his peaceful retreat from the worries of the world, his safe haven had been breached.

There were still issues of course. His son Donald was always a worry, whether he was here or at home in Kent. He had always been an unruly child. His behaviour now was to say the least, wild. He wouldn't settle down to a profession. Constance indulged him far too much; every time he spoke to her about it she made excuses for her son. "Plenty of time for responsibility; he's still so young". Herbert had reminded her on several occasions that Donald was older than he had been when they had married and he was, at that time, forging himself a successful career in banking.

The boy was overdrawn in London and was involved in gambling here. He had come to his father a few weeks ago extremely shame-faced, asking for money to settle his local debts. Added to that, it transpired that he had been seeing a prostitute, a common whore; he had admitted as much after she was found dead. For a short while it seemed that all would be well. The woman concerned had been attacked by a dog and died of her injuries. Thankfully it was all resolved bar the inquest which would be a foregone conclusion.

That was until the truculent Tester had the temerity to involve herself. He had asked her yesterday who she thought she was. She was a servant, a domestic underling in his home. He employed her, he fed her, he clothed her, he put a roof over her head and he brought her to their holiday home as part of his household. How did she repay him? She contacted the police, albeit indirectly through the pub landlord – oh yes – the local innkeeper if you will, to say she thought the whore had been murdered.

Was she taken seriously by the police, oh one could wager their last sovereign she was. An inspector was sent from Keswick to see her. And what did she have the barefaced audacity to say in his presence? She had said the woman was probably killed because she was blackmailing someone. He was speechless.

He had provided for her since she was little more than a child and for what? So she could spend her free time fraternising with innkeepers and bringing turmoil to his door. And today, today he had received a note from that blasted inspector from Keswick to say he was coming back and wanted to interview Donald that afternoon.

He has sent word to the family solicitor who would be present when the interview took place, in spite of the fact it was a Sunday. Obviously Donald knew nothing about the death so the whole process would be straightforward, although extremely tiresome and completely unnecessary.

After Tester had finished with her fantasy and the inspector had left, he had done the only thing he could do and dismissed her on the spot.

She had been so calm, damn her!

No begging, pleading or crying. She just stood there and asked him if he needed her help to sit down as he looked unwell. Looked unwell! That infuriated him even further, he was so apoplectic with rage he couldn't actually speak and just gesticulated towards the door and she turned and left. He was well and truly shaking after the encounter. He had lowered himself unsteadily into his chair. How could a mere servant reduce him, Herbert Knightley, to the point of collapse?

But was that the end of the distasteful business? Oh no, far from it! After about twenty minutes, just when his equanimity appeared to be returning, all hell broke loose. His house turned from a quiet tranquil retreat into something resembling a bawdy ale house.

His beloved wife Constance with whom he hardly ever had a cross word, appeared before him, white with fury.

'What is the meaning of this, Herbert? I have just heard that you have dismissed Tester. Have you gone mad?'

She actually squared up to him; looked him straight in the face as she shouted and pointed her finger at him. At one point actually jabbing him in the chest!

'My dear,' he had said in the most placating tone possible, 'she has brought scandal to our door. She dishonoured me and in fact the whole family. She has made the most outrageous accusations regarding the death of that local woman. If she had concerns she should have come to me; she did not. She has ideas above her station. We have had the police here and …'

'And you have dismissed her! Without consulting me, you have dismissed her and told her she could leave without a reference. All she did was to speak out and say she was worried about the cause of a woman's death.' Constance was tight-lipped with anger.

'She is a servant; she should not "speak out" as you put it. It is no business of hers to be having opinions. And that police officer was no better. I mentioned Sir Stanley Blake and he didn't bat an eyelid; insolence, pure and simple. No respect for their betters either of them. What is this world coming to? And did you know Tester has been fraternising with the landlord from the Blenthorne Inn? No I thought not; totally inappropriate.'

Herbert was quite pleased with that as clearly he had the upper hand, or so he thought, until Constance disabused him of the notion.

'As you well know, Mr Daniels came to her assistance when she was attacked by the dangerous dog that subsequently killed several sheep and that other poor woman. From what Crittle has told me, I believe Tester has subsequently made some clothes for Mr Daniels' daughters, as she felt indebted to him. It was a means of thanking him for his kindness to her. He is a widower I understand, so just what do you find inappropriate about that, Herbert?'

He had been a little taken aback but recovered himself quickly.

'Well all the same, it is unbefitting, her behaviour is incompatible with her position here and I have put a stop to it. She is to take the next train to London. From there she can go back to Westden and collect her things. She is dismissed without a reference.'

'No, I don't think so, Herbert. Employing and dismissing staff is my responsibility with the help of Mrs Luck. Since when did you involve yourself in such matters? Do you have any idea how difficult it is to find and retain a good lady's maid? No, I thought not and we have two, Crittle and Tester. If you dismiss Tester, I suspect Crittle will leave as well. They are related you know – oh you didn't know – yes they are aunt and niece and should you ever have bothered with either of them before, you would have been aware of that.'

Constance paused for breath but if Herbert thought she had finished he was mistaken.

'Furthermore, what will that say about us, Herbert, in society circles? Two of the best lady's maids in England leaving us simultaneously; how am I going to explain that? And mark my words, references or no references, both will be snapped up in less than no time. I am the envy of all London as both have had several offers to my knowledge but they are loyal servants, Herbert. Loyal to us and I cannot, I will not lose either of them is that quite clear? In addition …'

Constance's verbal torrent was terminated by a terrible tumult. There appeared to be a wailing banshee at large in the house. The door was flung open and the banshee appeared clutching her hair and screaming. For some time the sounds coming out of the creature's mouth were incomprehensible. She paused for breath and to collect herself a little.

'Papa, did you just take leave of your senses? Hemsley has told me that you have dismissed Tester. I will not have it. I will not have it,' sobbed Sophia, stamping her left foot as she collapsed dramatically onto the nearest sofa.

Herbert was about to reprimand her for the tone she was taking but didn't get the chance as his wife took charge.

'Hush child. It has all been a terrible misunderstanding. Your father was just upset because Tester had involved herself in something that was not her concern. It is all over now. No one has been dismissed. Have they Herbert? … Have they Herbert?'

Yes, at that point his elegant and dutiful wife was actually shouting at him.

So there it was; fait accompli, Herbert Knightley, successful banker, respected MP and pillar of society had turned and left the room, a beaten man.

He had called Donald to his presence in the study after supper. Donald appeared on the point of tears.

Herbert had apprised him of the earlier events.

'Do you have anything to tell me, Donald? Anything I should know about that woman, Grace Cork, because that policeman doesn't seem the sort to settle for an easy life. He will dig and delve like a ferret down a rabbit hole if he gets a whiff of anything which could lead him back here. She was found near to this estate wasn't she?'

'Yes, Papa, I believe she was. And in answer to your question, I swear there is nothing connecting me to her, other than the fact I have visited her on occasion, along with many others I might add.'

'I'm not bothered about the others. They are not my son; they are not my responsibility. They do not have to answer to your mother. Please tell me she knows nothing of this.'

'Of course not; I have been very discreet.'

'I hope so for your own sake. What I really don't want is another visit from the constabulary.'

As it turned out that was exactly what they were going to get later in the day. He just hoped that Donald cut a better figure this afternoon than he managed the evening before. If he wasn't able to convince his father that he knew no more than he was admitting regarding the dead woman, what hope did he had of convincing a trained police officer?

He turned from the window and left the comparative calm of the study to attend the family for their midday meal.

*

Nora had everything planned; thankfully they seemed to have forgotten about her in all that had happened recently. As usual George left her in the wood and she made her own way from there. As she approached the cottage she could smell wonderful aromas permeating the fresh air. He had the window open and she called out as she got nearer.

He looked out of the window, his shirt slightly open at the top and his dark hair damp from bending over the hot stove. He had made them a mutton hotpot and cold lemon cordial; simple fare but the food of Gods as far as Nora was concerned.

After they had exchanged their usual warm greeting they sat down on the bench at the wooden table to eat and he told her about his work since they were last together.

'What has kept you away?' he enquired looking at her, his deep brown eyes seeming to penetrate her soul.

'We have had all sorts of excitement at Highfields,' she explained animatedly. 'The police came to the house to speak to Tester, my maid. Well I was aghast! I mean what could she have done? It turned out she thought that local woman whom had been killed by the dog was actually murdered and had dragged a police inspector here, all the way from Keswick! Can you credit it? She's a servant for goodness sake. Well, Herbert my brother-in-law went mad as you can imagine and dismissed her on the spot. My sister Constance and my niece Sophia reacted like the world had ended and the upshot was Tester was reinstated with not so much as a warning; although I understand Constance left her to brood in her room for a while before telling her!'

'But you like her, don't you?' he asked looking at Nora intently.

'What? Like Tester? She's a maid! She's good at her job but I won't have need of a lady's maid for ever will I? I mean how on earth could we employ her here?'

They both laughed and then he asked about the police investigation, so Nora relayed the little she knew.

'So has he left now, the inspector?'

'Far from it, you know I have spoken of my nephew Donald, it seems he had a connection; a sordid connection to the woman who died and the police officer came back to question him this afternoon. It appears they now agree with Tester that the Cork woman was killed, as the police doctor has examined the body more closely. It's routine apparently to look at things twice, at least that is what we have been told. Inspector Bishop has

127

now searched the woman's house and has started questioning her … what would one call them? Clients I suppose. Apparently she kept a diary, well one would need to I expect, if one were in her particular line of business, to avoid double booking,' Nora giggled.

'Really, Nora, I'm surprised at you,' he said chiding her as he smiled indulgently into her eyes. 'When was she killed exactly?'

'They can't be sure; they think her body was found about three or four days after she died. I suppose any longer and the local wildlife would have feasted royally on her remains.'

He looked at her sharply. 'That's not a pleasant thought, Nora; I accept she wasn't exactly a respectable woman but even so …'

'I know, I'm sorry, my love, it was very cruel of me, heartless in fact. I know how sensitive you are. Please don't look at me like that; you know I can't bear it if I upset you in any way.'

He touched her shoulder reassuringly. 'So do you think the day she died could tie in with … what you saw?'

'Of course not, I mean, I didn't really see anything did I? It was probably just poachers; you know all the woods are full of them.'

'Even so, if you have any suspicions at all you should tell the inspector.'

'And explain what I was doing here at twilight and encourage him to trample his way all around the vicinity? Stumbling across the cottage and you; do you want that? How can you work if you are disturbed? I thought your privacy was the most important thing in your life − that is why we live like this isn't it − rather than announcing our relationship to the world and living properly in society?'

'Yes, of course you're right. Solitude is imperative for my work. No, I don't want anyone or anything to disrupt that. As you say, the chances of it being the same night are negligible at most. Now let's not waste any more time on matters so unpleasant; our time is precious, let's speak of happier things.'

*

Donald Knightley was examining his nails as a means of distraction. He was in a bit of a fix and needed money. He wanted to get away from here but he wasn't allowed to leave at the moment. Well, to be fair no one had actually said he was under house arrest but it would have looked suspicious if he had turned tail and ran like a common criminal. No, he needed to stay calm and all would be well.

At least one drain on his resources had gone so his allowance would go a bit further than of late. His mother had given him some to tide him over and his aunt Nora was inordinately kind but his commitments were substantial. One couldn't live on fresh air. How had circumstances contrived to reduce him to this? Clearly it wasn't his fault; it was a combination of misfortune and the mean-spirited, grasping nature of others.

He wouldn't risk gambling hereabouts again; by the time he got his allowance next month he would be back in London. No-one could have such a run of bad luck and their fortunes not turn around. He was one good bridge game away from putting everything straight. He looked at his nails again.

He wondered if he had been convincing when he had spoken to the policeman. He wasn't sure. The man was inscrutable.

He realised he was sweating a bit and wiped his forehead with his handkerchief. He knew what he had to do; he just needed to have more faith in himself and execute his plan of action. He was Donald Knightley of the merchant banking family after all; that meant something, didn't it?

*

At the same time as Lady Nora was visiting the cottage in the wood, Lizzie returned to Blenthorne to see the Daniels' girls. The pinafores were finished and the winter dresses were ready for fitting before final stitching.

Amid lots of joyful laughter, the girls had tried on their warm winter dresses and Lizzie promised they would be finished possibly by the morrow, if she could manage it. As she stitched, she took tea with Mr Daniels and told him of the events at Highfields. He was deeply concerned to learn that she had almost lost her job but sighed with relief when she said she would have come to see them before she left.

'Miss Tester, if you ever need a place to stay, Mrs Reilly near the green takes in lodgers and to be honest, I could certainly do with a housekeeper. I know it would be a comedown on what you are used to but it would tide you over until you got back on your feet.'

'Mr Daniels, your kindness knows no bounds and I do love it here in Blenthorne and so much enjoy walking the fells, although truth be told I haven't had much time to do that of late. However with my mother's health being so poor, I really do need to base myself in Kent, for the foreseeable future at any rate.'

'Just so that you know, the offer will always be there,' he said very softly.

She smiled at him and was about to say how much she enjoyed the time she spent with his family when the inspector walked in. She kept it to herself, as it would seem odd taken out of context, quite unseemly.

'Not disturbing you folks, am I?' he asked and sat down before waiting for a reply.

Obed looked a little put out but Lizzie smiled a warm greeting.

'Will you take tea, Inspector Bishop?' she asked formally. Then felt a little self-conscious at assuming the role of mistress of the house without being asked.

'Maybe the inspector would like something a little stronger?' enquired Obed.

'Well if you insist, Landlord, I'm sure my arm could be twisted,' said Albert Bishop as he settled himself onto the settee.

Obed Daniels left to go through to the bar.

'I am pleased to see you, Inspector; I wanted to thank you privately for taking my concerns so seriously. I feel I have done my Christian duty to Mrs Cork, whatever her profession and way of life. Even if it transpires that her death was accidental, at least it is being thoroughly investigated which is right and proper. May I ask how your enquiries are proceeding or are you not at liberty to say?' asked Lizzie sitting forward on her chair.

Obed returned at that moment with a bottle of brown ale and a glass.

'Not joining me? Oh I see,' said Albert Bishop eyeing up the two half-empty tea cups as Obed shook his head.

He sat with his beer in front of him but did not pour it. Lizzie thought maybe he was a little embarrassed to do so in her presence.

'Miss Tester was just asking me about my enquiries,' he informed Obed Daniels. 'I'm able to tell you that you were right, Miss, the police surgeon's revised post mortem report supports the conclusion that Mrs Cork died as a result of a knife wound to the neck. I had a look at her cottage this morning and I think she may have actually been killed there. You'll appreciate I shouldn't say why I believe that; I'll give the information to the coroner at her inquest.'

They both nodded and Lizzie hoped he would continue.

'I was also given a diary by Freda the maid with the names of Mrs Cork's – excuse me, Miss – clients.'

'Really, Inspector, I know quite well what she did for a living. I am far from naïve, as I am sure you can appreciate.'

Lizzie chose not to look at the landlord as she made this rather incredible statement. Had she done so, she would have seen he was quite unable to keep the small smile from his face or prevent his head from shaking almost undiscernibly as he and the inspector exchanged a glance.

'I understand that you came to Highfields again earlier this afternoon, Inspector. Was that to speak to Mr Donald?'

'Yes that's right. His father had the family solicitor present. The young man was quite evasive and very jumpy though. That in itself makes me wonder what he has to hide. I'm going to have him down to the police house for another interview, make it a bit more formal; see if that loosens his tongue. I have a strong feeling he knows more than he is letting on.'

'I suspect he just doesn't want his mother to know about his association with Mrs Cork,' said Lizzie knowingly, in her newly acquired blasé woman-of-the-world way. 'Where is the police house?'

'It's just along the road, towards the centre of the village. Tom lives there with his wife Edith and their son Gordon, who's the same age as May. These days the office seems to be Mrs Cummins' front room. Apparently she's taken it over with her knickknacks and knitting patterns but Tom clears a chair if needs be,' informed Obed Daniels with a smile as the inspector winced.

Lizzie finished her tea, packed up her needlework and took her leave.

*

The inspector seemed in the mood for mulling things over and Obed Daniels was nothing if not a good listener. He had had years of experience standing behind the bar of the Blenny.

'It seems the body was lying on Dundle Fell at the foot of a rock near the boundary of the Highfields estate. To all intents and purposes it appeared she was running from the dog, stumbled, hit her head and was then savagely mauled. However I have been to have a look at the spot and there isn't anywhere near enough blood; mind you, it has been wet of late so it's possible all traces could have been washed away. The police doctor now believes she would have suffered extensive blood loss causing death almost instantaneously; at least within less than a minute. On balance, I think she was moved after she died and dumped there,' the inspector confided. He paused, then asked his host a question.

'I'm glad of a word alone with you, Landlord; your nephew Ned, good lad is he?'

'Well, he needs to be kept on a tight rein, if you get my meaning. He's my brother's boy so I have a responsibility towards him. He had a rough start in life, my brother was a professional pugilist; money wasn't regular, they moved around a lot, usually just ahead of the bailiffs. Lived in rooms without water or cooking facilities. They often went without a hot meal for weeks on end. Really until I took him and his mother in, he had never had a proper home or reasonable standard of living. His schooling wasn't much either, so I have forgiven him the odd mix up with the takings, however as I say, I keep an eye out.'

'He was very vague at breakfast time this morning when I asked where he had been when he stumbled across Jem Mitchell just after he found the body. Can you shed any light? I'm only interested in the death, nothing else.'

A full minute passed. 'I think he was gambling; he's often out all night,' said Obed Daniels with a sigh. 'He visits Freshlea, a farm about a mile-and-a-half or so north east of Rowendale and would need to return that way, skirting round the Highfields estate, or through it knowing Ned, if he was coming home from there. They keep fighting dogs in a barn on the premises I believe. I suspect that's where the dog that attacked Miss Tester escaped from. There's cock fighting and bare-knuckle boxing as well. I've been asked to patch up the odd split lip and cut eye. I used to be a second for my brother so I know what I'm doing. I don't hold with it myself, but it is an old tradition and as long as they are not doing any harm to anyone else and not spending more than they can afford, then my motto is "live and let live". Who am I to sit in judgement? You never heard that from me though as I need to keep in with these people, it's my livelihood.'

'Rest assured, Landlord, I've heard nothing. One last question, did Donald Knightley frequent the farm, do you know?'

'If I were a betting man, I would say that was a certainty.'

They smiled briefly at each other as Obed Daniels left the room.

*

He was to have supper with the Cummins' that evening but before he did so, Inspector Bishop decided to request that Mr Donald Knightley come to Blenthorne the following day. He sent the constable over with a note, to the effect that Mr Knightley should attend the police house at ten o'clock in the morning; or as it was apparently known locally, Mrs Cummins' front room.

As it transpired, the summons would be in vain.

Chapter 8 – Suspicions in Absentia

September 1891

Monday morning dawned overcast and damp. Lizzie liked those days; she enjoyed tramping across the grass and the soft heather in the stillness and quiet. She hoped to be able to walk in the grounds during her free time later, after she had attended to her duties.

Miss Sophia was in petulant mood still.

'Tester, I can't believe you behaved so badly. I had to use all my powers of persuasion to prevent Papa from dismissing you; do you realise that? Really I have to be able to rely on you totally and you must be discreet; you will be with me for many years I hope, so let us have no more such indecorous behaviour.'

Lizzie had set out Miss Sophia's clothes for the day and was just getting ready to style her hair.

'Yes, Miss.'

'Why did you do it? You didn't know the woman concerned did you? So why make it your business to interfere?'

'Because she was a human being, Miss Sophia, and she couldn't speak for herself.'

'Really, Tester, you do have the strangest ideas at times.'

'If you say so, Miss.'

Sophia sat down at her dressing table pulling her silk dressing gown tightly round her.

'We'll just keep it simple today I think; I'm not expecting to see anyone of importance so a basic chignon will do.'

Lizzie picked up the hairbrush and arranged the appropriate hairpins in place ready for when she brushed out the tangles and had the hair correctly positioned at the nape of her mistress's neck for the bun to be formed.

Before Lizzie could be scolded further there was an urgent tap on the door and Lady Constance swished into the room, also in her dressing gown with her fair hair in a long plait to the right side of her neck.

Lizzie bobbed a small courtesy and bowed her head appropriately. Lady Constance ignored her.

'Have you seen your brother this morning, Sophia?' she enquired without bothering with the formality of a greeting.

'What, no of course not; I'm not in the habit of receiving visitors in my bedroom before I am dressed, particularly not my brother! Why?'

'According to Hemsley, the new valet has told him Donald didn't come home last night; his bed hasn't been slept in and to cap it all we have had a message from the policeman that he wishes to see Donald at the police house in Blenthorne this morning.'

'Mama, Donald is twenty-five years old; it really is up to him if he chooses not to come home. I would not trouble yourself; if we were at home in Kent and he didn't return one night you wouldn't think anything of it, you would just assume he had stayed with a friend or at his club.'

'Precisely; but he doesn't have any friends here does he and where would he stay? There is no suitable accommodation for miles around; no local families have houses of this standard.'

'I think the inn in Blenthorne has guest rooms doesn't it, Tester? If he had been drinking I'm sure he would not be too bothered if the standard of the accommodation was not up to snub. He's probably inebriated and sleeping it off. I'm sure he will be home before long, assuming he's sobered up of course,' said Sophia with an air of disinterest as she looked at herself in the mirror.

'Really, Sophia; must you be so coarse!'

Lady Constance turned on her heels and wafted out of the room as abruptly as she had entered.

Lizzie suddenly felt irrationally defensive regarding the accommodation offered by Mr Daniels.

'The guest rooms at the Blenthorne Inn are very nice indeed, Miss, very comfortable.'

'Tester, I don't even want to think about how you could possibly know that. Now, please can we get on?'

*

Inspector Bishop looked at his pocket watch which was attached to a chain and secured to his suit waistcoat. Five and twenty minutes past ten, nearly half an hour late and still no sign of Mr Donald Knightley; he dispatched Constable Cummins over to Highfields to fetch the little blighter. He tucked the timepiece back into his pocket. The Knightley's solicitor had tutted several times and finally left, announcing rather pompously that time equated to revenue regardless of the client.

Each time she had appeared in the doorway, the inspector had turned down offers of cups of tea and food from Mrs Cummins. She seemed quite put out that he had the audacity to want to use the office in the police house for its intended purpose.

He sat down behind the desk, having removed the aspidistra plant in its pot and placed it on the floor, in front of the window. He hung his jacket on the back of the chair after taking his pipe out of the inside pocket. He placed the unlit pipe in his mouth without adding any tobacco.

He had instigated enquiries into Donald Knightley's financial affairs and would wait to see what they elicited. He had found several witnesses to attest to the fact that Donald Knightley visited Grace Cork at her home regularly and had her own diary as supporting evidence.

Her property, Hope Cottage, stood in a prime location just at the mouth of Newbury Lane. From the window in the front room it was possible to see the village green and equally anyone standing on the green could see the front door of the cottage, so the comings and goings would have been obvious to the keen observer.

He was pretty sure the victim was killed in her home, having found dark staining in the cement between the tiles on the scullery floor. He had now had time to look at the information from the doctor more thoroughly. If he was correct in his interpretation of the report, it would appear that bilateral severing of the carotid arteries would have led to copious amounts of blood squirting from the long lateral wound like apertures from a fountain, spreading far and wide.

Whilst the floor had been cleaned adequately to the inattentive eye, there were tiny spatters on the whitewashed walls which were evident to anyone looking closely. When he visited the cottage the previous day, he drew this to the attention of Freda the maid who had been paid until the end of the month, so in the absence of anyone advising her to the contrary, was still diligently working her regular hours. She said she cleaned the floor "regular-like" and had not previously noticed that the cement was stained. She tended to wipe the walls down after doing the washing to try to remove the condensation. She had not seen any spatters the last time she did the laundry but with her mistress unexpectedly absent, she had not needed to fire up the copper for a while.

A close inspection of the rest of the property had revealed a clean and well-presented home; it was large for a cottage with four bedrooms upstairs and two reception rooms downstairs plus a kitchen with a pantry and scullery. Grace Cork had clearly used the second bedroom as her own with the largest bedroom being fitted out somewhat ornately, presumably for the purposes of entertaining. The clothes stored in the second bedroom were quite demure and sensible and in stark contrast to those in the closet of the main bedroom. These were brightly coloured, ostentatious and flamboyant. There was also a dressed blonde wig on a stand in the bottom of the closet. This was no doubt for those gentlemen who had a preference for this rather than the natural brunette of their hostess. There was running water in the scullery and the well-equipped kitchen boasted a top quality range. There were a variety of ornaments and keepsakes but no photographs, so no clues forthcoming as to family or friends.

Freda reported that Mrs Cork was a generous employer who paid her well and gave her hand-me-down clothes; although Freda confided they were not really to her taste being somewhat fancy for village life but she was usually able to reuse the material to make something serviceable.

'She didn't 'ave no uppity airs; she was a right thoughtful lady. She knew I suffers with me back like and always told me to take me time and leave the 'eavy stuff 'til I was feeling up to it.'

Freda confirmed her employer had never mentioned any relatives or had anyone to stay.

'Other than … well, I don't quite know how to put it, Sir,' Freda looked awkward.

'I understand. No one other than her clients,' he had responded helpfully.

Freda nodded with a small sigh. 'I liked her, Sir,' she volunteered.

'If she was a considerate employer then that's just as it should be in my humble opinion, Freda.' The inspector smiled at the maid, causing her to blush. Never hurt to keep servants on side.

With the help of the constable, Inspector Bishop had already managed to track down a few of the victim's clients; most were working men, a little shamefaced but honest enough. Grace Cork also attracted a few paying customers from further afield who would present more of a challenge. Nevertheless, he had set Tom Cummins the task of attempting to find these gentlemen.

He fervently hoped that his interview with Donald Knightley, when it took place, would prove fruitful as he was sure the young man was in possession of more information than he was currently admitting to. Possibly his father, Herbert Knightley knew something too, as whilst he didn't appear in Mrs Cork's diary as a client, he certainly took umbrage at the appearance of the inspector at Highfields.

There was also the question of the linear markings on the body. The doctor now believed these had been inflicted post mortem. He alluded to an implement being involved but didn't speculate as to what, other than that it was possibly a three pronged tool. Albert Bishop had had a look round the property and in the garden shed for anything that fitted the description but his search proved unproductive.

The Knightley angle was one possibility and the other line of enquiry of course had to be the goings-on at the farm; what was it called? Greenlea – something like that – he would need to check with Tom. If indeed there was illegal gambling or dog and cock fights taking place that might give a potential blackmailer a ready source of income.

A client with a loose tongue may have given Grace Cork information which she tried to use to her advantage; so she was silenced in a violent and opportunistic way. Whilst it was possible to wring a cockerel's neck quite easily and most country folk didn't have a problem with that, slitting an injured dog's throat would be another matter. It would need someone with the necessary skills. He wondered if that person would have any qualms if called upon to use their skills on a human being.

It was Monday and the inquest was set for Friday; at this stage it looked like it would be opened and adjourned, pending further enquiries unless he had an unexpected breakthrough prior to that. Now a confession from Mr Donald Knightley would be ideal at this time, however unless Tom Cummins had tracked him down, that didn't look too likely a prospect. On the other hand, could he see Donald Knightley slitting Grace Cork's throat? Not really. He came across as a bit weak; very weak in fact but he knew something, Albert would bet his pension on it.

He was still deep in thought and jotting down a few ideas when the constable appeared in the doorway of the police house office.

'No luck I'm sorry to say, Sir. Up at the big house, they told me Mr Donald didn't come home last night. They think he might have slept at the Blenny.'

'And did he?' asked the inspector.

The constable paused for a moment, clearly not sure how to answer. 'Did he what, Sir?'

'Sleep at the Blenny?' said Albert Bishop as patiently as he could.

'Well I don't rightly know; would you like me to go there and ask?'

Inspector Bishop swallowed his instinctive retort and instead said; 'I'll go myself, I could do with stretching my legs.

'I would like a report on what's-name farm, so anything you know or think might be useful, write it down and we will look at when I get back, as that is our second line of enquiry at present,' added the inspector.

'Yes indeed, Sir; that will be Freshlea Farm; John Busse's place.'

The inspector stood up and turned round to pick up the aspidistra plant.

'And get rid of this before I get back, as much as anything else there is no room for it in here, this is a place of work.'

Albert thought Tom Cummins was willing enough to write up a report on Freshlea Farm and what he knew of the activities there, he was also happily ploughing through the list of Grace Cork's clients. However, removing his wife's aspidistra from her front room, well that was altogether a different matter and he appeared terrified at the prospect; indeed he was almost squirming.

It did look for a moment as if he was going to appeal to the better nature of his superior officer but then clearly decided it would be futile to attempt to explain the dilemma of a married man to a confirmed bachelor.

He took the plant and left the room looking like he had the weight of the world on his shoulders. Albert followed him slowly, pulling his jacket on as he did so.

Albert stuffed his pipe into his inside pocket. He could kill two birds with one stone, see if the errant Mr Donald Knightley was at the Blenny and get something to eat at the same time. He had suffered at the hands of Mrs Cummins' gastronomic maladroitness once and to do so again would be foolhardy to say the least. He would enjoy a chat with the landlord and could manage a mutton pie accompanied by a small libation without too much persuasion.

*

Inspector Bishop made his way to the Blenny and found Obed Daniels behind the public bar. The inquest would be held in the other bar later in the week as that was seldom used by the locals. Presumably the landlord had intended to expand the business when his wife was alive and had had to rethink his plans upon her death. It couldn't be easy for a widower looking after two daughters and a wayward nephew.

'Afternoon, Inspector, how's your day going?' asked Obed Daniels cheerily.

'Oh fair to middling, Landlord, could be better; I need to find Mr Donald Knightley. I know this may sound daft as I'm staying myself, but did he sleep here last night? His family seem to think he might have done. I mean I didn't see him but then if he was sleeping off some over-excesses of yesterday, then I wouldn't have expected him to be rushing down to breakfast this morning.'

'He has done in the past but not last night that I know of; unless he's in the barn of course. I'll check with Ned. What do you want to see him about or can't you tell me?'

'I think it's fair to say I believe he can tell me a bit more about the events surrounding the death of Grace Cork than he is letting on. The fact he didn't turn up for an interview at the police house this morning makes me even more suspicious that he's got something to hide.'

'He wasn't drinking here at any point; not too many choices locally as you know so unless he went further afield … well that could explain why he's not back yet.'

'Do you know much about Freshlea Farm, Obed?'

'Only what I've heard. I think Jack Busse is keeping his head down. If I were him I'd remove all trace of any dubious activities as it doesn't take a genius to work out you'll be paying him a visit shortly. There could be a connection between the goings on there and a suspicious death I should think. There's little doubt in my mind the dog which attacked Miss Tester and was blamed for killing Grace Cork came from the farm.'

'Ever thought of joining the police force, my friend?' asked the inspector smiling at his host.

The landlord chuckled as he disappeared out the back to hunt for his nephew.

Ned Daniels appeared somewhat dishevelled from the living room behind the public bar. He was unshaven and his hair matted and clinging to his forehead. He wiped his hands across his chest as he saw the inspector observing him. His general demeanour was anxious and his nicotine-stained hands shook slightly. Albert wondered if he had a fondness for liquor; he wouldn't be the first bartender to do so.

'Can we sit down, Ned? There are a few questions I would like to ask you.'

'I don't know nothing, I don't, nothing about nothing.'

'Well as you don't know what I want to ask you yet, it's a bit premature to assume you can't help me isn't it?'

Ned seemed to be thinking about this but couldn't quite get his head round the concept and stared blankly at the police officer with his mouth slightly open.

They sat at a table in the corner affording a little privacy; however there were only two drinkers and they were at the other end of the bar.

'I would like to ask how well you know Mr Donald Knightley.'

'I don't know him.'

'Well I think you do; several people have told me they have seen you with him,' Albert lied with ease.

'He comes in here sometimes when the family's staying at Highfields that's all. I've served him a few drinks and we have talked a bit then I suppose. That's what bartenders are supposed to do, talk to their customers. My uncle employs me and I do the job he pays me for; there's nothing wrong in that; doesn't mean I know the man just because I've spoken to him now and again.'

'And what have you spoken about "now and again"?'

'Just the usual; weather and shooting, they have house-parties at weekends at Highfields, so he talks about that sometimes.'

'Gambling; betting on cock fights or dog fights?'

'I don't know nothing about none of that stuff,' said Ned twisting his hands together and looking down at the table.

'So you have never been to Freshlea Farm and don't know Mr Busse who owns it? That's strange as I understood you were coming home from there on the day Jem Mitchell stopped you to tell you he had found a body.'

Ned Daniels appeared agitated and looked over to the bar presumably in the hope his uncle would intervene.

'Let's have a drink shall we, Ned; are there any mutton pies going, my stomach couldn't stand another dinner courtesy of Mrs Cummins.'

Ned relaxed and smiled a little as he stood up. 'I'll fetch you a drink and a pie shall I? Brown ale is it?'

Albert Bishop nodded as he pulled his empty pipe out of his jacket pocket and stuck it in his mouth while he waited for Ned to return.

Over the next hour he and Ned had consumed two brown ales each, he had eaten his pie and they had chatted about football and boxing. Albert had also managed to ascertain that in fact Ned did know Donald Knightley and they had on occasion visited Freshlea Farm at the same time. However he would not be drawn as to what went on there. He also admitted when questioned, that he too had visited Grace Cork. He said he had not seen Donald Knightley for some days and didn't know where he was currently.

With that the inspector would have to be satisfied for the moment. He stood up to leave and as he did so he saw Obed Daniels disappear from behind the bar towards the back room. He waited to say goodbye before returning to the police house to see what progress Constable Cummins was making with his allocated tasks. He thought he could hear female voices from the living room, there seemed to be quite a hubbub of happy chatter and laughter.

The normally quietly spoken taciturn landlord reappeared looking animated and possibly even a little flushed.

'I'm off for now; I'll be back later, Landlord,' he called as Obed Daniels put up his hand in acknowledgement.

Albert wandered back through the village wondering what could have lightened Obed Daniels' spirit so noticeably.

*

Back inside the Blenny, Lizzie Tester had arrived as planned to take the girls back to Highfields for tea. It was a treat that she had been planning for a couple of weeks to coincide with the completion of the dresses. She wasn't sure if it would still be appropriate considering the amount of trouble she had apparently caused the family but Mrs Field agreed that if the girls had been looking forward to it, there was no reason to cancel; after all the family wouldn't even know they were there.

The drizzle from earlier had made way for a bright and relatively warm afternoon and having said goodbye to their father with the promise he would come to collect them at six o'clock, they set off happily with Lizzie in the direction of Highfields.

She planned to take them to the servants' quarters and then for a walk in the wood, being mindful to get back in time for their father to collect them later.

The girls had only seen the house from the road previously and both marvelled at how large it was. Lizzie explained it was nowhere near as big as the main family home in Kent. Even so, it took her nearly an hour showing them round the servants' rooms downstairs.

They entered via the backdoor at the rear of the house, where Obed Daniels had delivered Lizzie home on the day of her accident, some weeks before. From there she showed them the laundry room, explaining that when she entered service she was an assistant laundry maid and was about the same age as May at the time.

After that they went to the still room where jams and jellies were made. Further down the passageway they came to the cold pantry with its marble worktops where items were stored that needed cool conditions, such as butter, milk and eggs.

Next was the boot room, used for cleaning all items of footwear and from there they went across the passage to the butler's pantry where the silver was stored. Lizzie drew the girls' attention to a large book which she explained was called the wine ledger where Mr Hemsley itemised the wine in the family's cellar. The silver was stored in large locked cabinets covering the walls along with the serving dishes which were kept for best. Mr

Hemsley also kept the local merchants' accounts books in his pantry. Lizzie explained that in Kent, Mrs Luck the housekeeper would keep these but she seldom came on holiday with the family, instead staying behind to give the main house a jolly good clean while most of the occupants were away.

Next along the passageway was the door to the butler's sitting room which they did not enter and on the opposite side of the passage was Mr and Mrs Field's sitting room. They visited the servants' hall after that and the girls were impressed by the long wooden table.

They then came to the end of the passage and into the large kitchen with its central table. Lizzie was going to show the girls the larder and scullery but was waylaid by Mrs Reader who had been looking out for them. She was fishing hard boiled eggs out of the boiling kettle as they entered the kitchen. No doubt she would do her usual trick of using the same water to make the tea. It had taken Lizzie quite a while to get used to this strange practice but over time she had come to accept it and no longer believed she could taste eggshell when she drank her beverage.

'Has Miss Tester shown you how you can get to the top of the house without using the main staircase? No, well you ask her about that before you go for your walk.'

Prior to leaving the warmth of the kitchen, Lizzie explained to the girls that there were two sets of staircases within the house; one for the family which was a grand affair accessed from the hall leading from the front door and the other was the backstairs which were located near to the servants' hall. Bells would ring for the servants to attend the family and they could jump to their tasks quickly by using the backstairs to get to the main family quarters. Each floor could be accessed by a discreet door allowing the servants to enter and leave unseen.

They put their coats on as Mrs Reader said it might be chilly by the time they returned from the wood.

'You make sure you stick to the main paths; we don't want you getting lost.' She took Lizzie to one side and whispered, 'you know there are still some old mantraps in the wood to try to deter the poachers, so don't let the girls wander into the undergrowth.'

Lizzie promised they would be careful and they made their way across the yard to access the path a fair distance down the drive from the house but not before Mrs Reader had given each of the girls a glass of her special lime cordial.

She also told them to look out for a beech tree that was said to have the initials of Lady Constance and Mr Knightley etched into its trunk. They were said to have carved their initials in the bark in their courting days; so romantic. She had never seen it but she had heard it was somewhere in the wood.

They wandered happily into the woodland and both May and Lily said they wanted to try to find the special tree.

'What were Lady Constance's initials before she was married I wonder?' Lily asked.

Well Lady Nora is Lady Constance's sister and her surname is Kingsbury and she isn't married, so that would have been Lady Constance's name as well. So we are looking for a beech tree that has the letters "CK" for

Lady Constance Kingsbury and "HK" for Mr Herbert Knightley carved into its bark.'

They looked at the trees on their way and Lizzie was mindful to make sure the girls stayed in sight and on the main path. They listened to the birds singing and tried to identify the different breeds as they walked. Lily asked Lizzie if they had different birds in Kent. May laughed at her and told her to stop being so silly but Lizzie thought it was a fair question coming from a girl of nine who had never in her life been further than Keswick.

They were chatting happily when they heard another sound. It was a woman's voice clear but light. She was laughing and then talking to someone. Lizzie couldn't quite make out the other voice but could hear the sound of happy excited conversation. The realisation of who it was struck her after a moment or two. It was Lady Nora. She was talking with someone and in the quietness and tranquillity only infiltrated by birdsong, her voice carried on the breeze. The other voice must be deeper which was why Lizzie could not make it out clearly. A man's voice surely. She made up her mind quickly. After the fuss of the last few days she didn't want to bump into anyone from the family so she suggested they look for the tree in a different direction to that from which the sound was coming.

After another half hour of happy but unsuccessful searching for the tree they decided it was time to turn for home and Mrs Reader's afternoon tea. Philadelphia Crittle joined them and they sat down to egg and cress sandwiches, scones and fruit cake. The girls professed to love the lime cordial and Mrs Reader found another bottle for them to take home.

At six o'clock on the dot, Obed Daniels tapped lightly on the backdoor of Highfields. When Lizzie opened the door, both girls were trying to tell him at once about their adventure and were excitedly vying for his attention.

Lizzie had finished the dresses having spent the night before hard at work, staying up long after midnight to complete her task. Before he had arrived, the girls had tried on their newly made clothes in Lizzie's bedroom. She had wrapped them in brown paper afterwards and each clutched their treasured possessions as they prepared to leave. Obed Daniels looked over their heads and thanked Lizzie for her kindness. She waved away his renewed offer to pay for her time. He twisted his hat in his hands and looked like he wanted to say more but didn't.

Lizzie smiled and said it had been her pleasure. They would be returning to Kent after the inquest, so it was unlikely their paths would cross again, other than on the day itself of course.

They shook hands as they said goodbye. Lizzie felt sad after she had waved them off and shut the door as she had become very attached to the girls it seemed.

Fate is of course a strange master and as it transpired the paths of Obed Daniels and Lizzie Tester would cross again long before the planned return journey to Kent.

Chapter 9 – Alternative Angles

September 1891

Tuesday morning was cloudy with a hint of drizzle and Albert Bishop rose at six-thirty as was his wont. Obed Daniels was up and already clearing the bar of the previous night's detritus.

'Can't you delegate that to Ned?' enquired the inspector as he appeared at the bottom of the stairs, neatly booted and besuited ready for his day's work.

'Would be nice wouldn't it but the trouble is I want it done now and not at dinner time. He had a bad start in life and I do try to make allowances but to be honest ...' his sentence was cut short by a loud banging on the door.

The landlord walked forward and pulled back the bolts at the top and bottom of the heavy oak door and turned the key in the lock. He opened it slightly to see who the early morning visitor could be. He evidently recognised the liveried man standing before him.

'What is it, George? Is Miss Tester alright?' Obed Daniels asked urgently, as he admitted the footman.

'What, yes of course she's alright, why wouldn't she be? No, I've come with a note from the master. Mr Knightley I mean, for Inspector Bishop,' replied George giving the landlord a quizzical look, as he walked across the bar towards the policeman.

Albert Bishop noticed that his host let out an audible sigh of relief. Miss Tester was a fine woman, even he was aware of that, so it wasn't surprising the landlord was taken with her.

He took the note which bore his name as he sat down at a table and put his empty pipe into his mouth. The landlord had disappeared to start breakfast.

"Inspector Bishop. Come at once. My son Mr Donald Knightley has been absent for a second night. My wife and I are extremely worried and you need to present yourself to Highfields House without delay. Rt Hon Herbert Knightley MP".

Albert screwed up the paper and shook his head. Not for the first time he marvelled that the upper classes believed themselves superior in every way and common courtesy wasn't considered necessary when summoning a minion to their presence.

'Sir, are you coming?' asked George standing in front of him and looking increasingly worried.

'Firstly I'm going to enjoy the fine food that Mr Daniels and his daughter have kindly prepared for me and then I will be going over to the police house to review the case of Mrs Cork, whose inquest is to take place shortly. After that, I will send word to Keswick, London and Kent to ask them to make enquiries into the whereabouts of Mr Knightley. I was planning to do that today anyway if he hadn't turned up. Now what exactly

157

does the Rt Hon Herbert Knightley MP think I can do by foregoing my breakfast and running over to Highfields? Unless of course the family think Mr Knightley junior may be hiding in the shrubbery and his father wants me to look for him.'

George looked embarrassed but remained standing on the spot.

'Tell him I will call when time permits; in the meantime if Mr Donald Knightley should return of his own volition then please let me know, as I would like to speak with him as a matter of urgency.'

George left; clearly still unconvinced he should be doing so without the inspector in tow.

The landlord appeared from behind the bar with a beaker and coffee pot. He placed these along with some cutlery and condiments on the table in front of the policeman. He disappeared and returned almost immediately with the inspector's breakfast of eggs, bacon and devilled kidneys for which the policeman had a particular penchant and also half a loaf of bread for him to slice as he wished.

'My word, that looks good! Set me up until supper time. I don't know how poor old Tom Cummins stomachs what his wife puts in front of him.'

'Who does for you at home?' enquired the landlord, conversationally.

'I have a housekeeper who lives in; sometimes I feel like I'm a lodger in my own home, as she certainly rules the roost. I seem to be permanently in trouble but she's a good sort really.'

The inspector told his host of the contents of the note as he tucked into his breakfast. He pointed at the chair opposite his own and the landlord sat down.

'Tell me, Obed; what do you think of Donald Knightley? Does he often roam?'

'I don't know him well of course so I couldn't really say. However if that were the case I wouldn't have expected his father to be so upset now. As to his character, well feckless would be a good description I think. My feeling is that he's been spoiled by overindulgent parents and always had everything handed to him on a plate. Nothing unusual in that of course, many young men of his class could be described in that way I'm sure.'

'What about the family, the parents, Lady Constance and Mr Herbert Knightley? And there's an aunt living with them, isn't there?'

Obed Daniels gave the inspector as much background information regarding the family as he was able.

'My mother worked there as a kitchen maid when she was young. She used to go back to clean but she never lived in after she and my dad married, obviously. Highfields had been in the Kingsbury family for generations and Lady Constance's mother was particularly fond of the estate. It was occupied a lot of the time until she died but less so afterwards. However, the earl and his second wife still brought the family for holidays and house parties. I know my mother was fascinated when Mr Knightley first appeared on the scene when Lady Constance was a debutante. She described him as a steady young man who took himself very seriously. He had a brother who used to visit as well. He was also interested in Lady Constance I think. He was a different character all together. An artist and poet as I understand, my mother said he was a gentle soul. He was always polite. She was quite disappointed when Lady Constance chose Mr Herbert rather than his younger brother.'

'Does he still visit?'

'Not that I know of; he was never involved in the family banking business. I think he wanted to live abroad and pursue his own interests – now was it France or Italy? Sorry, I can't remember. Of course with a wealthy family behind him he didn't need to earn a living as such. He left ... oh it must be nigh on thirty years back, maybe a bit less but twenty-five at least. He still came to stay when the two eldest girls were young. It may be that he visits the family when they're in Kent. But then again, I suppose if his brother married his sweetheart, well some people take that sort of thing hard as I understand it.'

Albert Bishop nodded sagely. He had no empathy or much experience regarding affairs of the heart, never having a lot of time for that sort of thing. Bad enough placating a housekeeper; imagine if he was actually shackled by marriage! For a split second Mrs Cummins' face flashed before his eyes; he shuddered slightly.

He finished the beaker of coffee and thanked the landlord for his breakfast. He shoved his empty pipe in his mouth before making his way to the police house.

Hopefully Tom Cummins would be up and have completed his report into Freshlea Farm, its owner, Mr John Busse and his son Jack.

The inspector was delighted that he was correct in both his aspirations; Tom and his wife were in the kitchen when he arrived at the police house and Tom nipped quickly into the front room – office – he corrected himself, to find the report he had painstakingly written for his superior officer regarding Freshlea Farm. Albert Bishop accepted a cup of tea from the constable's wife, as he followed Tom into the office. Mrs Cummins came in with her own tea and settled herself on one of the chairs facing the desk. Albert looked at her enquiringly however it appeared she was not for moving and fully intended to contribute her pennyworth to the proceedings.

Albert adjusted the position of his pipe as he read.

"Report by Police Constable (516) Thomas Cummins into the Goings-On at Freshlea Farm

Freshlea Farm has been in the Busse (pronounced 'bus' as in 'omnibus') family for three generations and over the last twenty years some of the acreage has been sold off or rented out to tenants. The farm now consists of roughly one hundred acres, some of which is given over to crop production. They grow wheat, oil seeds, sugar beet and winter barley. Grazing pastures make up the rest with about one hundred and fifty head of sheep and twenty dairy cattle. They are in the process of constructing a new barn and have recently taken possession of a brand new threshing machine.

The farm buildings consist of the house itself, a two storey stone dwelling and several barns and outhouses.

Gossip surrounding the possibility of illegal activity in the form of card games, cock and dog fighting started to circulate around about the time old John Busse passed the running of the farm to his son, also called John but known as Jack. More recently there was a rumour being spread around about bare-knuckle boxing.

I (Constable Cummins) visited the farm on two occasions and had a look around both times but did not find anything untoward.

Subsequent to my visits, a dangerous dog attacked a servant from Highfields House (Miss Tester) and killed some sheep. However no proof has come to light that the dog came from Freshlea Farm, and when I called again Jack Busse denied he had ever owned such an animal and, whatever I believe in private, there is no firm evidence to suggest that the farmer is lying."

Albert sat back in his chair and removed his pipe.

'Excellent work, Tom, very commendable. I'm impressed,' he said truthfully.

'Well if you do go to the farm, Inspector, ask Jack Busse about that local lad. Clem Gibbs, here one day and gone the next,' volunteered the constable's wife.

'Oh Edith, don't start all that again. He wasn't a local lad any road; he was in the area for a while looking for work and then he left and there's nothing unusual in that,' said her husband clearly irritated by Mrs Cummins' interjection.

'Well he didn't tell Mrs Reilly that he was leaving, did he? Owed her a week's rent he did and left his possessions behind, such as they were. No, you mark my words; he was asking questions about the farm then all of a sudden he's flush with money, then the next thing you know, he's missing.'

This conversation was taking an unexpected twist and Albert was now quite pleased that Mrs Cummins had insisted on staying.

'Clem? Short for Clement do you think?' the inspector posed the possibility. 'Clem Gibbs. Do you know where he came from, Mrs Cummins? Who did he speak to about the farm? What was his interest do you know?'

'Well as a matter of fact I do,' said Edith Cummins sitting forward on her chair. 'Tom go and stick the kettle back on, there's a dear.' She beckoned the inspector closer to her.

He looked round, not sure who she thought was listening as Tom dutifully left the room to go and make more tea; at least that's what Albert supposed he was "sticking the kettle back on" for.

'It would be about four weeks or more past. I was in the post office and there was quite a group all talking about it, as I say Clem Gibbs had gone, leaving his possessions and owing for his board and lodging. When he first arrived he was looking for work and asked about Freshlea Farm. His landlady, Mrs Reilly said he didn't look like the farm labouring type, however he said he believed he could get "other" work there. He must have been in the area for about two months in total I think.'

'Other work; meaning what exactly?' Albert enquired, thinking Mrs Cummins might be a terrible cook but would make a very competent constable.

'Well it was round about the time that the boxing rumours were in full swing if you pardon my pun, so putting two and two together I think he may have got himself involved in that. What say you, Inspector?' said the constable's wife looking smug.

'Well it's certainly food for thought, Mrs Cummins. Now what can you tell me about the other goings on? What have you heard from the villagers in the shops? Someone with your skill at identifying important information is a godsend to an investigation, Tom is a very lucky man.'

Albert couldn't believe she would fall for that, he thought he might have overdone the blandishment. However he was wrong, as Mrs Cummins was clearly very amenable to flattery.

'My Tom says that. Well to be honest he says I'm a gossip, but at times it's useful to know what folks are saying. With regard the betting, I think they usually meet up twice a month, sometimes more – I think word gets circulated as to exactly when. There are card games as well as dog and cock fighting beforehand in anticipation of the main event. Bad business; I've heard that it is not uncommon for some of the animals involved to have to be destroyed.

'Now I also understand that some bets are taken in the village so there are people who don't attend but are still involved. You need to speak to Ned Daniels about that. I know for a fact when his uncle found out about it, he nearly threw him out – well in my opinion he should have done – a nasty piece of work and no mistake. As it was, I think he gave him a good hiding and told him he was on his last warning.'

She leaned closer still, Albert was worried the integrity of the desk would not be equal to the task should she be determined to insinuate herself any further in his direction.

'I think he feels a responsibility towards the boy; well not really a boy anymore, he must be early twenties now but still, what with his parents gone and everything.

'Mr Daniels blames himself for his brother's death you know,' said Edith Cummins conspiratorially, sitting back a little and folding her arms across her chest. He always looked after him during his fights. Oh, it was all professional and above board, so aught wrong with that. His brother took a blow to the head and seemed to be alright, but died a few days later. Mr Daniels feels he should have spotted something was wrong, but then as I said to him, "you're not an expert are you and if the doctor passed him fit to continue the bout, well what could you have done?"

'The other thing is, I understand young Mr Knightley from the big house has gone missing; well he was involved with what has been going on over at the farm. He seemed as thick as thieves with Ned Daniels. Not two people you would expect to see together, now something gave them a common interest, what could that be do you think?'

Albert was spared the need to try to answer, as at that moment the constable appeared with a tray of tea.

Albert accepted the proffered cup and saucer. He had plenty to be thinking about on his way to the farm and he also made a mental note to speak to the landlord tonight about Ned and hopefully after that, Ned himself.

*

By late-morning the inspector and constable were on their way out of the village. They used the pony and trap to get to the farm which took about twenty minutes. The drizzle had eased and it was by now a pleasant day for a trip out and Albert thought what a nice part of the world this was. If he had no better ideas in the years to come, he could do worse than to retire here. He suddenly realised his daydream was being infiltrated by the constable's voice.

'So I said to her, "Edith, you really shouldn't go round spreading rumours, after all you are the wife of an officer of the law". But did it make any difference? By heck it did.'

'Well from what your good lady told me she wasn't exactly spreading gossip, she was listening and taking a healthy interest. The Clem Gibbs angle gives us a good reason to visit the farm; pursuing enquiries regarding the whereabouts of a missing person. While we are there we can have a look round.'

Tom nodded in grudging fashion, clearly not convinced.

They arrived in the farmyard to a gaggle of geese, hens, ducks and dogs. Albert looked sharply at the dogs. They looked harmless, definitely nothing more than docile mutts. No sign of any bull-terriers but then they would hardly be running free in the yard, he reasoned.

'Yes, what do you want?' a course deep voice came from behind them in the direction of a barn which faced onto the yard.

'Hello, Jack; we wondered if you could give us a few minutes of your time. This is Inspector Bishop from Keswick.'

After wiping it down the sides of his grubby trousers, Jack Busse proffered a slightly less filthy hand in response to the gesture from the inspector. Albert saw before him a short but stocky man in his early forties with a balding pate and ruddy complexion, smelling slightly of slurry.

'What can I do for you gentlemen?' he asked, with less hostility in his voice than previously.

'Well several things actually, Mr Busse, could we go inside? I do appreciate you're a busy man and we'll keep this as brief as possible,' said the inspector in a friendly but firm tone.

Jack Busse said nothing and walked past the police officers towards the house. On entering, it took them a couple of moments for their eyes to adjust to the light in the rather dingy kitchen. An elderly man sat at the table and made no sign that he had noticed the visitors. The room smelled of grease and stale cabbage.

'Dad, these men are from the police; do you want to go in t'other room while I sort this out?'

Without speaking the elderly man rose and left the room. This would be John Busse senior thought Albert Bishop as they each took a seat at the table. Albert was concerned they might be offered refreshment and was already thinking up his excuses. However he need not have worried. Hospitality was clearly not on the agenda as far as Mr Busse junior was concerned.

'Now then, Mr Busse, what can you tell me about cock fighting and dog fighting?'

'Nothing.'

'What can you tell me about bare knuckle boxing?'

'Nothing.'

'What can you tell me about a bull-terrier that killed several sheep and attacked a lady on the road towards Blenthorne?'

'Nothing.'

'What can you tell me about the whereabouts of Mr Clem Gibbs and subsequently Mr Donald Knightley?' the inspector persisted.

'Nothing.'

'What can you tell me about the death of Mrs Grace Cork – and please don't say "nothing" as we are really just wasting each other's time. I could drag you off to Keswick, with the seriousness of the matters in hand that would be quite appropriate. I will then obtain a warrant and organise a search of the farm. This will amount to a thorough examination of the entire property, including the farmhouse, outbuildings and grounds by a team of policemen. In the absence of voluntary co-operation from a member of the public, in this case yourself, Mr Busse, this is indeed what should and will happen.'

The inspector's tone became increasingly sharp as he warmed to his theme.

'The issue I have, Mr Busse, is that the farm keeps cropping up and appears to be a common denominator in my investigations, so to speak.'

There was a noise behind them and John Busse senior reappeared, he was slightly stooped and his clothes probably fitted him better when he weighed more than was currently the case.

'He was here, Clem Gibbs, you must remember him, Jack,' said the elderly man looking towards his son.

'Dad, I'll handle this,' said Jack rising from his chair. The older man turned and left the room.

'Okay; yes, you just took me by surprise that's all. Clem Gibbs came here looking for work, when I told him I had nothing for him he left; that was that.'

'And Donald Knightley, how often does he visit the farm?' asked the inspector briskly.

Jack Busse thought about this for a moment before answering.

'He comes over occasionally when he's in the area with some others from the village. We drink and chat and have the occasional game of cards. Now and again we have the odd bet but there's nothing wrong with that.'

'As I mentioned earlier, both these gentlemen appear to be missing; can you throw any light on that?' asked the inspector.

'No.'

'And how often did Mrs Cork come here?' the inspector asked, as a shot in the dark.

If Albert Bishop was surprised by the answer, he gave no indication of it. His demeanour remained inscrutable.

'She came along once or twice. She was a good poker dealer. But I don't know anything about her death.'

'When was the last time she was here?'

'I don't remember,' said Jack Busse, his tone far less confident than previously.

'Mind if I have a look round? No, that's good,' clearly the matter wasn't up for negotiation.

'Constable; the barns I think,' said the inspector rising from his chair. We'll have a cursory look round and then call for reinforcements, as without any co-operation from Mr Busse we'll tear the place apart if needs be. I mean, missing persons, an allegation of illegal gambling and a suspicious death ...

'Oh and by the way, in what capacity does Ned Daniels work for you? Did you know he runs a book? What, you didn't know? In that case, he must have got himself a nice little side-line going. Most of the village seem to be involved didn't you say, Constable? Lots of them happy to talk; in fact we can't shut some of them up! Well I suppose if they think they are in a tight spot it's a case of anything to get out of a mess. Now then which barn did you fancy first, Constable Cummins?'

The inspector and constable made their way out of the farmhouse ahead of Jack Busse.

'You make a search of the barns and make sure you keep Jack with you; I want a crack at the old man,' said Albert Bishop quietly to his colleague. Tom Cummins nodded slightly.

'Right now then Jack where shall we start? What do you normally keep in this one?' asked Tom Cummins apparently informally.

Albert Bishop wandered off in the direction of the yard, seemingly to stretch his legs and when he saw that his constable had the farmer's attention, he doubled back to the farmhouse.

He entered the back door and found the older man in the kitchen, again sitting at the table where he had been when they first arrived.

'Mr Busse? May I join you for a moment? I'm not sure if you heard the constable introduce me, I'm Inspector Albert Bishop from Keswick.'

'Help yourself. Sit down,' said Busse senior waving at a chair.

Albert Bishop took a seat opposite the elderly man at the kitchen table.

'Will you be staying for a bite t'eat?' asked John Busse.

'Obliged, but in a while I'm gan yam for me dinner,' said the inspector, delving into the depths of his memory for an old Cumberland expression from his childhood that might just get the old man on side.

John Busse nodded with a small smile.

'Been in the area long, Mr Busse?' asked the inspector conversationally, already knowing the answer.

'I was born here, as was my father and his father before him. Not an easy life, farming. Winters can be hard so the sheep need to be tough; even so, we usually lose a few in the snow drifts. I still get pleasure after all these years from finding a ewe and pulling her out alive – little thanks for it though – they usually jump up and head-butt me!' John Busse smiled weakly.

'Bet you've seen some changes over the years, I understand that quite a few farmers are struggling to make a living and some have gone under. From what I hear you have tackled the problem by scaling back a bit, selling or renting off a few acres here and there.' The inspector leaned his elbows on the wooden table in front of him as if they were sharing a confidence.

'No choice. My grandfather had five hundred acres; we are down to a hundred now.'

'Presumably that has made a difference; I mean from what I hear you are making quite a good profit now; new barn under construction, well that must be costing a tidy sum.'

'Jack has the running of the place these days as I'm not as young as I was. I get tired very easily; dickey ticker the quack says. Jack was doing most things anyway so it made sense to hand everything over to him.'

'So how has he done it do you think? Turned a struggling farm into a thriving business once more? Just good management and sound husbandry, or has he diversified? Branched out so to speak?'

'You need to speak to him about that, Inspector. He has done what he's had to. He's kept us afloat.'

'Look, Mr Busse, I'm not interested in hounding anyone for a bit of minor law infringement, if you understand what I mean; we all like a bet don't we? Personally I like the occasional flutter on the horses,' he said, hoping he would not be questioned in any detail. He had actually never placed a bet in his life. 'I just need to be rid of the unanswered questions and that way I can clear away all the chaff and get to the wheat, to use a farming phrase. My only concerns are finding the killer of Grace Cork and the whereabouts of Clem Gibbs.'

'What Jack's been doing here at the farm, well I don't hold with it; but then again, what harm's it causing? I don't know the details honestly, Mr Bishop. I did know Mrs Cork. She was a pleasant lady; sharp mind, you couldn't put one over on her. She didn't miss a thing. She ran the card table for Jack sometimes.'

'When was she last here?'

'A couple of weeks before she was found I would say. Ned often saw her home, Ned Daniels that is. She lived at Hope Cottage, just along from the Blenny.'

'What part does Ned Daniels play in the proceedings?'

'He takes the bets.'

'And the cock and dog fighting; what can you tell me about that, just for my ears, as I said I only want to find a killer, nothing more.'

'I think they run the fights alongside the card games. Some people prefer blood sports; whereas some prefer just to gamble at the table.'

'Which does Donald Knightley prefer?'

John Busse hesitated; 'I wouldn't know, Sir.'

'The problem is, Mr Busse, Donald Knightley has gone missing. His family are frantic. So there is likely to be a full scale search of the area if he isn't found quickly. They have influence; you know what the landed gentry are, friends in high places. The whole area is going to be crawling with police; now whatever they uncover could be inconvenient or indeed incriminating for certain people. Of course if it does come to that, the whole affair will be taken out of my hands, so the more you can tell me now, the less likely it is there are repercussions later.'

After a few moments John Busse seemed to make up his mind.

'He comes here regular-like and gambles away his allowance every time he is staying at Highfields. He likes a game of cards and also the fighting; dogs, cockerels and the boxing. He was talking to Clem Gibbs the last night Clem was here. Now I don't know what that was about but … well I think they were obviously having a disagreement about something, you would have to ask Mr Knightley.'

'If only I could find the gentleman concerned, I would!' said the inspector with feeling.

'Have you tried the Blenny? If he was in trouble, he would go to Ned Daniels for help I'm sure of it; always together those two.'

A noise interrupted them and they both looked towards the door. Constable Cummins appeared with Jack Busse in front of him.

'You alright, Dad, what are you blathering on about? Wasting the inspector's time; he doesn't always think straight, you shouldn't mind anything he says. He won't remember later anyway.'

'On the contrary, Mr Busse, your father was extremely coherent. We were discussing farming and the challenges that the new century will bring to the old ways of life. I see you have a fine example of a threshing machine; you must save a lot on labourers, you can't need nearly so many.'

'It's the way forward. Wages have always been the bane of the farmer's life. Anything to reduce that well, I'm all for it,' said Jack defensively.

'Must have cost a bit?'

'We managed to get the money together through thrift and good management. Now officers, if you will excuse me, I have to get back to work.'

They left having made their farewells, with the younger of the two Busse farmers watching as they began their return journey towards Blenthorne.

'Was it productive, Sir?' asked the constable as they left the yard.

'Yes indeed, very and you?'

'Well I did find some staining on the floor of one of the barns and also some shackles and chains. Jack tried to explain them away; animals sometimes injure themselves apparently when they are indoors, particularly if they are tethered for any reason.'

'Well, I had a very interesting conversation with Mr John Busse senior. I think we need to speak to Ned Daniels fairly urgently.'

That they soon found out was easier said than done.

Chapter 10 – Heartbreak at Highfields

Late September 1891

George left Lady Nora at the usual spot and she made her way to the cottage. She had had the devil's own job to get him to bring her today because there was so much fuss over Donald. Off with some floosy no doubt but not exactly subtle. Why couldn't he wait until they were back home, he could do what he wanted in London or with a little more decorum, in Tunbridge Wells. Herbert had insisted that all the staff were to search the grounds; as if they would find him there! Constance would no doubt go to bed with one of her heads. The least sign of difficulty and she took to her room with a migraine. She had no idea what life could throw at a person if it chose. If only Constance knew what Nora's life was like year in and year out!

She knew she was a burden, a weight that had to be borne by the family; a drain on them, a social liability. Well not for much longer; if she had her way this would be the last time she would travel home to Kent with them. She would put her affairs in order, pack her possessions and come back here for good. So what if she lived like a peasant in a cottage? So what if her beau wasn't rich and they had to survive on fresh air and love. That was all they needed. Well that and her allowance of course.

By this time she had reached the door to the cottage. He opened it before she could even knock.

'Where have you been, my dearest Nora?' he asked with a worried expression, that dear sweet face with those deep brown eyes with his shock of dark hair falling over his forehead.

'Oh my word, you just would not believe the hue and cry my sister and brother-in-law have created over my nephew, Donald. He's a grown man for heaven's sake; just because he has gone off somewhere, anyone would think the world had ended. Wretched boy; he owes money I believe. I have often given him what I can spare but he is always asking for more. That was all very well in the past – now I need to save what I have as we will need some to live on. Yes, I know you are the least materialistic man in the whole world but we will need clothes and food. We can't be totally self-sufficient, though I have been reading up about growing vegetables. That sounds like fun doesn't it?'

She placed the bundle of food she had managed to scrounge from Mrs Reader onto the rustic table.

'Cod pie and cold potatoes,' she announced proudly, as if she had cooked the food herself. She eyed up the primitive facilities in the cottage. Well, needs must and she would have to learn how to cook even in these conditions! Maybe he would teach her, although she doubted he bothered much at all when she wasn't around. He was so very thin; he lost himself in his work and forgot to eat a lot of the time and she was always scolding him.

They settled into their familiar comfortable positions in front of the fire and watched the flames throw shadows all around the room. Life was good in their quiet corner of the wood Nora thought happily as the love of her life got up to serve their food.

*

Back at Highfields House, Lady Constance was beside herself with worry. How could he do this to them? Didn't he realise how much they loved him? Herbert only appeared to be mildly concerned but she really did wonder if anything fully penetrated that cold exterior. He was just … indifferent. Maybe that was to be expected, he had so many responsibilities to juggle. The House of Commons took its toll; his constituents seemed to think he was their property and could demand his attention at any time. There was the endless round of socialising when they were at home in Kent. Admittedly Herbert had the decency to spend some time at his club during the week but weekends were not their own. That was why it was so very important for them to get away twice a year and come to this tranquil bolthole.

Highfields certainly was not providing the respite they needed this year; what with Tester being attacked by a dog, one of their sheep being ripped to shreds and the terrible death of that poor woman. Then of course Herbert had taken leave of his senses and tried to dismiss Tester. What a calamity that would have been. Now, to make matters ten times worse, Donald, her darling baby boy, had gone missing. Maybe he had been kidnapped for ransom. Herbert dismissed this as preposterous as there had been no demand for money. But if he wasn't being held by force, where was he? Unless ... he was ... she almost allowed herself to think the unthinkable. No, it was ridiculous, he couldn't have fallen victim to the same fate as that Cork woman. They had no connection.

Herbert had demanded the policeman from Keswick attend them immediately and Mr Bishop had sent a message via George to say he would come when time permitted. Well finally that had spurred Herbert into action. He wasn't accustomed to having his authority questioned. Apart from the other day over the Tester business but then of course he was just being silly.

Herbert had ordered all the staff out into the grounds to look for Donald and sent a messenger to Sir Stanley Blake with a note telling him of the disgraceful behaviour of one of his police officers. He subsequently had the whole village looking for her son, her precious boy.

She had rung the bell twice now and no-one had attended her. What was this place coming to? Then she remembered they had resumed their search for Donald today. It was no good, she would have to go back to bed. They could send for the doctor later to prescribe her a tincture to calm her nerves. She got up, opened the door herself and made her way to her bedroom. Presumably Crittle was somewhere in the grounds and she would have to get herself undressed. Could things get any worse?

*

Lizzie and Philadelphia were entering the wood, picking their way carefully between the undergrowth.

'Surely he wouldn't be out here for another night would he?' Philadelphia asked her niece.

'Very unlikely; he's a bit of a wet rag isn't he? I can't believe he would be sleeping out of doors. No, I'm sure he will be looking out for himself. Nice and warm and dry somewhere while the rest of us search high and low and take the wrath of his anxious parents. He's highly irresponsible.'

'Really, Lizzie; that is no way to speak of your employer's son, where is your respect? What with that and your involvement in this murder. I wonder what has got into you recently.'

'Discontentment I suppose, Aunt Phily. I had always thought I might become a housekeeper one day but really I can't see myself in service for the remainder of my life. There are all sorts of opportunities in the cities now, there's factory and shop work. Not being at the beck and call of a spoilt little madam for ever.'

'Elizabeth Tester; your mother would have made you wash your mouth out with soap if she had heard you say such a thing. I think you need to get your head out of the clouds young lady. Do you know the conditions the factory workers endure? As for the shop girls, well they are far worse off than we are. They all live in; they have to sleep in dormitories and are not allowed visitors. They earn less than us and pay for their board and lodging. They wouldn't get the opportunity to spend weeks and weeks here every year; think how many times you have walked the fells and enjoyed sitting by the becks when the family is in residence at Highfields. You are well fed and warm and you wear fine quality clothing, what more do you want? No, you should thank providence for your good fortune my girl.'

'What's that place up ahead of us?' asked Lizzie feeling she had been told off as if she were five and desperate to change the subject. 'If you look between the trees, you can see it; maybe we can get to it.'

'Well I know there is supposed to be an old folly somewhere in the wood, maybe that's it. We had better take a closer look, not that it is fit for anyone to sleep in, I wouldn't think,' replied Philadelphia.

They were approaching the clearing where the folly stood when a cry went up and they heard footsteps behind them. George came panting along the narrow path.

'Come quickly, Miss Crittle. The mistress needs you now. He's been found. Mr Donald I mean,' he paused for breath bending over and touching his knees as he gulped for air.

'Praise the lord and thank heavens!' said Philadelphia then she noticed the look on George's face as he looked up at her from his bent position.

'He was found in the crypt at the church. His neck's been broken.'

'Broken? Is he dead?' asked Lizzie but, as she did so, instinctively knew the answer.

'Yes, Miss Tester. The doctor is examining him, well his body that is; so I don't know any more but I expect we will be told shortly,' he stood up as his breathing returned to normal.

The three of them made their way back to the main path and returned to the house as quickly as they could. It seemed to Lizzie that it looked like a place in mourning even before they entered. It had always been a sorrowful house. She kept quiet because Philadelphia had told her ages ago that she was being fanciful but now look at what had happened.

She had the terrible feeling that events had taken this turn as a result of her raising the alarm regarding Grace Cork's death. Oh goodness what had she done? She suddenly had a longing for her mother and the comfort of her arms. She wanted to be a little girl again; "Just remember you are very special, Lizzie," Rebekah Tester had told her. Well she didn't feel very special at that moment, she felt wretched and forlorn. Her thoughts strayed to Blenthorne and the Daniels girls and if she was honest, Obed Daniels' calm, reassuring presence.

The house was as quiet as the grave when they entered. Lizzie suddenly had a terrible urge to laugh hysterically at her simile but thankfully no sound came out of her mouth. Lady Constance was in her room Hemsley informed them and Philadelphia took off her coat, changed her shoes and made her way directly to her mistress.

Lizzie went to the servants' hall to await a summons from Lady Nora or Miss Sophia. Neither came. In fact, when Lizzie went outside for some air, she saw Lady Nora wheeling herself along the path from the wood.

Lizzie hurried over to help her.

'This is intolerable; I told George when to be back for me and he wasn't there. Do you realise I have had to get myself all the way back from the wood?' she demanded of Lizzie.

'Yes, Lady Nora. It isn't my place Ma'am but I think the family have had some distressing news. George has been engaged in other duties these hours past,' said

Lizzie as she moved towards the back of the chair and took the handles.

'What distressing news, what's happened? Has Donald turned up? What sort of scrape has he got himself into this time?' asked Lady Nora as she tried to turn round to look at Lizzie.

'Lady Nora, you must ask the master.' Despite the protestations from her mistress, Lizzie wheeled her directly to the front door without saying another word.

Hemsley came rushing out in response to the bell and took Lady Nora directly to the master who was in the morning room. Lizzie made her way back downstairs.

She wondered what would happen with regard the inquest which was planned for Friday, the day after tomorrow. She assumed it would be cancelled, or what was the other thing; adjourned? Yes, that was it. However without instruction to the contrary she would attend as requested to give her evidence, such as it was.

She heard the doorbell chime. Hemsley was nowhere to be seen, nor were George or Mr Field. She had done it before when she was a parlourmaid so she presumed it would be alright for her to answer the door under the current circumstances. She made her way up the stairs and through the green baize door into the hallway. She smoothed the front of her frock and opened the front door and found Inspector Bishop standing in front of her with his hat in his hands. She felt strangely comforted by his presence.

'Good afternoon, Inspector Bishop; please do come in. I will advise the master you are here.'

'Miss Tester, it is indeed a pleasure to see you again; although clearly the circumstances are far from ideal,' said the inspector quietly.

Lizzie took his hat and coat. She was not sure Hemsley would have done so, the inspector not being out of the top drawer so to speak; however, he was a professional gentleman going about his duty and she decided it was appropriate to extend the courtesy his office deserved. She felt her actions were not lost on him.

She left him in the hall as she went to the morning room to tell the master of the inspector's arrival. She opened the door quietly and bobbed a courtesy. Lady Nora had presumably been taken to her room as the master was alone. She kept her head down as she announced the policeman. Mr Knightley absentmindedly told her to let the inspector in.

She did so and went downstairs again to the servants' quarters, whereupon she heard Miss Sophia's bell and veered off to the left to mount the back staircase to reach the family's bedrooms.

*

'Who found him?' asked Herbert Knightley as he stood in front of the fireplace. The inspector stood in the middle of the room, not having been invited to sit.

'The vicar; he uses the crypt as a storage facility and he went in earlier today, not having been down there for a while. He found Mr Donald Knightley on the floor and raised the alarm immediately. It appears Mr Donald had been planning to stay there. There is a door round the back of the church which leads directly to the crypt. It is normally kept locked but the mechanism is easily breached and I understand it has sometimes been used in the past by vagrants particularly when it's cold. So initially the vicar thought that was the case however, when he approached he realised it was your son and that sadly, he was dead.'

'How long ago was he killed? I suppose what I mean is, if you had attended when I summoned you yesterday morning, he might have been saved. In fact I felt I had no choice but to organise a search by my staff and the villagers. Sir Stanley Blake will hear of this, Inspector, and of your gross incompetence. When I have finished you will be lucky if you are still employed as a beat officer.'

'The village doctor believes he was killed yesterday, probably in the early hours but there will need to be a post mortem to ascertain the cause of death and also of course, an accurate time. I will conduct interviews with both him and the vicar in the morning. As to my actions, I was pursuing enquiries which directly related to your son. He decided not to be candid with me when I interviewed him previously and the consequences of that decision may well have led to his death however, that remains to be seen. I will of course give a full report to Sir Stanley or a senior officer of his choosing, should it be deemed necessary.'

Herbert Knightley's shoulders suddenly seemed to slump. He dropped into a chair and waved at the inspector to sit opposite him.

'What do you think happened to him, Inspector?'

'It is my belief that your son had knowledge or information pertinent to the death of Mrs Cork. Some other information has come to light with regard a young man by the name of Clem Gibbs. Your son was seen in a heated conversation with Mr Gibbs at Freshlea Farm, a place I understand they both visited regularly and subsequent to that discussion, Mr Gibbs disappeared. It might well be that this and Mrs Cork's death are related, either way, I have a strong feeling that your son knew something of material importance which may be the reason he was killed.'

'Find out what happened I implore you; he was my only son. His mother will never get over this. At least if we know what happened we can perhaps come to terms with it somehow.'

'Sir, I will pursue your son's killer relentlessly. No human being deserves less. Someone recently reminded me of that; Miss Tester to be precise.'

'What's that – who?' Herbert Knightley looked confused.

'Miss Elizabeth Tester, your daughter's personal maid, Sir.'

However Mr Knightley was clearly no longer listening and seemed to have drifted away into his own world. The inspector took his leave. It was imperative that he speak to Ned Daniels and Clem Gibbs, if the latter could be found.

He hoped for some unknown reason that Miss Tester would see him out but Hemsley had clearly resumed his duties and was on hand to give him his coat and hat. He did so with a disdainful look that implied he wished he could have passed the apparel to its owner on a shovel rather than have to touch the items. He shut the front door firmly behind the police officer.

The inspector was walking up the drive when he heard his name being called. He turned round to see the subject of his recent thoughts running in his direction.

'Inspector, oh I'm so sorry to bother you; it's just that on Friday, will the inquest be going ahead? Has it been cancelled in view of what has happened?'

'No bother at all, Miss Tester,' said Inspector Bishop, raising his hat. The coroner will have it in his diary so it will be opened. In light of recent events I strongly suspect it will be adjourned. However you still need to be present in case you are called. Would you like me to send the pony and trap for you?'

'No indeed; I will enjoy the walk. Oh I mean well, not "enjoy" as such … Oh dear,' Lizzie flushed at her insensitivity.

'That's alright, Miss, I fully understand what you mean; blow the cobwebs away, as they say.'

'Thank you, Inspector; you are most kind.'

'At your service, Miss Tester,' he turned and tipping his hat once more, made his way down the drive.

Lizzie watched him leave. He seemed to be walking with more of a spring in his step than before she had stopped him. She wondered why that would be. She dismissed the thought and went back inside the sorrow-filled house.

*

Inspector Bishop arrived back at the Blenthorne Inn a little after five o'clock. He knocked on the backdoor, the inn itself being closed at that hour.

Obed Daniels answered the knock almost immediately and let his guest in. The inspector gave him a brief overview of the events at Highfields after they had gone into the back room and sat down. The discovery of the body was already widely known in the village. Speculation was rife as to the perpetrator of the crime.

Inspector Bishop looked at his host gravely.

'Obed, I'll be frank with you; I think Ned might be up to his neck in this business. I'm sure the deaths of Grace Cork and Donald Knightley are linked. There is also the question of Clem Gibbs who appears to have gone missing after taking part in boxing bouts at the farm. I really need to speak to your nephew as he seems to be linked with every aspect of this case.'

'I haven't seen him all day. He's not the most reliable of people.'

'I understand you knew about him running a book on the fights at Freshlea Farm.'

'Then I assume you also know I stopped him once I found out. He knows he is on his last warning; I can't afford to harbour someone who bends the law to suit himself. I have my daughters to think of, if I were to lose my licence, how would I provide for them? If I knew where he was, Inspector, I would surely tell you; on that you have my word.'

'If I'm not here, get word to me the minute he returns, Obed.'

'Again you have my word.'

The inspector duly stuck his pipe in his mouth and adjourned to a corner table with his newspaper to look forward to his supper.

*

An early start on Thursday, the day prior to the inquest, saw the inspector make his way to the police house. From the puddles on the pavement, there had clearly been a substantial downpour overnight but the day looked set fair with no more than a few clouds on the horizon. He didn't have to knock as Mrs Cummins was clearly window-watching and opened the door as he approached. She gave him a conspiratorial nod as she showed him into the office. He went round behind the desk and sat down in the chair. He noted that the aspidistra was back and pushed it to the side. He wondered fleetingly if he could shove it onto the floor and claim a tragic accident however his cunning plan was thwarted by the entrance of the constable from the hallway.

Tom Cummins looked a little flustered and was evidently still in the process of getting dressed. The inspector watched as the constable buttoned his tunic and licked his hand prior to smearing it across his head in a vain attempt to flatten his wayward greying hair. Albert discreetly averted his gaze and addressed his comments to the filing cabinet.

'Tom, we need to get some officers over to the farm; I want the corpses of the animals that were destroyed found. I want the body of Clem Gibbs found; if indeed it is a body we are looking for. Above all, I want a full confession from Jack Busse about his part in this business, so bring him in if he tries to be obstructive. We will start here and take him to Keswick if we have any bother.'

'Do you think he killed Mrs Cork, Sir? And do you really think Clem Gibbs is dead?'

'I don't know the answers to either of those questions Constable. But someone does and that is our task, to find that someone or work it out for ourselves.'

Tom looked perplexed when considering both options.

'Oh yes, I've just got hold of the financial records you asked me for, Sir. With regards Mrs Cork, as you can see, she had a healthy bank balance. I assume she dealt mainly in cash. She certainly settled all her bills in the village promptly.'

'That's as we expected. I suspect when we are apprised of the details of Donald Knightley's affairs we will find a different picture; quite the reverse of Mrs Cork, unless I am very much mistaken. It will be interesting to know just how bad things were for him financially.'

The inspector changed tack. 'I want to go back to the church crypt as the vicar had been called away when we first looked at the body; what's his name again? I also want to see if the village doctor has had a chance to come to any conclusions prior to the police surgeon getting his dubious hands on our victim; if his last performance is anything to go by, he'll probably say Donald Knightley died from natural causes!'

Tom Cummings looked a little nonplussed and was clearly unsure whether he was supposed to agree with his senior officer or not.

'Reverend Jolion Mayhew; he's been the vicar here getting on for the best part of thirty years. Not much about the locals he doesn't know I'll be bound. If you go to the vicarage just along yonder, Sir, he will accompany you; I told him I expected you would want a word this morning,' said Tom Cummins proudly, again trying to flatten his hair.

'Meantime, can you go over to Mrs Reilly's place and see if she still has Clem Gibbs' possessions; if so, bring them back to the office and we can go through them to see if there is anything that will help us find him,' instructed the inspector.

Tom Cummins nodded quite enthusiastically and almost bounded out of the office. The inspector thought he appeared to be relishing the opportunity to get his teeth into some real police work. The inspector got up from the chair and, picking up the offending aspidistra, handed it to Mrs Cummins as he left.

Inspector Bishop went the way he was bid and found the vicar, Reverend Mayhew without difficulty.

He was a man close to sixty years with the countenance one would expect of a man of the cloth. His suit had seen better days; his cuffs were a little threadbare but he had an air of authority coupled with a quiet aura of calm competence.

Without complaint, the vicar accompanied the police inspector to the crypt under the church of St Mary the Virgin Blenthorne. The church, the reverend explained as they walked, had a tower of early Norman architecture. Parts of the building dated back to the fourteenth century with the addition of a vaulted porch in the fifteenth or early sixteenth century. The single spire was constructed of beech and oak shingle. There were eight bells in the tower and bell-ringing was an activity pursued enthusiastically by some villagers. He had a soporific voice which had a very calming effect on the policeman and for a moment Albert almost forgot the macabre reason for their visit to the crypt.

They circumnavigated the church and Reverend Mayhew took the inspector round the back to an almost hidden door down five stone steps which formed the entrance to the crypt.

'How many people would know of this place, would you say, Reverend?' asked the inspector as they entered the dark, dank room under the church.

'Most of the village I would imagine. I'm sure you've heard that we do from time to time get the odd homeless soul sleeping here. Whilst I don't encourage it, I can't begrudge the needy a roof over their head occasionally and goodness knows there are no home comforts to be had here, Inspector.

'I'm sorry I had to rush away yesterday, I had a dying parishioner to attend. I sincerely hope that your investigation has not been unduly delayed by you having to return today to speak to me.'

'No indeed, Reverend; I wanted to see you here in the crypt as it's often the case that witnesses remember small details if they're taken back to the scene of a crime after the initial shock has worn off.'

'Yes, I see …' the vicar paused. 'You know, I'm not sure if it's relevant but now I cast my mind back, there was something … I noticed a strange smell when I first entered the crypt prior to discovering the body.'

'Early putrefaction do you think or human waste?' offered the inspector helpfully.

'To be honest, Inspector, after what I subsequently found, those odours would not have struck me as odd. No, I would say if pressed, it was a type of cleaning agent. I'm not sure where it came from or how it's relevant.'

Albert Bishop's eyes were now accustomed to the low light given off by the two candles the vicar had lit and picking up one candlestick, studied the floor. The vicar reiterated his statement from the previous day, when he confirmed he had not touched the body or the surrounding area. Donald Knightley had a change of clothes and provisions for several days, so it was safe to assume it was his intention to stay holed up for a while.

The inspector had looked through Donald Knightley's pockets when he first attended the body the day before and among other things, including some loose change and a handkerchief, found a small bottle of organic solvent, which was consistent with what the vicar had now told him. There had been no signs of a struggle and no blood. However, in the hands of an expert, breaking someone's neck was a swift and clean execution.

He judged the vicar to be a shrewd and astute gentleman of learning and asked for his opinion on Donald Knightley, Grace Cork and Ned Daniels.

As they left the crypt, the vicar said Mrs Cork attended church regularly and contributed generously to the collection. He understood her to be a widow without family. She had been vague about where she lived and worshipped before or indeed where she had been married. He said no more on that subject clearly allowing the inspector to make his own interpretation of what had been said and left unsaid.

He described Obed Daniels as the salt of the earth and Ned as the cross he had been called upon to bear. The vicar had heard the gossip surrounding Ned and whilst he had no first-hand knowledge of his affairs, he believed Ned had chosen a path which would never lead him to a godly life.

Donald Knightley attended church occasionally with his family when they were in residence. The vicar did not believe him to be a committed Christian. He came along because it was expected. Indeed the vicar couldn't imagine Donald Knightley was much concerned about anything but himself.

'We are all different, Inspector; we have all been put on this earth in all our forms and guises; we make of ourselves what we will. We may choose a path compatible with a respectable and decent life; or we may allow ourselves to deviate from that path and choose aberrance. We alone make that choice and can blame no-one but ourselves.'

Albert Bishop considered himself a fairly intelligent man with a reasonably broad education who was doing well in his chosen profession but blowed if he could understand what the vicar was alluding to. Upon asking what he had meant, the vicar smiled sanguinely and said; 'Just that.' So the inspector was none the wiser.

He took his leave and made his way to the doctor's surgery which was situated in a large house on the edge of the village. The consulting and waiting rooms made up the front of the property with living quarters at the back.

When he arrived, Dr Rufus Danes had just finished morning surgery. He was a small, affable type and ushered the inspector into his consulting room, anxious that his wife would not be disturbed.

'She has a delicate constitution and is easily upset,' the doctor explained in a low voice as he adjusted his spectacles.

Albert Bishop thought ironically it was always the well-bred who had "delicate constitutions", those that had to earn their living just got on with it.

He took a seat opposite the doctor's large mahogany desk. He instinctively started to feel nervous, which was ridiculous because the doctor was certainly not going to stick a needle in him or attempt any form of intimate examination.

'Now that you've had a chance to examine the body, are you in a position to confirm your original theory as to the cause of Mr Donald Knightley's death, Doctor?'

'Indeed I am. I believe he was killed in situ; that is the body was not moved after death. He was approached from behind, I suspect and his neck was twisted by means of grasping the jawbone in the left hand with the right hand being placed on the left side of the head and jerking sharply. This caused fractures at the craniocervical junction and also possibly the second cervical vertebra; the post mortem will confirm or disprove that obviously. An amateur trying to perform such an act could well cause injury, leaving the victim paralysed but probably still alive. I think your killer knew exactly what he was doing, he knew how much pressure to apply and where its impact would be fatal.'

'You are very knowledgeable, Doctor,' said the inspector, impressed by the clarity and conciseness of the information imparted to him. He again thought of the police surgeon who had needed two attempts to identify a slit throat.

'For a simple village sawbones you mean! Yes, well I served Queen and Country and saw action in Southern Africa. Every type of atrocity you could imagine, on both sides.'

The inspector took his leave from the "simple village sawbones" and made his way back to the Blenny. He sat at the desk in his room and looked though his notes; he was making progress, albeit slowly. As he put away his fountain pen he could have no possible idea what the following forty-eight hours had in store for him.

Chapter 11 – Admissions and Denials

Late September 1891

After an hour's work Albert went downstairs to the bar. He caught the eye of the landlord who shook his head in answer to the unspoken question regarding the whereabouts of Ned.

As he returned upstairs to freshen up before supper, he contemplated the events of the morrow. He had told Lizzie Tester that the inquest was likely to be opened and adjourned. He hoped he was correct as he felt he was moving forward in the investigation and didn't want to lose the momentum he had gained during the past few hours.

He responded to the quiet tap on the door and found May Daniels standing on the landing with a pitcher of hot water and fresh soap. He thanked her and twenty minutes later appeared in the public bar ready to eat.

The locals were getting used to his presence and were beginning to talk more freely in front of him.

In response to his seemingly casual question about Clem Gibbs, it appeared he had arrived in Blenthorne about three or four months back and blended into the community well. He was quietly spoken and affable. He was always ready to stand his round but no-one wanted to be drawn on how he made his money.

'Well I heard he did a bit of boxing,' Albert Bishop threw the comment out into the ether to see if there were any takers. 'Didn't he work for Jack Busse taking on all-comers? I heard he and Donald Knightley had a few issues. Now who's for a drink?'

Over the course of the next hour-and-a-half he had consumed a mutton pie and mash, two brown ales, bought several more rounds and found out quite a bit about Clem Gibbs.

It appeared he'd never spoken of any family and had travelled around after originating from London. He had mentioned serving in the navy for a time and subsequently doing manual labouring work in various factories in the north. He was in his late twenties, fair haired, of average height with a strong build and had tattoos on both forearms.

No-one of course had any first-hand knowledge of any bare knuckle boxing and furthermore none had ever placed a bet on the outcome of dog and cock fights but several had heard that such things happened. One said he did overhear Clem Gibbs talking about the need to be flight of foot if one wanted to be successful in the boxing ring.

One day Clem just wasn't around anymore. People didn't think that was strange as he was obviously a bit of a rover and clearly had decided to move on.

As a result of his conversations, Albert decided to go back to the police house to see if Tom Cummins had managed to retrieve any of Clem's possessions from his erstwhile landlady, Mrs Reilly. It was by now fifteen minutes before ten o'clock.

When he arrived at the door the place was in darkness; clearly the Cummins family retired early and Tom didn't consider himself a policeman twenty-four hours a day. It would seem that women didn't appreciate that sort of approach to the job. Maybe that was why Albert Bishop had never married. He tapped lightly on the door but wasn't surprised when he got no answer.

He was walking back down the path when the door opened and Tom appeared in his nightshirt. That was definitely a sight Albert could have done without but he turned politely and told the constable he would return in the morning, he had just called to ask about Clem Gibbs' possessions.

'Well I can save you the trouble, Sir; Mrs Reilly didn't have any of Clem's possessions as she'd had a clear out so that she could rent the room again. She sold off what she could. She found a note though in one of the pockets which she kept as she wasn't sure what to do with it. I suspect she was going through his clothes looking for money but if she found any, she kept quiet and took it in lieu of rent.'

The inspector retraced his steps back along the path and stood by the door, assuring the constable he didn't need to come in; he had a sudden terrible premonition that if he did so he might find Mrs Cummins similarly clad and that would play havoc with his digestion.

Tom Cummins retreated inside and fetched the note from the office. He handed it over to the inspector.

'I don't suppose we're in luck and it's from Donald Knightley?' said the inspector, tongue in cheek.

'No, Sir, I think that would be hoping a bit too much. Next best thing though; it's from his father Mr Herbert Knightley asking Clem to attend a meeting in the grounds of Highfields.'

'Good lord! So we have our connection, albeit not the one we expected. See you in the morning, Tom.'

Albert Bishop made his way back to his billet thinking that tomorrow should prove very interesting.

*

The next morning, Friday 25 September 1891, was again overcast with the threat of rain. The coroner duly arrived and settled himself in the corner of the comfortable, little-used lounge bar of the Blenny. He readily agreed to the landlord's offer of a small nip of brandy before proceedings got underway. Those called as witnesses had gathered as requested. However after establishing the name and address of the deceased, her age and occupation – given as hostess – the coroner adjourned proceedings at the request of the senior investigating police officer, pending further enquiries.

Lizzie breathed a sigh of relief. She had never been involved in any sort of official proceedings before and whilst confident in many ways, was very nervous regarding what might happen that day.

She had been welcomed by the landlord upon arrival; he seemed very pleased to see her and asked if she would care to remain afterwards to partake in refreshment. She thanked him but explained she needed to get back to Highfields as the house was in a state of flux due to the terrible events that had befallen the family.

Inspector Bishop kindly offered to accompany her back to the house as he said he needed to speak to Mr Herbert Knightley. They left the Blenny and walked in companionable silence for a while and then discussed some well-known local walks; the inspector confided that he enjoyed rambling across the fells and stayed in Keswick whenever possible. However, Lizzie's curiosity was aroused and she wondered if there was a way she could subtly ask the purpose of his visit.

'Why do you need to see Mr Knightley, Inspector?' she blurted out before she could stop herself. The inspector didn't seem perturbed at her directness but posed a question of his own.

'Miss Tester, have you ever come across a man by the name of Clem Gibbs? Apparently he had a connection to Freshlea Farm and also to the Knightley family. Mr Herbert Knightley sent a note asking Mr Gibbs to meet him. It would be a few weeks back now; maybe shortly after you arrived here for the family's summer holiday.'

'No indeed, Inspector, the name means nothing to me, I'm sorry. The master wanted to see him you say? What sort of a man is he?' asked Lizzie as she looked across to her companion.

'A bare-knuckle boxer by all accounts,' said the inspector with a reticent smile.

Lizzie tried not to look shocked. 'Oh my goodness me; no, I have not the faintest idea what connection he could have with the family … unless of course it was something that Mr Donald had got himself involved in.'

'My thoughts exactly!' said the inspector with feeling.

They reached the front door of Highfields and Lizzie took her leave of the police officer. Rather incongruously, she walked around the back of the house to the servants' entrance and he pulled the bell chain.

As Lizzie entered, Mr Hemsley was walking towards the stairs leading to the baize door in answer to the bell.

'That's Inspector Bishop, Mr Hemsley,' called Lizzie as she took off her bonnet and shawl in the hallway.

'Really the nerve of some; when will that man learn it is not his place to expect admittance via the front entrance to the house. He is a policeman after all, he has no right,' said the disgruntled butler as he straightened his collar.

'Well he's investigating two murders so I suppose he thinks that gives him the right. He is an inspector, Mr Hemsley; it's not as if its Constable Cummins getting above himself and Mr Bishop does need to see the Master. I hardly think Mr Knightley will want to talk to him in the servants' hall,' said Lizzie probably more sharply than she intended.

Mr Hemsley looked down the stairs disapprovingly. 'It appears you are very well informed, Miss Tester, you not only know who is ringing the bell, you know why. Maybe you would be better suited to my job than me.'

His demeanour clearly conveyed he felt it was not just the jumped up policeman who was getting above their station.

Lizzie allowed herself a small smile. She had obviously annoyed Mr Hemsley. My goodness, the very idea of a female butler! What next, a female prime minister? What an outlandish notion; that would never happen.

*

The inspector was shown into the hall by the affronted butler who didn't offer to take his hat and coat. He didn't seem surprised to see the police officer and Albert Bishop wondered if Miss Tester had advertised his arrival.

After a couple of minutes the butler reappeared to say that Mr Knightley could spare him ten minutes in the study.

'Very hospitable,' said the inspector, although he felt the irony was lost on the butler.

'Well, Bishop; what is it? This is a house in mourning; I assume you have a good reason for being here when you should be pursuing my son's killer,' said Herbert Knightley as he stood in front of the fireplace.

'That is the reason I'm here, Sir. Some new information has come to light regarding Clem Gibbs, I mentioned him the last time I was here. What can you tell me about him?

'What? Absolutely nothing, why?' snapped the master of Highfields.

'Well, because you sent him a note arranging to meet him in the grounds of this house and he hasn't been seen since.'

The timing was actually wild speculation on the part of the inspector but he thought it was worth a try. As it turned out, he was rewarded.

'Sit down.'

It appeared to be a command rather than a request but the inspector was quite pleased to do so; he was holding his hat in his hands and removed his coat, as he did so he looked round pointedly for somewhere to put them.

His host rang the bell.

The butler appeared as if he had been waiting on the other side of the door.

'Take the inspector's things, Hemsley. He's a guest in my house for heaven's sake,' said Herbert Knightley with an impatient wave of his arm.

The butler bowed slightly and took the items proffered by the police officer, clearly extremely irritated and not meeting the policeman's gaze.

'Inspector, a man in my position ... I can't afford any scandal to be attached to my family, to my parliamentary party or to the business ...' Mr Knightley said slowly.

'I may just be a simple policeman,' interjected Albert Bishop, 'but I do understand the need for discretion and you can rest assured all I'm interested in is finding out who killed Mrs Cork, your son and the circumstances surrounding the disappearance of Mr

Gibbs, because it seems to me, Sir, that the three things are connected. Nothing will come out that isn't pertinent.'

'Well you clearly already know about Freshlea Farm as you mentioned it at our last meeting.'

'Yes. My officers are continuing their search of the property today. I am hopeful that Mr Busse will cooperate and we will not need to dig up the whole hundred acres but we will if necessary to get to the truth.'

'My son found out about the place a couple of summers ago and started going there to gamble. He had run up debts in London and nearer home in Kent. He thought, in common with most gamblers, that he would be able to pay off all his creditors with one good win. I pleaded with him to stop; I was worried his mother would find out. I now understand he had been begging money from her and my sister-in-law, Lady Nora Kingsbury.' Mr Knightley shook his head despairingly.

'And his association with Mrs Cork, what can you tell me about that?' asked the inspector sitting forward in his chair eagerly awaiting the answer, which as it turned out was a little bland.

'Well, Inspector, you know what she was, how she made her living.'

'I understand she also dealt cards at the farm, Sir.'

'I know nothing of that,' said Mr Knightley quickly.

'Maybe that is where they first met; I mean, someone of her … social standing, well they moved in different circles surely?' said the inspector as delicately as he could.

'Inspector, are you being deliberately naïve, or do you really not know that people of her "social standing" as you call it, make the majority of their money from men like my son. I believe he visited her at her cottage in the village. He owed her money too, I was amazed that she would give him credit; a very charitable whore!'

The inspector allowed himself a brief knowing smile.

'I dare say she knew her money was safe. I mean all she had to do was threaten to present herself at the front door here; Mr Hemsley is clearly very particular about whom he admits but her very presence would cause a stir wouldn't it? I don't suppose she was averse to using a bit of what shall we say, leverage, if the need arose. How much did he owe her?'

'He came to me and asked for twenty-five pounds.'

'What! Goodness gracious how many times a week did he visit her if he managed to rack up a debt of that magnitude? That's more than a lot of people earn in a year!' exclaimed the inspector incredulously.

'He assured me he only visited her occasionally,' said Mr Knightley.

'Well then, how did he explain away that sum? Surely if he came to you for that amount of money you must have asked?'

'He wouldn't say; he just begged me to give him the money. I refused; it happened at around the same time as the Clem Gibbs business and really, to be frank with you, I'd had enough. I had bailed him out more times than I care to remember and it was always the same. He would make amends; he would never transgress again but of course he always did; as soon as I gave him what he wanted the pattern continued. In my wisdom I thought I was teaching him a lesson. Maybe that is what led to his death.'

'Mr Knightley, if Mrs Cork was a blackmailer, I have to consider the possibility that your son killed her. After all, a dead woman can't call in a marker,' said the inspector shrewdly.

'He isn't … wasn't capable of that sort of attack.'

'But he patronised a venue where blood sports took place on a regular basis. He watched as cockerels and dogs tore each other apart. He also watched as men fought bare-knuckle boxing bouts, potentially inflicting serious injuries or worse. Maybe we will find Clem Gibbs buried at the farm.'

'You seem to have forgotten that my son has also been killed, Inspector,' said Herbert Knightley his face pallid and his lips taut.

'No, Sir; I haven't forgotten that. Do you think Mrs Cork was blackmailing him?'

'Well as you say, twenty-five pounds is an awful lot of money; so yes, if I'm completely honest. Would you care for coffee or tea, Inspector?' He consulted his watch, 'or maybe something stronger?'

'Well if the sun is over the yard arm I'll join you, thank you very much, Sir.'

Herbert Knightley got up and moved across to the decanter. He poured an equal measure of scotch into two glasses and returned to his chair, handing one to the inspector as he did so. During this process, the inspector looked round the room at the photographs placed on the mantelpiece, the top of the bookcase and the occasional tables.

'Lots of pictures of happier times I'll be bound.'

'Yes indeed; the family as they were growing up. I have three daughters and just the one son. We spent some happy times here over the years. In fact before we were married my wife's family invited me and my brother Charles to several house parties here. We were all young and carefree in those days; good thing we didn't know how things would turn out. My wife has always loved this house. I bought it from her brother the earl, you know. I'm not sure she will ever want to set foot in it again.'

'Yes, a bad business indeed.' The inspector paused to allow an appropriate time to elapse after the sombre moment they had shared. 'Did your son give you any indication or hint as to what sort of hold Mrs Cork might have over him?'

'No, Inspector, none whatsoever; as I said, I specifically asked him why he needed such a large sum and he wouldn't tell me. I told him he would have to pay off what he owed from his allowance, get himself a job or find a rich wife.'

'And how did he react to that?'

'He screamed at me and rushed out of the room. Things were not easy between us after that.'

'I see. Moving to the matter of Clem Gibbs; you wrote him a note asking him to meet you, why was that?'

'I might as well tell you, what harm can it do now? Donald had persuaded Clem Gibbs to throw a boxing

208

bout. He planned to place a bet on Mr Gibbs' opponent and he believed that this would provide him with sufficient funds to clear some of his debts which were accruing interest by the day. Mr Gibbs wanted payment to oblige. He said he would feign injury and retire from the bout for fifteen pounds or alternatively allow himself to be punched around the head and body for thirty pounds. Apparently people bet more during the bout if there is sufficient blood and gore.' He paused and drained his glass before continuing;

'Donald didn't have the money to give him prior to the bout and said he would pay Mr Gibbs from his winnings. That wasn't good enough. Gibbs turned on Donald and threatened him for wasting his time; told him he wanted recompense or Donald would face the consequences. Donald came to me for help. I arranged to meet Mr Gibbs but he never turned up. That's the truth, Inspector, before my maker.'

'I keep coming across people who tell me that your son had a connection with Ned Daniels, the nephew of the innkeeper. Can you throw any light on that, Sir?'

'Only that I believe he was equally enamoured of blood sports but then I assume that many of the locals were as well, so if there was a particular link between the two of them, I could not speculate as to what that might be.'

After a few minutes Inspector Bishop took his leave of the bereaved father and made his way back to Blenthorne, having been reunited with his outer apparel on his way out.

As he left the front of the house he cast a glance towards the direction in which Lizzie Tester had walked earlier. She was nowhere to be seen. He admonished himself for even hoping she might be. This place was beginning to affect him in a very strange way. He needed to close this case as soon as possible and get back to normality.

As he walked along the narrow road towards Blenthorne he was pleased with the information he had secured during the interview with Mr Knightley senior. If Donald Knightley was scared of Clem Gibbs, then that could be a reason he was in hiding in the crypt at the church.

Did Clem Gibbs catch up with Donald Knightley and kill him? Unlikely, he wanted money from Donald or his father but he wouldn't get any if Donald were dead.

He was sure Grace Cork was blackmailing Donald Knightley but why? Blackmail was a clear motive for murder, either by Donald or another and from what he now knew of the personality of Donald Knightley, he didn't see him having the stomach to murder anyone.

There was still that nagging connection between the Knightley boy and Ned Daniels. No, Donald's death only made sense if the motive was to stop him from imparting what he knew about the death of Grace Cork.

He needed to find Ned Daniels, in the inspector's opinion he was the key to this.

Something the vicar had said had been bothering him but he could make neither head nor tail of it; the more he pondered, the more he wondered. Also something old John Busse had said made him think; he didn't pay much attention at the time, but now, well … A thought suddenly struck him … what if …? He stopped dead in his tracks as he let the possibility embed itself. Good

Lord; that might just make sense. To be sure, he needed to speak to Freda, Grace Cork's maid. He would do that this afternoon if Ned wasn't found.

As he walked back towards the Blenny, Tom Cummins waylaid him with an urgent wave of his arm.

'I've just got back from the farm and Jack Busse is singing like a canary. When he saw that we weren't going to give up, he finally took us to the burial ground. About thirty animal corpses I would say. Dogs in the main, he admitted they burnt the cocks. The bodies were in varying stages of decay but from the look of them, it was clear some had had their throats cut and some had had their necks broken. Jack told me Ned Daniels took care of the injured animals. He "dispatched them efficiently and then disposed of them" was the way Jack put it.'

'So he knew how to snap a neck; that puts him right in the frame for Donald Knightley. Any sign of the body of Clem Gibbs?'

'No, Sir; Jack swore he was not buried on the farm, to his knowledge at any rate. He said the last time he saw Clem, he was alive. I'm inclined to believe him to be honest, he's pretty scared.'

'Well, as I told him I'm not interested in prosecuting him; as long as the illegal operation is shut down. We won't tell him that for a while though, let him sweat a bit. Maybe he is telling the truth about Clem Gibbs but if he does know something, then perhaps a day or two to contemplate possible imprisonment might make him have a sudden epiphany.'

'Yes, Sir,' said Tom looking very confused.

'As we have the use of a team of officers, once things are finished at the farm, I suggest we concentrate on a search of the area for Ned Daniels. Maybe he can lead us to Clem Gibbs.'

'Are you certain Gibbs is dead, Sir?'

'No, not entirely but if he's alive, why did he leave without his possessions and why did he fail to keep his rendezvous with Mr Herbert Knightley?'

The inspector relayed his conversation of earlier with the master of Highfields to which the constable nodded sagely.

'Gibbs had been promised fifteen pounds at least or thirty if he was prepared to allow himself to be used as a punch bag. He must have been hopeful that Mr Knightley senior would pay him to throw a fight. It would have been less if he was just paying Gibbs to stop him carrying out his threat to beat his precious son to a pulp but still sufficient to tide the boxer over for a while,' the inspector paused and then changed the subject.

'I need to speak to Freda, Grace Cork's maid; do you have any idea of her situation now?'

'Yes, Sir, she will be working over in the vicarage for a while; their regular is laid up with lumbago,' said the constable; clearly keeping his ear to the ground with regard the health of the villagers.

'After I've been to the vicarage, I'll go back to the Blenny and have a word with Obed Daniels; he must have an idea where Ned goes when he's away from the inn.'

The inspector and constable parted company, with Tom Cummins going back to Freshlea Farm to collect some officers to start a search for Ned Daniels. Albert Bishop glanced at the window of the office at the front of the police house. He noted the aspidistra was back.

He made his way to the vicarage and tapped lightly on the door. Freda herself answered and took him through to the kitchen. They spoke briefly for a few minutes. She nodded her silent ascent to one question in particular that he posed. He left, satisfied that his hunch was correct.

Inspector Bishop had the feeling he often experienced when a case started to make sense. With any luck this might be his last night in Blenthorne, not that he hadn't been made welcome at the inn, Obed Daniels was a competent host but he wanted to get back to his own house. He very much liked this village though and indeed some of the residents. Well if he was honest, one in particular … he pulled his thoughts back to the present as he entered the public bar and ordered his supper.

Chapter 12 – Astonishing Revelations

Late September 1891

Inspector Bishop was waiting patiently for a word with his host. He had spent the morning at the police house putting his theories down on paper, aided by some enlightening information he had received by telegram the evening before. He liked to work in a methodical way as it made it easier when he came to write his final report. Obed Daniels was mindful of his presence and as soon as there was a lull of dinnertime patrons he beckoned the policeman to the far end of the public bar.

'I'll be straight with you, Obed; I fear Ned is responsible for the death of Donald Knightley. Jack Busse is spilling his guts to save his own skin. Ned has the skills to break the neck of a muscular dog; to my mind that suggests he would be more than capable of breaking the neck of a man. I think Grace Cork was murdered because she was a blackmailer and I believe I now know the motive. However I have precious little evidence. I still have no idea as to the whereabouts of

Clem Gibbs. I don't know if he's a victim or a potential perpetrator in league with another.'

Obed Daniels wiped his hands on the cloth that hung from his belt.

'Maybe I've been too lenient with Ned but he's not all bad. He loves the girls, makes them things and buys presents for them. He has told me more than once how much he appreciates being part of a family. Yet there is another side to his personality; he can be furtive and at times dishonest. It's like he's two different people. Maybe it's something that is beyond his control; I don't think anyone knows enough about the workings of the brain to be able to explain what may be wrong with him. Maybe they never will. I'm not trying to excuse him but somehow I still feel I need to try to protect him.'

'Even if he's committed murder?' the inspector asked, looking closely at the landlord.

'If it can be proven that he's a murderer, then no, I can do no more for him,' said Obed Daniels spreading his hands wide and then laying them face down on the bar and looking the police officer straight in the eye.

'I believe ...' started Obed only to be disturbed by Tom Cummins rushing in through the door of the public bar.

'Sir, he's been sighted. Ned Daniels, he was seen by a villager making a run for it across the fells and then he ducked into the wood on the Highfields estate. I'll round up the men doing the house to house enquiries shall I and we will follow you?'

'Let me come with you; I might be able to persuade him to give himself up,' said Obed looking at Albert Bishop imploringly. The inspector nodded his assent.

The landlord announced that due to unforeseen circumstances, he had to close the bar and ushered the slightly disgruntled drinkers out. Within ten minutes he had locked the door and the inspector had collected him in the pony and trap. They kept their conversation to a minimum, both clearly preoccupied with their own thoughts on their way to Highfields House.

Upon arrival they pulled the bell chain which Hemsley answered after a short delay. The inspector advised him sharply that he had no time for ceremony or pleasantries and told him to fetch his master. Taken aback but clearly still determined to retain control over who should be admitted to the house, the butler told them to wait while he enquired if the master was at home.

Inspector Bishop was not renowned for throwing his weight around but at times, particularly if he was pushed to the limit of his tolerance level, he reacted. This was such an occasion.

'Get out of my way man unless you want to be arrested for obstructing a murder investigation,' he said as he moved towards the door, causing the obdurate butler to step back quickly to avoid being shoulder-charged.

Herbert Knightley appeared from the passageway which led off the hall, most likely as a result of the commotion at the front door.

'Begging your pardon, Sir, but these … gentlemen are requesting to see you …'

The inspector stepped forward and addressed the master of Highfields.

'Mr Knightley, we need to make a search of your property as we have reason to believe a suspect has taken refuge in the wood on this estate. To be honest this is a courtesy call but in view of the circumstances …'

'Do whatever you feel is appropriate, Inspector. I just want an end to this terrible business. Can I or my staff be of any assistance?' asked Herbert Knightley wearily.

'Someone who knows the wood would be useful if they could be made available,' observed the inspector.

Herbert Knightley looked at his butler.

'Well if I may, Sir, I would suggest George knows the wood as well as anyone; he takes Lady Nora there for her walk most days,' said the butler giving the inspector a withering glance as he did so.

'Fetch him please,' said the inspector.

The belligerent butler remained rigid and looked at his master.

'Do as you are asked Hemsley; bring him to the hall,' said Herbert Knightley impatiently.

'Mr Knightley, do you know of any buildings or structures in the wood where someone could hole up? We'll eliminate those first,' said the inspector.

'There are one or two old buildings left over from the days of crofting. Also a semi-derelict folly; my brother Charles used to have it as his art studio. Since he went to live abroad it hasn't been used for anything. However I imagine it's as good a place as any to start.'

George appeared looking apprehensive and was apprised of the situation. He was then asked to accompany the party to the wood.

'I understand there's an old folly? Does that mean anything to you?' asked the inspector.

Yes; I've never been that far previously but I think I know where it is, in fact Miss Crittle and Miss Tester were approaching it when we were out looking for Mr Donald, that would have been on Wednesday. I called them back to tell them the news … about the crypt and Mr Donald I mean …'

'Where do you take Lady Nora?' asked the policeman sharply.

'Only to the end of the path proper and then she wheels herself to wherever she wants to go after that. I think she just likes to wander around as she said the wood makes her feel alive and allows her to be free. She often takes a picnic. So much food sometimes it's a wonder she can manage her supper when she gets back,' confided George somewhat gratuitously.

'Can you find this folly do you think? We'll eliminate that first,' said the inspector.

George looked a bit uncertain. 'Well to be honest, I sort of stumbled across it last time and followed Misses Crittle and Tester back but I'll do my best, Sir.'

'Take Tester with you George; that will save time if you are uncertain,' commanded his master.

'Mr Knightley, Sir, I hardly think it's a suitable environment for a woman,' Obed Daniels appeared from behind the inspector, actually taking the words out of the mouth of the policeman who felt vaguely vexed.

'Who are you? Oh it's Mr Daniels isn't it from the Blenthorne Inn? Why are you with the inspector?' asked Mr Knightley.

'Because it's my nephew they're pursuing and it was felt I might be able to persuade him to give himself up. It's a bad business and one which needs a resolution. However he's only a suspect, not a convicted killer, as nothing is proven against him yet,' said Obed Daniels defensively.

Herbert Knightley nodded briefly.

'Go and ask Tester, George but make it clear there is no pressure on her to accompany you; heaven knows from my limited dealings with her, she is quite redoubtable,' conceded Mr Knightley placing his hands on his hips and shaking his head slightly.

George disappeared before either Inspector Bishop or Mr Daniels could protest further.

Five minutes later an unlikely quartet made up of the police officer, the inn landlord, the lady's maid and the footman made their way towards the wood.

'Why do you think he would head to the wood?' the inspector asked Obed Daniels. 'Is there a way out the other side?'

'Well there's the cut through to Blenthorne but I don't suppose he's heading in that direction. He would know the police were looking for him. There's a tarn to the west under Rundle Ridge but there's no route through. Apart from that there's Hallows Gap, an outcrop to the south which is nigh on impossible from that side. The only man I knew who tried it became cragfast. Rescuers tried to reach him but he could move neither up nor down until he finally fell and perished. I can't believe Ned would try to scale it but then there's no knowing what a desperate man might do. I need to persuade him to give himself up, if I can,' said a determined Obed Daniels.

'Miss Tester, after you have identified the folly, I would like you to return to the house with George,' said the inspector as he turned towards Lizzie.

'There is something I think you should know, Sir; Lady Nora is in the wood. She likes to come at all times of the day, sometimes nearly nightfall. I think it's a bit creepy but she says she loves the patterns the trees throw in the twilight,' George volunteered from a few steps behind the others.

'She's out here you say? Oh my God,' exclaimed the inspector, 'begging your pardon, Miss Tester.'

Lizzie smiled as she breathed heavily, trying to keep pace with the men who unlike her, were not encumbered by their apparel. She held her skirt up as much as decency allowed. The going under foot was soft and spongey as they had had significant rainfall in recent weeks.

'He won't take her hostage if that's what you are worried about. He wouldn't be that stupid,' said Obed Daniels but without much conviction in his voice.

'Lady Nora was in the wood the day I brought May and Lily for a walk; do you remember, Mr Daniels? It was Monday, the day they came to tea in the servants' hall,' said Lizzie a little breathlessly.

'Indeed I do, Miss Tester; the girls still talk about it. They loved their guided tour and are so very pleased with their new clothes; I am greatly indebted to you,' the innkeeper smiled down briefly at her.

'It was my pleasure, Mr Daniels,' said Lizzie even more breathlessly as she gathered her skirt slightly higher around her ankles to prevent it getting tangled in the brambles.

Albert Bishop felt like an outsider eavesdropping on a very private conversation. A strange sense of dismay came over him and he couldn't understand why.

'What was she doing? George seems to think she just wanders around,' the inspector said.

'I don't know; to be honest we didn't actually see her we just heard her laughing and talking to someone. I don't know who, as I couldn't hear his voice properly,' replied Lizzie.

'Why do you think it was a man?' enquired the inspector.

'Well because we could clearly hear Lady Nora's voice but not that of her companion. So I think it must have been much lower in tone; a man's voice,' reasoned Lizzie as she turned towards the inspector.

'So you think she meets up with someone in the wood?' Inspector Bishop sounded sceptical.

'Well it would explain the attraction of going out in all weathers wouldn't it? George said the wood made her feel free, didn't you, George?' said Lizzie turning round slightly. 'What if there was someone whom she actually visited, someone who made her laugh and made her happy. I think that's rather wonderful actually. She has a very tough life. Not really fitting in. Not quite having the same social status as her sister. Always on the outside looking in like a spare part that no-one really wants.'

'Does she ever confide in you, Miss Tester?' asked the policeman.

'Good gracious no never, it's just intuition. Lady Nora is the most private person I have ever met. To be honest I have tried to draw her on the subject; but she never drops her guard. I think she assumes the role expected of her in most aspects of her life and when she is here with her beau, she is carefree and joyful. It's her secret and no-one should begrudge her that.' She broke off as they reached the end of the main pathway.

'The folly is this way gentlemen; Miss Crittle was with me when we were searching for Mr Donald and we spied a solid-looking building a short distance in front of us. As we got a bit closer to the bend in the narrow path, we could see it was in a bad state of repair but we didn't actually get as far as the door.

'Mr Knightley's brother used to have it as an art studio I understand,' said the inspector.

'That would be Mr Charles. I don't think he has been home for years though; not in the time I've worked for the family at least,' said Lizzie.

'There must have been some almighty falling out for him to leave and break off all contact,' remarked the inspector.

'Indeed but as I said, it was well before my time,' repeated Lizzie.

'Nearly thirty years didn't you say, Landlord?' queried the inspector.

'Well that would be the last time he was here at Highfields; as to whether he visited the family when they were in Kent or wrote to them, I couldn't comment,' answered Obed Daniels.

'The folly is just around the bend up ahead in a bit of a clearing if I've got my bearings correct. Wait ... what's that noise? Can you hear something? Like a low moaning sound,' said Lizzie. 'I think it came from this direction.' She started to head away to the left.

'No, Miss, please, you agreed to go back with George once you'd identified the folly,' said the inspector urgently.

'I don't believe I did, Inspector, and some sort of living soul sounds to be in trouble ...' remarked Lizzie over her shoulder.

'Lizzie, for once please just do as you are bid,' said Inspector Bishop, completely forgetting himself in his form of address to the lady's maid. 'Now I don't want to be a harbinger of doom but whatever is making that noise is not fit for your eyes.'

'He's right, Miss Tester; we'll attend to this. Go back with George,' said Obed Daniels firmly.

The inspector and landlord made their way past Lizzie who looked after them.

George had remained silent for several seconds. Clearly he was very uncomfortable with the situation and looked like he wanted to be anywhere other than in the wood at that particular moment.

'Come with me, Miss Tester,' he implored, urgently beckoning her towards him as he turned back in the direction of the house.

'Look George, we are so close to the folly, we might just go and check to see if anyone has been there recently. That will save Inspector Bishop some time,' suggested Lizzie.

With that she walked purposefully round the curve in the narrow clearing in the direction of the building. She could distinctly hear the inspector's whistle in the distance summoning the other officers, so they had obviously found something or someone.

George hung back and only moved forward tentatively as Lizzie turned round to see where he was.

In the event, George's reluctant progress was so slow that Lizzie was at the entrance before he could reach her to advise caution before going in. She gave the door a gentle shove and it gave way immediately ...

*

Nora was sitting contentedly in the cottage. They had enjoyed a pleasant meal together and as usual he had made her laugh and lightened her spirits. There was no laughter at Highfields now. Nora wondered if there ever would be again. How she longed to be away from them all. Her sister Constance wearing her mourning black almost triumphantly as a symbol of her despair and weeping into her handkerchief, devoid of jewellery and unable to speak. Her brother-in-law Herbert walking around like a ghost, solemn and solitary, silently grieving for his son. Sophia petulant and moody as usual, frustrated and particularly irritated that for once she was not the centre of attention.

He had suggested a walk later; that would be nice, they would ramble slowly, as her limitations allowed but he didn't mind. He would walk next to her, guiding her and taking her arm if the ground was particularly uneven.

A sudden noise broke in on her thoughts.

'Did you hear that?' she enquired looking at him in alarm.

'No one comes here, it must be an animal, I expect …' he said, his voice sounding anything but convincing.

The door opened, Nora saw someone standing there; a woman silhouetted in the doorway. She looked from the woman to her beloved who had moved across to the far wall and was standing against it. Inexplicably, he seemed to be smiling at the woman as he stretched out his arms towards her, an expression of gentle recognition on his face.

What was happening? He was shrinking before Nora's eyes; his outline was becoming blurred and she could hardly make out the shape of his body. He was disappearing and she was transfixed by what she was seeing. It was as if some form of osmosis was taking place. The wall seemed to have become porous and was enveloping and absorbing him until he vanished completely.

There was nothing left. He had gone. She stood alone in the silence.

*

'Lady Nora? Is that you? Are you alright? What are you doing in here? This place is horrible. You need to come with me now; there is a dangerous man in the wood. Let me take you to safety,' implored Lizzie.

She moved across to the bewildered-looking lady in front of her. She glanced round as she did so.

The room was almost round in shape with an old easel to the left and a bench to the right. There were spiders and dead flies in cobwebs attached to the rafters. A solitary crow flapped around in the roof space. A wooden table stood in the middle bearing a mountain of decaying food which appeared to be moving, as if alive. Then she realised the movement was due to feasting vermin. Rats were everywhere; on the bench, on the easel, scurrying across the floor in front of her. Bottles were scattered around and there was an abundance of broken glass. The stench of rotten matter and animal excrement was intense and Lizzie put her hand to her mouth to stop herself from retching. There was a pile of filthy rags near the table on the brown stained floor.

'What have you been doing here, Lady Nora? This place is filthy and you could injure yourself; look out for the glass. Come with me now please,' said Lizzie urgently as she stepped tentatively towards the older lady and held out her hand.

She looked round for George who seemed to be hanging back, unhappy to cross the threshold.

As she did so, Lady Nora rushed towards her with her hair flying loose around her shoulders and across her face. She caught Lizzie off guard and pushed her to one side, causing her to stumble and fall against the wall. It took a moment or two to recover her composure.

'Are you alright, Miss Tester?' enquired George, appearing to be rather shamefaced regarding his reticence as he helped her to stand up.

'Where did she go? She can't have got far, she's on foot. Quickly we need to find her, you go to the left and I'll go to the right,' instructed Lizzie, ignoring George's question.

George looked very unhappy but did as he was told.

Lizzie pushed her way through the low undergrowth close to the folly. If she was finding it difficult in her frock to make headway then surely Lady Nora couldn't have made much ground, as she had the added complication of her disability. However she clearly knew this wood well.

'Lady Nora; Lady Nora, please come back. It's not safe here. Please tell me where you are,' called Lizzie.

Lizzie suddenly heard a sound to her right, near to some worn stone steps leading to higher ground, above which a tall strong beech tree stood. There was a scrabbling sound and mumbling coming from just beyond. Lizzie lifted her skirt so that she didn't fall as she mounted the moss covered steps. Maybe they were the remains of a former dwelling that had stood on the site in bygone years.

She reached the tree. 'Oh my goodness!' she exclaimed aloud, for she had found the tree with the carved initials "CK-HK". Constance Kingsbury-Herbert Knightley – so it did exist! This must have been her employers' courting place. She was pulled out of her thoughts by a clawing sound several feet away on the other side of the tree.

When she slowly tiptoed round the trunk, she witnessed an incredible sight, so much so she could hardly believe her eyes. Lady Nora was on her knees, digging and scratching at the soft ground with a knife in her right hand and using her bare left hand to make a hole; she was digging down deeper and deeper and making a strange noise as she did so. The recent rain had clearly made the ground soft.

'Milady, what are you doing? Please get up. You will hurt yourself. Look you are getting all muddy,' Lizzie said gently as she approached Lady Nora.

She bent down and whilst it was unseemly to do so, gently touched her mistress's arm. Nora shrugged her off.

'Get off me. Leave me. Go,' she hissed. When Lizzie tried again Lady Nora turned towards her.

She stood awkwardly and moved menacingly towards Lizzie, who involuntarily backed away. The crippled woman leapt forward and shoved Lizzie with incredible upper body strength, presumably gained from years of pushing herself around in her wheelchair. Lizzie fell backwards and her head hit something hard. She felt dazed as she tried to sit herself up.

Lady Nora was continuing to make a strange moaning noise as her hair flopped all over her face. She pushed it away with her muddy hands. She moved back to her hole, leaned forward and plunged down deeper and deeper.

Lizzie managed to pull herself to a sitting position.

'Help,' she yelled. She realised this would alert Ned Daniels if he were still in the vicinity but she didn't know what else to do.

'Help us please; George, Mr Daniels, Inspector Bishop, please, Lady Nora and I need help,' shouted Lizzie at the top of her voice. She then inserted the index finger and small finger on her left hand into her mouth to give the shrillest whistle she could. Strange to think that was something she hadn't done since childhood and a skill she probably thought she would never need again.

Nora dropped the knife and left what she was doing to hobble over towards Lizzie.

'Shut up; shut up; why are you here? Why couldn't you leave us alone? We weren't hurting anyone. It's happening all over again. Just like before. People couldn't leave us alone, we were happy and meddlers destroyed that. Well no more! And you, you, you're nothing but a flyblow. You shouldn't be here, you shouldn't exist!'

Lizzie found herself covered in spittle from the woman bending down and hissing over her.

Without warning, Lady Nora lunged at her maid and before she had time to react, the older woman was suddenly astride Lizzie with her hands round her neck. Lizzie fell backwards as she tried to loosen Lady Nora's grip around her throat and managed to let out the type of scream that is only possible when one's life is in mortal danger.

Within seconds Lizzie was struggling to breathe, she could see dark spots before her eyes as her consciousness faded away. Blood fizzed and coursed through the veins in her temples as she tried to gulp for air. Her lungs were silently screaming as the life began to drain out of her. Then all at once, the weight on her body was lifted and the hands around her neck were gone. She lay still while her body's autonomic system kicked back from the brink causing her to involuntarily cough and gasp. The world was spinning round her as she opened her eyes and shapes slowly came into focus.

Obed Daniels had Lady Nora held firmly by the arms as he dragged her away.

'Miss Tester, are you alright?' he asked looking over the shoulders of the woman he had tightly in his grasp.

Lizzie had the most amazing déjà vu moment. All of a sudden she was back on the road to Blenthorne and the innkeeper was dragging a dangerous dog off her. This time it was a deranged woman.

Lizzie sat up and realised her hair was in nearly as bad a state as that of her mistress.

'Yes I'm fine but Lady Nora is unwell. I found her in the folly. It's in a terrible state. There are rats and rotting food everywhere. That must be where she has been coming to. She rushed passed me and came here to this tree. She was digging over there,' Lizzie pointed and Inspector Bishop who had just appeared, walked over to the spot.

George was standing a little away from the group and the inspector told him to go and find the other officers; however at that moment Tom Cummins and another constable arrived. Obed Daniels handed Lady Nora over to their care.

'Take her to the house and stay with her,' instructed the inspector. He then knelt down in front of the hole. Obed Daniels had pulled Lizzie to her feet and she thanked him as they made their way towards the hole together.

'No, Miss Tester, please don't look,' said the inspector as he put his hands up in front of his body.

'What is it?' asked Obed Daniels who was half a pace ahead of Lizzie and standing slightly in front of her to act as a barrier.

'There's a body down here,' said the inspector grimly.

'Clem Gibbs?' enquired the landlord.

'Lord no; it's been here for years, it's no more than a skeleton,' said the inspector looking again into the hole.

'Who can it be?' asked Lizzie trying in vain to see round the large human blockade in front of her.

The inspector looked from Lizzie to the landlord; 'At a guess and it is just a guess mind, I would say we've just found Mr Charles Knightley.'

Chapter 13 – The Shattering of Illusions

Late September 1891

Lizzie arrived back at a little after five-thirty. She had felt shaken and her legs didn't want to work as they left the wood. Mr Daniels must think she spent her life courting disaster. However as before, he helped her when she was at her most vulnerable. He offered to carry her but she insisted she could walk. He gave her his arm and supported her as they made their way out back to Highfields House.

'Did you find your nephew, Mr Daniels?' enquired Lizzie as they made slow progress through the trees.

'Yes, Miss, we did. He was caught in a mantrap,' said the landlord quietly.

'Oh my goodness yes, Mrs Reader warned me about those when I took the girls into the wood. But surely Ned would have known where they were and been able to spot them, after all he's lived in these parts for years.'

'Yes but he was panicking and badly injured. You see, he had been stabbed in the abdomen.' Obed Daniels swallowed deeply.

'Clem Gibbs?' asked Lizzie tentatively.

'No, it was Lady Nora. It seems she saw them; Ned and Mr Donald when they were disposing of Mrs Cork's body. They were near the clearing at one point and then seemed to change their minds and left her on the nearby fell. He was in the wood today and went to the folly after he spotted Lady Nora going in; I don't know what was in his mind, maybe to try to reason with her, however he has killed twice so I think he was probably going to silence her too before making a run for it.'

'He killed both Grace Cork and Mr Donald?'

'Yes, Miss Tester, he did. He was close to death and admitted as much when we found him,' confirmed the landlord.

*

Obed Daniels had no intention of giving his female companion the gory details of the distressing scene he had witnessed at the small clearing in the wood where he and the inspector had found Ned. His nephew was lying on his side with his left leg ensnared in the deadly iron mechanism; its teeth embedded a couple of inches above Ned's ankle. The rusty metal had penetrated his skin and was buried deep within the tissue of his leg; probably to the bone, if the previous stories Obed had heard were true.

He also had a gaping wound to his abdomen, about an inch below his waist, down a little from his umbilicus. The knife wound had been deep; tearing away his muscle wall allowing some of his intestines to protrude.

The inspector had blown his whistle to summon help. Obed had taken off his jacket and made it into a wad to try to stem the flow of blood however even as he did so, he realised it was a futile gesture. Ned looked pleadingly into his uncle's face, his own pallor already deathly grey with sweat running from his forehead.

As he had spoken a small trail of saliva and blood appeared in the corners of his mouth. Even so, Ned managed to answer the questions the inspector put to him. Finally he grabbed his uncle's arm.

'It was madness, Uncle Obed; Donald talked of killing Grace. I told him I wouldn't be any part of it but he tried anyway. He planned to bash her brains in and make it look like she'd fallen out on the fells. He cornered her in her cottage and hit her over the head with a rock but not enough to kill her and she was still alive when I arrived. He made a complete mess of it. I had to finish her off. It was his idea to make it look like an animal attack. That was the worst thing I've ever done, using a hoe to tear into her flesh. We took her to the edge of Highfields to start with but then carried on going and dumped her on the fell. It made me feel sick. I wanted to …' his voice had trailed away.

Obed's heart felt heavy as he relived the moment his desperate nephew slumped before him; he wondered if he would ever be able to forget it. He realised Lizzie was speaking again and pulled himself away from the painful memory.

*

'Lady Nora attacked Ned with a knife you say? Well to be honest I can well believe it; she leapt at me like a madwoman,' said Lizzie with feeling.

'It seems he entered the folly and found her there. He was a bit disconcerted by what he saw. She appeared to be talking to herself, like she was in conversation with someone. She grabbed a knife and caught Ned off guard. She managed to lunge forward and stab him. He staggered off but he thought she was coming after him and stumbled into the mantrap. So that was the noise we heard, Miss Tester, when the inspector and I left you, with the strict understanding that you were to go back to the house.'

'Well George and I agreed we would just take a look in the folly to save the inspector some time,' said Lizzie feebly, realising how unlikely it sounded.

'Yes well, knowing George I'm sure you had a job to stop him,' Obed Daniels said ironically.

Lizzie smiled in spite of herself.

'Where is Ned now, Mr Daniels?' asked Lizzie looking concerned.

'He died where he was. One of the constables went for the doctor but there was nothing to be done. He lost a lot of blood from the knife wound and also his left leg was badly damaged. Mantraps are wicked things; they've been illegal for over fifty years but with so many hidden in the undergrowth in the past, it would be well-nigh impossible to locate them all.' He swallowed deeply and then continued;

'It's supposed to be a deterrent to keep the poachers at bay. It's possible Ned that might have died as a result of the injury to his leg anyway. Even if he had survived both that and the stomach wound, well it would have been the gallows.'

'Oh, Mr Daniels, you have my utmost sympathy for your loss,' said Lizzie with feeling.

'To be honest, I think it was always going to end this way. He wasn't all bad you know, at times he was gentle and somehow a bit lost. But the bad side seemed to outweigh the good on so many occasions. It was one thing after another. No two ways about it. I did my best but I think the damage was done well before he came to live with me. Maybe he was born that way; I mean look at Mr Donald, had everything he could ever want handed to him on a plate and he still turned out to be tarred with the same brush.'

*

As they arrived at the house, Philadelphia Crittle was waiting on the drive and came running towards her niece. She put her arms around her and Lizzie's resolve to be strong melted. It wasn't quite her mother but it was the next best thing.

'Aunt Phily; oh my goodness, I don't know what has come over Lady Nora. There is a body out there by the tree with the initials carved in the bark. The inspector thinks it might be Mr Charles Knightley. If that's true, he didn't go to live abroad after all. He died here and has been buried in the wood all these years.'

'Yes, that makes sense,' said Philadelphia Crittle softly almost to herself.

Lizzie was puzzled that her aunt didn't seem shocked. In fact, if anything, she looked like she had the answer to a riddle.

'Thank you, Mr Daniels, for bringing my girl safely back home. Please, you must come in and have some refreshment.'

'Thank you kindly, Miss Crittle, but I need to get back to Ned. I have to find Inspector Bishop to see what's what.'

Lizzie allowed herself to be guided in through the backdoor of the house. She turned and smiled at Mr Daniels. She hadn't thanked him properly but he smiled in return. She hoped he knew how grateful she was to him yet again.

He really was a very nice man.

*

It was agreed that Lady Nora Kingsbury would stay at Highfields House for the night in the custody and care of her brother-in-law Mr Herbert Knightley and then travel to Keswick with Inspector Bishop the following day, once the appropriate arrangements were in place.

She didn't appear to understand what had happened and had not spoken to anyone since she was taken into custody. Mr Field had taken her to her bedroom and Mrs Field had cleaned her up. She said that Lady Nora was muttering to herself and wandering round her room, apparently looking for something or someone.

As Lizzie was being cossetted by her aunt, the inspector arrived at Highfields having attended to matters in the wood and was taken directly to the master. He outlined the sequence of events that had taken place

237

that afternoon and told Mr Knightley that in view of the statement made by Ned Daniels before he died, Lady Nora would be charged in connection with his stabbing. The inspector also mentioned that Ned had been ensnared in a mantrap when he was found.

The body found in the wood would be removed for examination. There were a few personal items in what remained of the top garment, presumably a suit jacket. There was a diary; damp and mouldy with the pages stuck together. Those that could be prised apart revealed ink staining only. Time had washed away the entries, making the contents illegible. A pocket-watch and chain were also found.

When shown them by the inspector, Herbert Knightley identified the items as belonging to his brother Charles.

'Tell me about your brother, Mr Knightley,' the inspector said as they sat in the morning room. Hemsley had brought in a decanter and offered the inspector a drink on a silver salver with a discreet bow, again making sure to make no eye contact.

'He was an artist; a poet; a dreamer. He was highly intelligent but not remotely interested in the business, he just wanted to paint. To be honest he would have been hopeless at banking. When we first met the Kingsbury family, I think it was an open secret that my wife Lady Constance was initially attracted to Charles. He was handsome and witty. I was the steady one. Doing my duty to the family, leading the life they expected of me.'

'Constance's father had remarried after the death of her mother and he had a son with his second wife. I think both Constance and Nora became rather a tiresome burden after that. Pressure was brought to bear on Constance to make the correct decision. With me she would have security, a position in society and respect from her peers. With my brother, she would have had to live on his allowance. As it was, he decided to leave and go abroad. It was agreed that a lump sum would be settled upon him. It was then up to him to make a success of his chosen career, such as it was.'

'So the idea that he was broken-hearted when Lady Constance chose you over him didn't drive him away?' asked the inspector.

'No, no he continued to visit for several years after our first two daughters were born. It was a bit of a scandal with a local girl that drove him away in the end I believe, Inspector. I never knew the details; my wife took care of it you understand. I just signed the cheque,' commented Mr Knightley with a small smile.

'Didn't it surprise you that your brother broke off all contact? Never came back or wrote over the years, even if it were only to ask for more money?'

'Well yes; I think I probably expected him to spend what money he had been given and then come back cap-in-hand for more. To be honest I was rather impressed that he didn't. I hoped that meant he had made a success of his life. As to why he never wrote, well he was quite self-absorbed and if his life was running smoothly, he probably wouldn't have even thought of it.'

Herbert Knightley broke off for a moment and then a thought appeared to strike him.

'What made you think it was my brother even before I had identified the items you have brought with you?'

'Well his name had cropped up a couple of times so I made enquiries; it seems the money you settled on him hadn't been touched. I got my constable to liaise with the Reigate police who contacted Mr Knightley's bank and I received a telegram yesterday advising me the account hadn't been active for years. That made me think he wasn't in a position to access it. It also transpired no-one had had any contact, not even a letter. Being of a suspicious nature, I'm afraid I assumed he was probably dead,' said the inspector logically.

'I see, yes; well you have been proved correct, Inspector,' Herbert Knightley looked at the policeman clearly with a heightened degree of respect.

'Mr Knightley, this is rather a delicate matter but I think we now have reached the point of being candid with each other. The fact that Lady Nora knew where the body was ...'

'Yes, Inspector, I see what you are implying. The inference is that she killed my brother and from what you've just told me, created the illusion that he was alive and living at the folly; whereas in fact he was actually buried a few feet away.' Herbert Knightley crossed his legs and spread his hands in front of him.

'What can I say?' he continued, 'I assume after all this time there would be no supporting evidence and it will remain conjecture. The fact remains she was involved in the death of Ned Daniels, although I imagine that mitigating circumstances might be put forward in her defence. Either way, she has clearly lost touch with reality so it will either be prison or an asylum, would you agree?'

'That will be for doctors and, if the evidence warrants it, a court to decide but I suspect they will be compassionate,' the inspector said quietly and they sat in contemplative silence for a few moments. The inspector then continued; 'of course there is also the attack on Miss Tester. There could be a charge there; if Mr Obed Daniels hadn't intervened, I've no doubt the outcome would have been very different.'

'Miss …?? Oh yes of course, Lady Nora's maid, well I don't think, Inspector that we really need to worry …'

The inspector silenced the master of Highfields with a cold stare.

'Well of course, that will not be for me to decide,' murmured Mr Knightley. He then changed tack; 'Ned Daniels, did he kill both Grace Cork and my son?'

'Yes, because Grace Cork was, as we suspected, a blackmailer. It was Ned's idea that your son should lie low in the crypt and then make his way to London. He apparently used the servants' stairs to leave the house unnoticed, having helped himself to food from the pantry. Before he died, Ned told his uncle and me that Donald Knightley was very jumpy. He was present when Grace Cork was killed and it was only a matter of time before he cracked so Ned broke his neck. He said he went to the folly today to silence Lady Nora because she had seen him and your son with Grace Cork's body. As it was, Lady Nora turned the tables on him.'

Inspector Bishop decided not to elaborate on what Ned had told them in the wood. Bad enough for the man to know as much as he did about his son, without being told he had been complicit in murder.

'You said Grace Cork was a blackmailer. Was she blackmailing my son, Inspector?'

'Indeed she was, her bank balance was very healthy and growing each month, corresponding more or less to what your son was withdrawing from his account; I suspect she kept enough cash to pay her bills and then deposited the rest for her retirement. After all, her way of life had its limitations, once her looks had gone or she put on weight ...'

'So what was the reason, do you know, was it because he was a client of hers or because of his gambling?'

'Neither, Sir; I stumbled across the motive rather by accident. There were two things; firstly, something that John Busse the farmer told me, he said Grace Cork was very astute and missed nothing when she worked for his son as a card dealer. I thought at the time he was referring to her ability to spot a card sharp but I now think he actually meant she was just generally perceptive.

'Secondly, the vicar made some cryptic reference to people choosing a path compatible with a respectable life or choosing aberrance. I didn't understand what he meant at the time but later, putting the two things together, I believe I made sense of it.' He paused, this was difficult.

'To be certain, I went to see Freda, Grace Cork's maid who is currently working at the vicarage. I put a certain question to her and she confirmed my theory. In addition she gave me some further information.'

'Which was what, Inspector?'

'Do you really have no inkling, Sir?'

'Please just tell me.'

'I asked Freda if Grace Cork entertained your son and Ned Daniels herself … or if she well, left them alone together. Freda confirmed that usually Ned and Mr Donald visited at the same time and spent a couple of hours in each other's company on almost every occasion. I also believe your son was a similar size to Mrs Cork …' the inspector added quietly.

Herbert Knightley looked blankly at his companion.

'From what Freda told me, I think Mrs Cork may have encouraged your son to indulge in certain role-play activities … for a fee.' He paused hoping his host might understand his meaning without the need for further explanation. However he soon realised he would have to elaborate.

'Freda told me that your son liked to dress in Mrs Cork's clothing and she also kept a blonde wig for his use. He liked Mrs Cork to call him "Dulcie" as I understand it, Sir.' He paused while Mr Knightley senior gulped and exhaled sharply.

'Even before he became involved with Ned, Grace Cork was encouraging your son to visit her and they would dress similarly, share makeup and nail polish, chat and take tea together. That was what he was paying for in the beginning. I found these in your son's possession at the time of his death, Sir.'

The inspector took the small bottle of organic solvent out of his pocket and a red-stained handkerchief and showed them to Herbert Knightley.

'The vicar noticed a smell that he described as a cleaning agent when he entered the crypt. For a while I couldn't understand why Mr Donald would have these items with him. However it made sense in light of what Freda told me. It obviously wasn't practical to dress in female clothes after Mrs Cork's death, so most likely he just painted his nails in the privacy of his room and kept the solvent with him so that he could remove it quickly when he needed to. He probably cleaned his nails just before he was killed, hence the smell of the solvent and the nail polish on the cloth.

'It's my guess that Grace saw your son with Ned Daniels at the farm. She watched their interactions and picked up on certain … nuances. Being the shrewd person she was, she probably saw another lucrative avenue to exploit your son's … inclinations and offered them a meeting place, for a price. Freda told me her mistress used to help clean the silver when they were there, as a way of passing the time.

'From the start of this investigation it was difficult to understand what the two of them had in common, apart from their gambling habit but well … I think we both understand now don't we? They were engaged in … certain practices.'

'Yes, yes I fully understand, Inspector. To be honest, there was an incident when Donald was at school; a boy was almost suffocated during some sort of game. However that was years ago I thought he had grown out of it. Just a phase; often happens when they are away at school, all part of growing up. Frankly, I was quite delighted when I discovered he was visiting a doxy. I never dreamt he was pursuing insalubrious practices, wearing women's tawdry clothing, painting his nails and calling himself Dulcie to boot. Oh my God ...' he gasped and then collected himself.

'My wife doesn't have to know this does she, Inspector? She is in pieces already without knowing her son was a ... well least said and all that.'

'She'll hear nothing from me, Sir. I'll write up my report; no need to turn out the dirty washing in public.'

'Good man. You mentioned that Ned Daniels got entangled with a mantrap in the wood. Obviously that forms part of my property; will I be prosecuted in connection with that?' asked Mr Knightley looking worried. 'A gentleman in my position ...'

'That's not for me to decide, however I suspect not. Many estates still have such devices scattered around. As you know, they have been illegal for many years now so if I could make some mention that you are attempting to clear them from your property, well I should think that would be sufficient.'

'Thank you, Inspector. Tell me, what happened to Clem Gibbs?'

'That's actually the only fly-in-the-ointment. He isn't buried at the farm and I don't believe he was involved with either murder, so what happened to him will remain a mystery. I can't explain why he didn't keep his rendezvous with you; he was clearly motivated by money so maybe he got wind of a better payday elsewhere and took off. He is just one of thousands of itinerants who travel the country making a living where they can and being completely anonymous; no attachments, no commitments. I don't suppose we will ever know,' said the inspector with a sigh.

The inspector took his leave for the night and arranged to return in the morning with Constable Cummins to collect Lady Nora for the trip to Keswick.

*

Lizzie had allowed herself to be looked after by her aunt and Mrs Field after her return from the wood. They fussed over her for the remainder of the day. She was aware of the inspector arriving and leaving.

The talk in the servants' hall suggested that as soon as the police released Mr Donald's body they would be leaving Highfields. She wondered if they would ever return. She would miss this place. She loved the area and didn't want to think this might be the last time she would see it.

Speculation regarding Lady Nora was rife. George was interrogated mercilessly by the staff. "Did you never suspect anything?" seemed to be a recurring theme. He had been told to hold himself in readiness for the following day in case the police wanted to question him regarding Lady Nora's visits to the wood.

Lizzie wondered if she should go to Lady Nora. Philadelphia had already told her that Miss Sophia was spending the night with the Misses Mackenzie, the daughters of the retired vicar of Blenthorne, as she was distraught and couldn't face remaining at home. They employed a general maid who would "do" for her.

However her aunt told Lizzie she had already attended Lady Nora.

Lizzie insisted she was fully recovered from the events of the afternoon however by nine o'clock decided she would retire for the night as she was feeling strangely emotional.

When her aunt turned in at nine-thirty Lizzie was still awake.

'Can't you sleep, Lizzie? Do you want some warm milk?' her aunt asked gently as she stroked her hair.

'Yes please, Aunt Phily. The thing is; there is so much I don't understand, my mind is in a whirl. Not least the fact that you didn't seem very surprised when I told you that Charles Knightley was dead.'

'That's because I wasn't surprised, my dear,' she replied softly. 'I'll go down for the milk and then when I return, I will tell you the whole story but whatever you hear stays within these walls, you must promise me that.'

It was chilly when her aunt returned about fifteen minutes later. Lizzie was sitting up in bed with her dressing gown around her shoulders listening to the rain beating upon the window panes and feeling the draughts which had found their way through the curtains.

Philadelphia Crittle got the eiderdown from her own bed and putting it round her shoulders, settled down with her back against the iron footboard of Lizzie's bed. She tucked her legs under the covers at her niece's behest. They wrapped their hands around the warm beakers. Over the coming hour, Philadelphia told Lizzie her tale.

'Lizzie, there is no point beating about the bush so I'll just tell you; Charles Knightley was your father.'

Lizzie wondered for a moment if she had heard her aunt correctly.

'I'm sorry what did you say, Aunt Phily?' said Lizzie incredulously. 'Fred Tester is my father.'

'Fred Tester was paid by the family to marry Rebekah after I went to Mrs Reader and we approached her Ladyship following Mr Charles' disappearance. Lady Constance arranged it all. You were born five months after the marriage.'

Lizzie suddenly remembered what her mother had told her when Lizzie had asked how one knew they had met the right man. She had had a far-away look in her eyes; clearly the person she was thinking of wasn't Fred Tester. She realised incredulously her aunt was telling her the truth.

'Please go on, Aunt Phily.'

'Rebekah and I started in service much as you did at the age of thirteen. Rebekah was two years younger and so started two years after me. After I had worked my way up, I got a job as a housemaid with the Knightley family and then she followed me to Westden, when a vacancy for an assistant nursery maid arose. Rebekah looked after Miss Prudence and Miss Anna, the first two Knightley children. Mr Charles was a regular visitor, both to Westden and here at Highfields.

'I don't know how they first met, Charles and your mother. He probably attended the nursery to play with his nieces; whatever happened, a strong mutual attraction formed. Theirs was truly a love story; the young man from the rich influential family and the girl from the labourer's cottage. Charles was not a materialistic man, he was creative and imaginative, non-judgmental, maybe unworldly would be a better description; he cared nothing for social hierarchy or ascribed positions through birth. He could see no barriers to their being together. They planned to leave and live in Italy where he would paint. They were to be married the night before they left.

'Reverend Mayhew had only recently arrived in the parish; he was a pleasant young man and he readily agreed to perform the service, under special licence. I was to be a witness as was the reverend's wife. The plan was for Charles and Rebekah to leave together in the morning, after spending the night at the vicarage. Rebekah and I got to the church early in the evening expecting Charles to be waiting. He wasn't there.

'At the time I felt that he had panicked and run away. However Rebekah was adamant, she insisted he would not leave without her. She trusted him, she loved him and she knew he loved her. I admired her loyalty but at the time, felt it was misplaced. I believed Charles was out of his depth and had bolted.

'She told me of her pregnancy a few weeks later. She had kept it secret but realised the truth would be bound to come out. Mrs Reader and I went to Lady Constance and she spoke to her husband; I don't think she went into detail but I think he was made aware that Charles was responsible for a certain situation. As I told you earlier, Fred Tester was given money to marry Rebekah. He couldn't believe his luck; he wasn't a bad young man, just apathetic and ineffectual. The money bought respectability for Rebekah but I suspect Fred drank it all away within a year or two,' said Philadelphia grimly.

'The sparkle went out of Rebekah the night Charles went missing and it never returned. As time went by, I think we expected to hear word as to where he was and what he was doing but it never came. Rebekah always maintained he must be dead; nothing else would have kept him from her. So strong was her conviction that as time went by I began to believe she was correct.

'Tonight I was helping Lady Nora get ready for bed and she was quite lucid. Lady Constance came in to sit with her. Lady Nora told her sister that she had spent time with Charles both at Westden and here in his painting studio, the old folly. He used to let her sit and watch him work. She had fallen in love with him probably because he was one of the few people in life to be kind to her.

'One fateful day his kindness was his undoing, he didn't want to disappear without explanation, so he told Lady Nora he was leaving to live abroad and was taking Rebekah Crittle with him as his wife. Much as with Ned today, she picked up a knife and stabbed him.'

Philadelphia paused as Lizzie gasped and clamped her hand over her mouth.

'There is something else, Lizzie. It's a truly terrible thing. But you are a strong, sensible woman and I believe you should know the whole truth. Lady Nora told her sister tonight that the stab wound wasn't immediately fatal. She said she tended him for several days in their special place; I assume she meant the folly. She admitted earlier tonight that Charles died with your mother's name on his lips. Afterwards, somehow Lady Nora managed to drag him outside and; "wrap him in love and bury him under our tree" as she put it.

'Frankly, Lizzie I'm not sure how I kept my countenance. Lady Constance and I just looked at each other. When we left the room, Lady Constance took me to one side and made me promise never to breathe a word of what I'd heard to a soul. I just nodded. However, my dearest, I've thought about it and you have a right to the truth, as does your mother.'

'Lady Nora is very strong, at least in her upper body, I found that out when she attacked me this afternoon. Yes, I can see that she would be capable of dragging a body and burying it.

'Rest assured I won't tell anyone … but … I can't believe she made no attempt to get help. She tried to look after him herself with no medical knowledge and no medicines, not even morphine? He must have been in agony from the wound as infection set in; do you think he begged her to fetch someone?' whispered Lizzie.

A physical pain swept Lizzie's body and she clutched her chest, breathing deeply. Silent tears rolled down her cheeks as the rain beat relentlessly against the window panes.

A thought suddenly struck her.

'There was a pile of stained rotting rags in the folly; you don't think they could be what she used after she stabbed my father do you? And the floor, was that his blood under nearly thirty years of filthy rubbish and animal waste? Oh, Aunt Phily; how could she? Lady Nora said she loved him yet she let him suffer and die, crying out for my mother; what sort of love is that? It's the cruellest thing I could ever imagine. She's inhuman.'

'Don't torture yourself, Lizzie,' replied Philadelphia as she shook her head. 'She was unbalanced, who knows what was in her mind. Maybe she hoped she could nurse him back to health and he would be so grateful he would stay with her forever. I suppose in a way he did.'

'You told me Lady Nora said "our tree". Yet it bore the initials of Lady Constance and Mr Herbert. Why did she consider that to be a special place for her and Charles?' asked Lizzie, looking puzzled.

'Think about the initials; CK-HK,' said Philadelphia looking at her niece closely.

'Yes, Constance Kingsbury and Herbert Knightley,' replied Lizzie.

'No, Lizzie; Charles Knightley and *Honora* Kingsbury; Nora is a shortened form of her name. She carved the initials herself after she buried Charles all those years ago,' said Philadelphia quietly.

'Oh my word, do you think she did that so she could remember where she had put him?' Lizzie blurted out almost hysterically.

'No, I imagine she thought about where she had put him every day of her life henceforth. That was why she created an imaginary world while she was here. He was still alive and living in the wood and she visited him whenever she could. It was probably the only way her mind could cope with what she had done,' said Philadelphia.

'You said my mother had a right to know, will you tell her?' asked Lizzie as she wiped away the tears from her eyes.

'Oh yes of course, but not about the manner of his death, that would be heartless. But she has been waiting all these years. She has never given up hope of finding out what happened to him.' Philadelphia got up from the bottom of Lizzie's bed.

'A letter would be too blunt. I will leave for Kent tomorrow. In spite of her initial reluctance, Lady Constance has given me permission to go. After what we both witnessed tonight, she really didn't have a choice. I will stay while Rebekah has need of me and the rest of the household will return to Kent in a while I expect.'

'Lady Nora called me a "flyblow". She told me I shouldn't exist. I think she knows who I am,' said Lizzie suddenly remembering Lady Nora's words in the wood.

'Well I wouldn't be surprised; you favour your father in looks. That must have been the final straw for her, you invading her private space in the folly where she lived out her fantasy. You are the daughter of the man she loved. The child he had with another woman. I imagine in that moment she wanted to kill you too.'

'What will happen to Lady Nora do you think, Aunt Phily? Will she face any punishment for her crimes? I mean, if he'd lived, Ned Daniels would most likely have been hanged.'

'Most likely not; from what I have heard downstairs, I believe that the inspector fully intends to charge Lady Nora but no doubt the family will employ a clever and very expensive lawyer and she will be treated sympathetically by the authorities. At the end of the day, Lady Honora Kingsbury is a member of the aristocracy; who was Ned Daniels? He was just an easily led lower class young man of dubious character. No, the law won't worry too much about Lady Nora's culpability. She will no doubt end up in some sort of sanatorium but for how long is anyone's guess. I can't imagine the family will rush to have her back though, can you?'

'But surely Lady Nora should be held accountable for Ned's death?'

'Yes, Lizzie, I agree with you but I have my doubts; I would not be surprised if she escapes justice.'

When aunt and niece finally blew out the candles it was nearly midnight. They both had a difficult day in front of them.

At six o'clock Philadelphia Crittle got up, washed and dressed and then packed her bag. She then went downstairs to make breakfast for Lady Constance. Lizzie washed and dressed and went down to prepare Lady Nora's breakfast. Upon completion of their tasks, Philadelphia Crittle proceeded from the backstairs along the landing leading to the master suite of rooms and Lizzie Tester made the shorter journey from the backstairs along to Lady Nora's room.

She unlocked the door. Not finding her mistress in her bedroom Lizzie went into the adjoining bathroom.

Lady Nora was in the bath.

She was wearing her nightgown and was lying just below the waterline. Her hair was floating, spread out around her like pond weeds.

After spending some time checking that there were no signs of life and doing what needed to be done, Lizzie closed and locked the door; she then raised the alarm.

Lady Nora Kingsbury's wretched fantasy-filled life had ended.

Chapter 14 – Resolution

Late September 1891 – Mid February 1892

The morning after the terrible tragedy passed very slowly as the horrors of the night were discovered and digested. The inspector was duly summoned.

He was shown into the morning room and Lizzie was called up from the servants' hall.

'Miss Tester, thank you for seeing me, this must be a terrible shock for you; particularly on top of everything that happened yesterday.'

'To be honest, Inspector, I think I am quite numb and firmly believe that nothing else will ever shock me again,' said Lizzie with conviction.

'If you could just tell me of the sequence of events as you remember them this morning,' he asked gently.

Lizzie sat stiffly on the edge of the sofa opposite the policeman as she described in detail her morning routine. She had made Lady Nora's breakfast and taken it up to her room at about eight-fifteen. She would normally prepare Miss Sophia's breakfast as well if she wished to take it in her room rather than downstairs but she was staying with the Misses Mackenzie in the village. Lizzie unlocked the bedroom door and went into Lady Nora's room which she found empty. She placed the breakfast tray on the chest of drawers and called out Lady Nora's name. Getting no answer, she walked towards the adjoining bathroom which Lady Nora normally shared with Miss Sophia.

'Plumbing had been installed just a few years ago; the room was originally a dressing room but it is so much better now, as it means servants no longer have to carry heavy buckets of water up the stairs for the purpose of bathing … oh dear, Inspector, I am so sorry, I am gabbling, please forgive me.'

'Not at all, Miss. What happened after that?'

'Well I opened the door and went into the bathroom and found … well I found Lady Nora floating in the water. I don't know if she meant to kill herself or if it was an accident. She was wearing her nightgown so it is possible she just slipped I suppose; however it seems unlikely. There would be no reason for her to have run a bath in the middle of the night and even less reason for her to be in a position to slip in accidentally, so I think she must have climbed in deliberately,' said Lizzie in a measured tone. 'I initially tried to get her out then realised she was dead.'

'Thank you. I agree; it seems clear that Lady Nora decided to end her life. Her future would have been bleak anyway.'

'Would she have gone to prison or been hanged? My aunt seems to think not?' asked Lizzie softly.

'Depends on whether or not she could have been charged with causing the death of Charles Knightley as well as Ned Daniels. It seems unlikely on the surface as there is no evidence against her. In fact it's doubtful an actual cause for Mr Knightley's death will be found after all this time,' said the inspector frankly, 'unless there is a bullet wound in his skull or ... oh forgive me, Miss Tester, I shouldn't be so indelicate.'

Lizzie was unperturbed. 'But what if she confessed to killing Mr Charles; I mean how else can one explain how she knew where his body was?' persisted Lizzie.

'Well, that would be a different matter ... still, I don't think she would have gone to the gallows, not with her mental state; probably would have been committed to an asylum. Yes, maybe this is for the best,' he concluded pragmatically.

When the inspector was satisfied with what she had told him, Lizzie stood up and took her leave. He said he would like to speak to her again after he had spoken to Mr Knightley and would see her downstairs.

Lizzie said she would ask Mr Hemsley to tell the master that the inspector would like to see him.

Mr Herbert Knightley was in the study looking drawn as Albert Bishop entered and he waved the inspector towards a seat.

'Did you check on Lady Nora at all during the night, Sir? In particular did you hear anything, the bath water running for example?' asked the inspector.

'No. I did check her door was still locked, about four o'clock this morning, no idea why it shouldn't be, but I suppose after all that had happened … However there was no sound at all, I assumed she was asleep,' said Mr Knightley. The inspector didn't speak and he continued.

'I was having a restless night myself but nothing unusual in that. I'm a bit of an insomniac I'm afraid, it comes from years of working on speeches mentally in the middle of the night, that sort of thing. I always seem to be able to think more clearly when the house is still. The events of the last few days were whirling around in my head so I decided to come down and get a book.'

'I found what I wanted quickly and came straight back upstairs. The rooms my wife and I share are quite a distance from those of my daughter and Lady Nora, so I wouldn't expect to have heard the bath being filled. I suppose my sister-in-law just woke up and decided to … well take matters into her own hands so to speak. It was a pretty sad life all in all.' He shook his head contemplatively.

The inspector took his leave and asked if he might have one final word with Miss Tester. The master of Highfields looked blank for a moment and then appeared to remember who she was. He summoned Hemsley to take the inspector to the staff quarters.

'I just wanted to say goodbye,' said the inspector rather awkwardly, as he was shown into her sitting room by Mrs Field.

Lizzie had been waiting for him and rose from the chair as he entered. 'Inspector Bishop; it was indeed a pleasure to make your acquaintance. I don't expect we will meet again, other than at Lady Nora's inquest I suppose,' she said extending her hand with a small smile.

'Likewise, Miss Tester, although obviously the circumstances have been less than ideal,' he paused clearly wanting to say something more. He cleared his throat and spoke, with less confidence than normal.

'I was wondering … do you think you might possibly be in Keswick at any time in the future? If so, it would be my pleasure to show you round the area. I know you enjoy walking and the views from the summit of Skiddaw for example are breath-taking.' He looked hopefully at Lizzie.

'Mr Bishop, that is so very kind of you, however I will be returning to Kent as my mother is frail and I need to live close by so that I can attend her when she needs me. As much as I love this part of the country, I will be going back to Westden Chase after the formalities have been completed. But thank you so very much for your generous thought. I wish you well for the future.'

The inspector shook Lizzie's hand gently. 'And you, Miss Tester,' he replied softly.

She accompanied him to the back door and watched as he walked slowly up the drive.

At the time Albert felt strangely forlorn but later when he gave the matter a bit more thought, he realised that he had been fortunate in the extreme that she had declined his invitation. He couldn't imagine what had come over him. A woman in his life; what a ridiculous notion – he was totally committed to his job – wasn't he?

He pulled his pipe out of his jacket pocket and stuck it between his teeth.

*

Lizzie in turn was thinking of the inspector as she climbed into bed that evening. If only he knew. She could scarcely believe it herself. Her thoughts turned to the events of the night before.

After her conversation with her aunt she couldn't sleep, she kept tossing and turning. The phrase "I would not be surprised if she escapes justice" kept repeating itself in Lizzie's mind.

She could not get the thought of her mother and Charles Knightley out of her head.

Had they married as planned in the village church in Blenthorne, Lizzie's life would have been totally different. They may not have been rich but she certainly wouldn't have been a servant. She would have been brought up perhaps in a village somewhere in Italy; their lifestyle would have been ... what was the word? She had read it somewhere ... Bohemian, yes that was it. She would have been encouraged to read, paint, learn the language and choose her own path in life. She would have had two parents that not only loved her but loved each other.

Maybe her father would not have made sufficient money to support his family; maybe he would have had to return to ask for assistance if they faced financial ruin but at least they would have had the opportunity to try.

As it was, her mother had been trapped in an emotionless marriage with the burden of pregnancy forced on her every year or two until her body was worn out and her spirit crushed. She herself was in service at the age of thirteen; working for the very people who had indirectly robbed her of the life she should have had.

For some time she lay and stared at the ceiling; an idea was forming in her mind but could she carry it through? If she did, would she be caught? If she was, did it matter? She said once that everyone deserved justice; now was her chance to prove she believed that to be true.

She rose a little before four o'clock, pulled on her dressing gown and left the room quietly so as not to disturb her aunt. The rain was still pounding against the windows of their room and the house was making strange creaking noises.

She walked quietly down the backstairs in bare feet so she could move almost without sound and she gently pushed open the door connecting the servants' staircase to the family's bedroom corridor. Her heart had increased to a rapid rate, it was beating loudly in her chest and there was a thumping sound in her ears.

She paused; maybe she didn't have the courage to do what she intended. Then she pictured her mother excitedly getting ready for her wedding, putting on her dress, Phily brushing her long blonde hair and putting a posy of violets in her hands. Her father saying goodbye to Lady Nora, to whom he had clearly been very kind. And how she repaid him!

In spite of her disability or maybe because of it, Lady Nora had become a deranged and jealous woman. She had taken Charles' life. Worse still, she had kept his body concealed in the ground. No coffin for him and no Christian burial. He was not resting in peace. He was hidden in the damp mouldy earth in a wood while his murderess played out her hellish fantasy a few feet away for over a quarter of a century.

She took a few steps along the corridor; she had no light so was feeling her way in the darkness. Her courage faltered and she stopped. She thought back to the photographs of her father here at Highfields and likewise at Westden Chase. She was always drawn to his picture, now she understood why. Because when she looked into his face she saw a reflection of her own. She thought of her mother, so burdened and beleaguered, defeated by life. Her resolve returned.

She heard a door open and the sound of footsteps. From the direction they were coming, it must be the master. She had to think quickly. In common with Westden Chase, Highfields had a sluice cupboard on the landing and Lizzie ducked into it before she could be seen. Since the introduction of the plumbing it was not needed for its original purpose and now housed cleaning products to save the maids from having to carry everything up from the scullery each day. She held her breath as Mr Knightley walked past. He stopped outside Lady Nora's room; Lizzie wondered if he was going to turn the key and enter but after trying the knob he continued on his way down the main staircase.

What should she do? The whole household knew that the master was a poor sleeper and often wandered the house during the night, so there was always a possibility of this happening. She waited for what seemed like an age and then heard the plodding footsteps returning from whence they came. Mr Knightley walked steadily along the landing and disappeared down the corridor leading to the master suite.

Lizzie waited for what she judged to be five minutes and then left the confines of the cramped cupboard.

She walked purposefully to the door and, turning the key in the lock, entered the room quietly. She locked the door behind her and could hear Lady Nora breathing evenly. Lizzie reached up and turned the nearest wall light to a low setting. She had tended this woman for years. Bathed her, dressed her, styled her hair and responded to her every command. All that time she had been serving her father's killer.

'Come along, Lady Nora. It's time for your bath,' she said in as normal a voice as she could manage.

Lizzie went through the connecting door to the bathroom and started to run the water. The taps were situated in the middle of the bath which meant that Lizzie had to lean over its width to test the temperature of the water.

Lady Nora came limping through from her bedroom, clearly unperturbed that it was still dark. Once the bath water had reached a sufficient level, Lizzie guided her mistress towards the tub. She turned to the door leading to Miss Sophia's room and checked it was locked.

'No, don't worry about taking off your nightgown. Straight in, that's it, it's just the right temperature,' Lizzie's voice was smooth and calm but with an underlying edge of steel.

Lady Nora looked at her oddly in the dim light but did as she was bid.

Once she was in the water Lizzie moved to the foot of the bath and rolled up her sleeves. She leaned into the water. Her nerve almost failed her; the faces of her parents again flickered in front of her. Without further ado, she grasped the older lady firmly by the ankles and pulled upwards and towards her.

Lady Nora was taken by surprise and tried to grab the sides of the bath. As it was, she couldn't get any purchase and for what seemed like an age, she spluttered, splashed and writhed around with her head becoming submerged time and again beneath the waterline. Occasionally she bobbed up and gulped for air but before she could take a proper breath she disappeared again due to the superhuman strength Lizzie suddenly seemed to possess.

Lizzie thought the noise would surely wake the household.

The flailing woman scratched at the sides of the bath and attempted to lever herself up by the elbows. However, unlike earlier in the wood, her strength was no match for this new vengeful Lizzie. Nora's hair was hanging over her face in long brown and grey strands; it gave her a wild witch-like appearance as she struggled and spat. Lizzie held her legs firmly for as long as she could.

When the splashing had finally abated, Lizzie gave a final tug of her ankles and Lady Nora's head and torso disappeared from view one last time. The waves gently subsided and all was still. When she was satisfied her task was complete, Lizzie released the legs which then dropped and hung limply over the end of the bath until she pushed them back into the tub.

Before she left the bathroom she spoke softly to her dead mistress.

'That was for Charles and Rebekah you wicked, evil woman.'

She unlocked the door, left the bedroom and re-locked it from the outside.

In the morning she made breakfast for her mistress and took it to her room. She went into the bathroom and mopped up the excess water from the floor and smoothed out Lady Nora's hair so that it no longer covered her face, in the hope it looked less likely a struggle had taken place. When Lizzie was satisfied she had done as much as she could, she raised the alarm.

If Philadelphia Crittle had woken in the night and noticed that Lizzie had been missing or that her dressing gown was soaking wet before the body of Lady Nora was discovered, she said nothing.

*

Three days after Lady Nora's death, Lizzie had visited the church for a pre-arranged meeting with Reverend Jolion Mayhew. She asked him about the night nearly thirty years ago when her parents had planned to marry. He confirmed what Aunt Phily had told her.

'Yes, I remember them well; Charles Knightley and Rebekah Crittle. He was an unusual young man; unconventional. It meant nothing to him that he and his intended were of different social classes and I have no doubt theirs was a true love match. He was very clear in his intentions and I was in no doubt he planned to take care of your mother. I was very surprised when he didn't arrive for the ceremony. I never saw Rebekah again, what happened to her?'

Lizzie told the vicar of her mother's burden-filled life in Kent with Fred Tester. He shook his head sadly and offered to pray with Lizzie. She declined. It was clearly inappropriate; in view of the fact that she had committed a mortal sin.

She accepted that the death of Lady Honora Kingsbury would remain on her conscience for the remainder of her days and wondered with foreboding what sort of blows fate would rain down on her by way of retribution.

*

Grace Cork's inquest was reopened and those of Donald Knightley, Edward Daniels and Lady Honora Kingsbury took place in that order over the following three weeks. The verdicts of unlawful killing were delivered in the first two with the perpetrator being identified as Edward Daniels.

It was ruled that the statement made by Edward Daniels prior to his death should be given no credence. The verdict therefore in the case of Edward Daniels was recorded as accidental death as a result of an injury inflicted by Lady Honora Kingsbury in self-defence. An inquest into the death of Charles Knightley was to be convened shortly. Lizzie was only called upon to give evidence regarding her discovery of the body of Lady Honora Kingsbury and her actions thereafter. The coroner outlined the circumstances in which the deceased had been found and the results of the subsequent medical examination.

Lizzie's heart was pounding as she described how she had tried to get her mistress out of the bath, having found her submerged. At the time she didn't realise this was a futile gesture.

She was asked if she noticed any discolouration to any part of the body and she replied she had not and volunteered the suggestion that she had possibly caused damage to the body in her vain attempt to help her mistress.

The coroner then called the doctor and asked about the discolouration on Lady Honora's upper arms and around her ankles. Dr Rufus Danes from the village had examined the body in situ and it had been he who had originally drawn attention to the ecchymosis caused by bruising. The coroner asked if this could have been caused by the actions of Miss Tester in her attempt to get Lady Honora out of the bath.

Lizzie started to panic a little as Dr Danes gave his reply.

'I feel that to be unlikely. Ante mortem bruising can appear post mortem; however bruising sustained after death is highly unusual as blood circulation ceases once cardiac function fails. In my experience, the only way post mortem bruising could occur would be the result of a violent trauma. That did not fit with the chain of events as described in this instance.'

The doctor's voice droned on, clearly warming to his theme.

'In this case the ante mortem bruising caused damage in the form of swelling of the epithelial tissue, coagulation and infiltration of ... '

Lizzie's could no longer concentrate on the doctor's evidence, as her anxiety levels were rising alarmingly. It was clear her attempt to explain the injuries to Lady Nora were being dismissed. Any minute now, the inspector would be instructed to arrest her, she was sure.

'... This could quite likely be due to post mortem artefacts,' concluded the doctor.

The coroner thanked the doctor for his succinct and insightful testimony.

Inspector Bishop was then called to the stand but although Lizzie could hear his articulate and familiar voice, she had no idea what he said. She thought she was going to be sick. Her hands were shaking and her mouth had filled with excessive saliva, the exact feeling one has just before bile and vomit force their way up the gullet and out of the mouth. She swallowed rapidly several times and breathed deeply, hoping she gave the outward appearance of being composed and that no one would notice that she was sweating.

The coroner sat thoughtfully at the conclusion of the evidence and then delivered his verdict.

After the inquest was brought to a close a cacophony of noise filled the air as everyone relaxed and began to chat to each other.

The inspector made his way over to Lizzie.

She felt frozen to the spot. 'What is happening, Inspector? Are you going to arrest m … make an arrest?'

'Make an arrest? What makes you think that, Miss Tester? The coroner's verdict was accidental death. Didn't you hear?'

'What? Well no not really, I was confused. I thought he said I couldn't have caused the bruising when I tried to get Lady Nora out of the bath after she was dead; so that means someone must have injured her before she died.' Lizzie realised her voice was shaking in terror.

The inspector looked at her quizzically.

'There was no suggestion that anyone else was involved. I gave evidence to that effect just now. The doctor said Lady Nora might have had a change of heart and tried to get out of the bath herself. She probably thrashed around and got tangled in her nightgown and bruised herself in the process. There was no way of knowing exactly what she was thinking. The doctor said some small veins might have been damaged as you tried to get her out of the bath which also added to the discolouration of her skin, "post mortem artefacts" he called it. Are you sure you're alright, Miss Tester?'

'Goodness, was that what the doctor said? Oh dear, so much has happened; I can't really take it all in. Maybe I'm not as tough as I thought,' she said dropping her felt purse and gave the inspector a weak smile when he retrieved it from the floor.

'Allow me to escort you back to Highfields, Miss.'

'No, I'm fine thank you, Inspector. I am to return with Mr Knightley in the carriage; an honour indeed,' she said weakly.

She left the inn quickly as she couldn't trust herself not to blurt out a confession. She would wait for her master by the carriage with the coachman. Such was her haste that she did not see Obed Daniels trying in vain to catch her eye.

*

It was Thursday 29 October 1891, the family and staff were all packed and ready to leave Highfields House. Life had returned to something like normal after the inquests. Mr Herbert Knightley had returned to London a week earlier as Parliament was sitting again after its summer recess.

After completion of the formalities, the body of Charles Knightley was to be re-buried near the family home in Reigate Surrey, alongside his parents. In the absence of any evidence, the inquest took less than half an hour and an open verdict was recorded by the coroner. Lady Nora was to be taken to the Kingsbury family estate in Middlesex to be interred in the family vault and Donald Knightley's body was to be returned to Kent.

The family and staff were to accompany Mr Donald's coffin on the journey. Lizzie was to travel with the entourage to London and there she would take her leave of the Knightley household.

She was to take up a new position as lady's maid to Lady Frances Forward, a well-known society hostess who lived in opulent splendour and comfort in a villa in Kingston-upon-Thames. Lady Frances had been trying to persuade Lizzie to take up her proposal of employment for over six months and had continually increased her offer. Aunt Phily would pack Lizzie's things and send them up from Kent.

Lady Frances was planning a trip to America early in the new-year and this would give Lizzie the chance to travel abroad on a boat … passenger liner, she corrected herself. She would be foolish to turn down such a chance.

After all, there was nothing to tie her to Kent any more. Everything changed for her upon receipt of a letter from her dear Phily. It arrived three days after the inquest into the death of Lady Nora.

She took it out of her felt purse again and sat down on the bed to re-read it.

'My Dearest Lizzie,

It is with deep sorrow that I write to tell you of the death of your mother, Rebekah.

I broke the news regarding Mr Charles Knightley's body being found and she sat back in her chair and smiled; a small almost happy smile, maybe of vindication. "I knew he would never have left without me," she said quietly.

Over the coming days she seemed to gently withdraw, it was as if her body was shutting itself down. She was waiting here on earth to find out what happened to the love of her life and once she had done so, she had no further reason to stay.

She slipped peacefully away at the weekend. She was very calm and composed and dying held no fear for her.

She wanted me to tell you how much she loved you but you know that already, don't you?

Let's hope that she and Charles are together in death in a way that they couldn't be in life. I look forward to hearing from you soon, my dear girl.

All my love,

Aunt Phily

PS: Please find enclosed a drawing that I found among your mother's things. I think it says more than any words.'

Lizzie wiped her eyes again as she looked at the charcoal sketch in front of her. The paper was slightly yellow and quite coarse. The drawing was a portrait of a girl with her hair flowing across her shoulders. Her eyes sparkled and almost danced off the paper as she looked

271

directly at the artist. She had high cheekbones and a gentle loving smile. The artist had signed it on the front and on the back there was a simple message: "*To my dearest Rebekah – my love, now and always, Charles*". This was her mother, drawn by her father. No matter how many times she read the letter and looked at the drawing, she always wept. After a few minutes she regained her composure and put the letter and drawing back in the envelope.

Everything was prepared for the trip.

Lizzie needed to make sure Lady Constance was ready; she had been looking after her and Miss Sophia since Phily went to stay with Rebekah in Kent. She managed adequately as Lady Constance spent most days in her room, refusing to get dressed. Miss Sophia devoted herself to engineering invitations from friends in order to have suitable audiences for her grief and had rarely been in residence since the tragedies.

Lizzie wouldn't be sorry to leave this house. She had always felt it concealed a tragic past. Little did she imagine that her father's body was secreted in the grounds, no more than a mile away; or indeed that a member of the family could be harbouring such an unbearable burden. Maybe that was what she intuitively felt; the very presence of Lady Nora tainted the whole house with her torment.

Both Lady Constance and Miss Sophia were distraught at the prospect of losing Lizzie, particularly as Sophia and her fiancé had just broken off their engagement by "mutual agreement". The talk around the servants' dining table was that the "dead uncle" and "barmy aunt" would be enough to put anyone off and Sir

James understandably was not keen to marry into a family beset with scandal.

She was just about to go up to look in on her mistress when George found her.

'Miss Tester, there's a gentleman here to see you.'

'To see me, really how strange, who is it?'

'It's Mr Daniels, Miss.'

'Oh my goodness I really should have gone to see him to thank him for helping me the day that his nephew died.'

Lizzie hurried downstairs, smoothing her thick dark hair as she did so, to make sure it was still firmly within the confines of its neat bun.

She went to the backdoor and found Mr Daniels standing in the yard, his hat in his hands.

'Mr Daniels, how nice to see you won't you come in? I do apologise for not paying my respects and for thanking you properly for helping me that terrible day in the wood. With my aunt back in Kent, I've since been fully occupied with my duties. Her Ladyship hasn't been entertaining you understand but still seems to need me every hour for one reason or another.'

'I fully understand and no thank you, I would rather stay outside if it's all the same to you. Could we sit on the seat maybe, Miss Tester?' said the innkeeper awkwardly.

Lizzie nodded and they walked across the yard to the seat in front of the wall to the kitchen garden.

'The thing is,' said Obed Daniels twisting his hat in his hands, 'I've heard from the talk in the bar that you weren't remaining with the family now that your mother has sadly passed away. I was terribly sorry to hear that of course, please accept my condolences.'

'Thank you, Mr Daniels; it was what they call a happy release I believe. She had been ailing for years and maybe she has found a form of happiness in the next life that she was denied in this. I am to take up a new position in Kingston-upon-Thames. A delightful place I believe. You see there is no reason for me to return to Kent now.'

'No, well that being the case ... however I can see the attraction of a new life for an intelligent lady such as you. But the thing is ... maybe I shouldn't take up your time ... the girls though ... I can't go back and face them until I have at least asked,' Obed Daniels suddenly stood up.

'Asked what, Mr Daniels?' enquired Lizzie looking slightly puzzled. She was suddenly transported back to another yard and another man standing in front of her many years previously. She wondered almost incredulously if this conversation was going to take the same course.

Would she give Obed Daniels the same answer as she had Horace Blackford? How different her life would have been had she accepted Horace's offer when she was seventeen. He was talking again and she dragged her attention back to the present.

'... I mean it's a much more simple life I suppose, no grand house to live in; there's no comparison really ...

but against that there are people here who would take care of you and … provide for you … and …'

Lizzie stood and faced Obed Daniels. 'Are you again offering me a job as your housekeeper, Mr Daniels?'

'No, Miss Tester, I'm not.' Obed Daniels pulled himself up to his full height and his voice held a degree of authority, which Lizzie didn't think she had heard before. Unlike Horace, Obed Daniels was a head taller than her. 'I am making so bold as to ask you to become my wife.'

Lizzie thought of living in Richmond-upon-Thames, having an assistant, being served her meals by the junior staff, having a salary that was the envy of all London, going to America … straight forward decision, surely?

'Well, that actually depends, Mr Daniels.'

'On what, Miss Tester?' he asked looking down straight into her eyes.

'On whether you plan to call me "Mrs Daniels" after our marriage or if you will finally acknowledge that I have a Christian name. After all, even Inspector Bishop called me Lizzie once!'

When the meaning of the reply became clear to him, Obed Daniels smiled from ear to ear and threw his hat in the air.

'Lizzie,' he said quietly.

*

It was mid-February 1892 and Inspector Albert Bishop had just returned home from Blenthorne. Obed and Lizzie Daniels had invited him to their wedding in the village. He was pleased he had gone as it had been a

275

grand day. They made an impressive couple and knowing Lizzie, she would take the Blenthorne Inn and turn it into one of the best establishments in the whole of Cumberland. He looked forward to visiting from time to time.

If he was honest, something still bothered him about the day of Lady Nora's inquest. Lizzie's reaction after the verdict was very odd to say the least. She was normally so composed yet for a brief moment she was as white as a sheet and had seemed scared out of her wits. Surely she hadn't ... no, he wouldn't even entertain the idea and pushed the nagging thought from his mind. She was a fine woman and that was the end of it. Where was his pipe?

He finally admitted to himself that he admired Lizzie very much. Maybe things might have been different if he had been more forceful. As it was, his feeble attempt at courtship really didn't amount to much. Obed Daniels had offered her marriage; he had offered to show her around Keswick and take her for a walk to the top of Skiddaw! Oh well, once a confirmed bachelor always a ... something caught his eye in the newspaper.

A bare knuckle boxer by the name of Clement Gibbs had been found dead the morning after an alleged illegal fight. It was suggested that during the bout he had apparently not been himself, unable to fend off blows he would normally parry without a problem. He was discovered in his room by his landlady. He had thirty pounds in his pocket.

Well, well, well; the last loose end in the Cork and Knightley case. He finally found his pipe and stuck it firmly between his teeth.

Chapter 15 – Afterword

For the reader interested in history, genealogy and outcomes or indeed for those who are just curious, it is worthwhile to mention that historical records show that a marriage did indeed take place between Obed Joseph Daniels, widower and Elizabeth Louise Tester spinster, in February 1892.

Local newspaper articles give testimony to the fact that the Blenthorne Inn soon began to prosper from a steady rise in patronage and its sparingly-used lounge bar rapidly became the focus of many a local gathering. With a little sprucing up, the guest rooms began to attract visitors from the lower middle classes who wanted an affordable base for their annual holidays. Mrs Daniels' natural air of quiet competence and immaculate manners made every guest feel special and repeat bookings meant they had more enquiries than they could handle for the summer months.

Encouraged by her stepmother, May Daniels' culinary skills were honed and refined; in time her flair and confidence had more than a little to do with the inn's steady increase in clientele and profit margin.

Obed and Lizzie Daniels' son Charles was born in January 1896 and was christened in March of the same year. His godfather was a family friend, Albert Bishop.

Charles won a scholarship to advance to grammar school in 1907. His parents and latterly his godfather paid the fees; his mother in particular being insistent that he should continue his schooling. When subsequently interviewed for a professional journal he paid tribute to their dogged determination to ensure he completed his education.

From obituaries, it appears that Obed Daniels died unexpectedly in 1909, with the cause being recorded as acute interstitial nephritis. It was said in the village that his widow's reaction was one of quiet resignation. She believed her beloved husband's sudden passing was fate taking its ugly revenge but she would not be drawn as to what she meant.

Having distinguished himself at school, Charles Daniels' entry to university was delayed by the Great War. Military records show that Charles served with distinction in the trenches. He was wounded in action during the Battle of the Somme and sent home for a time in July 1916 but returned to the front line upon recovery. He was again wounded in February 1918 and awarded an honourable discharge with the rank of sergeant in May 1918 when it became clear the injury he had sustained to his patella and surrounding tendons had caused permanent damage to the left knee.

He subsequently went on to study in Manchester in 1919 and became a medical doctor in 1924. After completing his mandatory training, Dr Daniels specialised in psychiatry and became an eminent authority in the field of dissociative personality disorder and schizophrenia, with papers published on both sides of the Atlantic.

In 1938, at the age of forty-two he fulfilled a long held ambition to have an exhibition of his paintings in London. When interviewed for a national periodical about his prestigious amateur talent, Dr Daniels suggested it was probably inherited from his maternal grandfather. However extensive research failed to find any surviving works attributable to Frederick Tester.

Census records from 1921 indicate that Miss Philadelphia Crittle, occupation: retired lady's maid was resident in Blenthorne at the same address as her niece. Miss Crittle's death was recorded in August 1922 at the age of seventy-nine from septicaemia.

Prior to moving to Blenthorne, Philadelphia Crittle remained in the service of Lady Constance Knightley. Sir Herbert Knightley, as he became, did not stand in the general election of 1895, deciding to leave political life to concentrate on the family banking business. Henceforth, the couple lived quietly at Westden Chase in Kent. Sir Herbert retired in 1908 and died in 1910 at the age of seventy-one. Thereafter Lady Constance lived in a small manor house in Tonbridge attended by a staff of twelve and died in 1918 at the age of seventy-five.

Social commentators noted that after the autumn of 1891 the Knightley family never returned to Highfields House. It remained in their possession under the care of Mr and Mrs Field however the property, other than the faithful retainers' living quarters, was closed up and shrouded in white linen for the following eighteen years. It was subsequently sold in 1909 to a Mr Theophilus Ravens whose family had made their money in the railway industry.

Miss Sophia Knightley had four broken engagements before finally marrying a diplomat from the foreign office. They lived in several locations, during which time gossip columnists of the day linked her to at least three marital scandals in various parts of the globe. She and her husband returned to England and retired to the south coast prior to her death in 1929 from a riding accident near Eastbourne.

May continued to live at The Blenthorne Inn until 1945 and ran the establishment with her husband, Gordon Cummins, after the death of her father. They had two daughters and subsequently retired to a cottage in the village.

Lily Daniels married Robert Barton, a local farmer and had ten children. The ownership of the farm remains in the family to this day.

Both May Cummins and Lily Barton were ably attended in all their confinements by their stepmother. It didn't take long for word of Lizzie Daniels' proficiency to spread. By the early twentieth century, if one found oneself with-child in the local area, then it was given that Mrs Daniels would be booked for the delivery.

Lizzie Daniels it appeared had a natural aptitude for midwifery and all things obstetric. She was competent, capable and kind and most importantly of all, she charged much less than the doctor.

In addition she understood the problems faced by working class women burdened with the perpetual cycle of pregnancy, the cost of child-rearing and the cramped conditions in which many families lived. It was rumoured that the birth rate in Blenthorne and the surrounding area fell for several years but if the local doctor was aware that this could be due to anything other than natural phenomena, he turned a blind eye.

In December 1913 marriage records show that Elizabeth Louise Tester Daniels, widow married Albert James Bishop, bachelor at St Mary the Virgin Church in the village of Blenthorne. Local women looked on in dismay as she temporarily left the village to live with her husband in Carlisle.

Census records for 1921 indicate that Albert Bishop, occupation former detective superintendent of police, gave his residence as an address in Blenthorne, thereby fulfilling a promise of his wife to return to her former home after his retirement. However during his time as a serving police officer he investigated many interesting cases, often with input from his enthusiastic wife and it is just possible dear reader, that in time some may find their way into print.

Upon her return to Blenthorne, Lizzie Bishop re-established herself in her former role. However, any discreet services she provided for multigravidas beyond ante natal and obstetric care were few and far between, in deference to her husband's former occupation and indeed his police pension. If he knew of his wife's unorthodox gynaecological skills Albert Bishop, in common with the village doctor, also developed myopic vision.

After a happy marriage and subsequent retirement, Albert Bishop died at Blenthorne in 1933 from emphysema.

Lizzie continued to live in the village and was visiting her son in wartime London during June 1944 to celebrate his engagement to a consultant neurologist.

This coincided with the launch of the enemy V-1 "doodlebug" bombing campaign. The property next to Professor Daniels' London home suffered a direct hit during the second night of the bombardment, less than five hours before he had planned to take his mother back to the relative safety of the Lake District. The blast was sufficient to kill them both instantly.

Many of the older residents of Blenthorne, who live there to this day, can remember a formidable but fair lady who rejoiced in the name of "Granny Daniels", despite her name being Mrs Bishop for the last thirty years of her life. Some suggest that it took nothing less than the full might of the Luftwaffe to finally bring her life to an end.

Elizabeth Tester Daniels Bishop, her son and both her husbands are buried in the churchyard in the village of Blenthorne, near a large oak tree. RIP.